PRAISE FOR
MURDER AT HATFIELD HOUSE

"Meticulously researched and expertly told, *Murder at Hatfield House* paints a vivid picture of Tudor England and a young Princess Elizabeth. Amanda Carmack's talent for creating a richly drawn setting, populating it with fully realized characters, and giving them a tight and engaging narrative is unparalleled. An evocative and intelligent read."
—*New York Times* bestselling
author Tasha Alexander

"An excellent start to a new historical mystery series."
—*Romantic Times* (top pick, 4½ stars)

"Amanda Carmack writes beautifully.... I enjoyed *Murder at Hatfield House* and recommend it; it is a cozy excursion into Tudor times with a lively heroine."
—Historical Novel Society

"A great historical suspense with a solid murder mystery and very enjoyable heroine."
—Mysteries and My Musings

"I enjoyed this novel, with the rich descriptions and the lively and interesting cast of personable characters. I think that this is going to be a great series to follow and I highly recommend it to those who enjoy a bit of history to their mystery!"
—Sharon's Garden of Book Reviews

"We see the action unfold through [Kate's] eyes, but the most exciting revelation is not the unveiling of the mystery, but the unveiling of Elizabeth."
—Heroes and Heartbreakers

ALSO BY AMANDA CARMACK

The Elizabethan Mystery Series

Murder at Hatfield House

MURDER AT WESTMINSTER ABBEY

AN ELIZABETHAN MYSTERY

AMANDA CARMACK

AN OBSIDIAN MYSTERY

OBSIDIAN
Published by the Penguin Group
Penguin Group (USA) LLC, 375 Hudson Street,
New York, New York 10014

USA | Canada | UK | Ireland | Australia | New Zealand | India | South Africa | China
penguin.com
A Penguin Random House Company

First published by Obsidian, an imprint of New American Library,
a division of Penguin Group (USA) LLC

First Printing, April 2014

Copyright © Ammanda McCabe, 2014

OBSIDIAN and logo are trademarks of Penguin Group (USA) LLC.

ISBN 978-0-451-41512-7

Printed in the United States of America
10 9 8 7 6 5 4 3 2 1

Somehow, this book came to be the tale of strong women forging their own destinies against great odds, at a time of enormous social change and upheaval! Women both historical and fictional, I loved spending time with them all—Queen Elizabeth and her mother, Anne Boleyn, Frances Grey and her daughters, Madame Celine, Mary Everley, and especially my new bff, Kate Haywood. None of them would have been possible without the example of my own favorite strong, loving woman, my mother. This book is for her. . . .

PROLOGUE

I will be as good unto ye as ever a Queen was unto her people. No will in me can lack, neither do I trust shall there lack any power. And persuade yourselves that for the safety and quietness of you all I will not spare if need be to spend my blood.
— Elizabeth I on the eve of her coronation

London, January 1559

"Out of my way, you foul hedgepig! Ain't you ever been told to give way to ladies before?" Nell shoved at the thick crowd clustered ahead of her, using her elbow or a well-placed heel to wriggle her way in. She had never seen a real-life queen before, and she wasn't going to miss it.

Nell's grandmother, who had been a toothless old crone when Nell was a toddler, good for nothing but sweeping the floor and boiling the linen of the bawdy house, once saw this new queen's mother, Queen Anne Boleyn, ride past in her own coronation procession. She'd told Nell all about it, and Nell remembered it now. Her grandmother's stories of Queen Anne's gown, all silver and gold, sparkling as she sat up high in her chariot with her black hair loose and twined with jewels. The music and the flowers, the wine that flowed free at every fountain.

"There were few enough to cheer for her, Nellie," her grandmother had always finished the tale, with a rueful shake of her gray head. "For all that they drank her wine enough, there were too many as missed good Queen Katherine of Aragon. But she was a glorious sight to see. She knew how to put on a show, did that one. They say she started from naught, too. Think what you could do, my Nellie, with the right man. . . ."

"And look where 'the right man' got Queen Anne in the end!" Nell's mother would cry, stumbling into the kitchen in her stained smock, her lip paint smeared and her eyes shadowed. "Better an honest whore than a dead queen. Don't go filling the child's head with strange fancies, Mother."

Fancies died quick enough in the stews of Southwark, no doubt about it. A girl had to eat, and dreams of jewels and white chariots wouldn't fill a hungry belly. Nell's grandmother was long dead now, her mum too, and she worked hard to keep their old room at the bawdy house for herself and her sister.

But she still remembered those words, the image of Queen Anne in her gold and silver gown, and she wanted to see a queen for herself. When Queen Mary, daughter of "good Queen Katherine," came to the throne five years ago, Nell was still just the scullery girl of the house at the Cardinal's Hat, too young to be a proper whore, and she couldn't escape when the others went to see Mary come into the city after vanquishing the men who would have overthrown her.

"Wasn't anything to see, anyway," the girls sniffed when they came back from Mary's procession. "Her jewels were fine enough, and her gown fancy, but her face—

I would just as soon have looked at her horse. She never smiled, neither. A queen ought to smile."

This new queen, Queen Anne's daughter, was sure to be different. And Nell was going to see her, even if she had to clout someone over the head to do it.

"Out of my way!" she screeched. It was a cold day. Frost lay thick on the lanes, a silvery white layer over the mud and muck, making the ground slippery underfoot even as it cut some of the sickly-sweetish stench of the streets.

Nell had never seen London like that before, even though she had lived there all of her days. For over a month, people had been working day and night to dress the drab, crowded streets in their finest for Queen Elizabeth. Windows that had never seen soap before gleamed in the pale, watery winter sunlight. Trash middens were cleared away, drainage ditches flushed down to the river. Brightly colored banners hung from every house, snapping in the wind.

Here by the river, where soon the queen's barge would pass as it went from Whitehall to the Tower, the cold didn't reach its icy fingers through the close-packed crowds. Everyone jostled shoulder to shoulder there, shopkeepers, ferrymen, the clergy clutching their new English Bibles, beggars, merchants' wives in their pretty hats, children perched on their fathers' shoulders. They all waved small green-and-white banners, clutched flowers to toss to their queen.

Even common whores like Nell, who rarely dared venture from the narrow warrens of Southwark, were a part of it. The everyday world of grime and grit and heaving work, of grasping desperately for every drink of wine, every stick of firewood, fell away before the magic of the day. She was just another English person, like anyone else, and she was about to see the queen.

If those bloody cod-pigs would get out of her way!

"Nell!" she heard someone shout, and suddenly a gloved hand shot out from the jostling crowd and grabbed her arm. Before she could think, she was pulled to the front of the throng, right up to the edge of the riverbank.

Gasping for a breath, she looked up to see one of her regulars grinning down at her from beneath his fine pearl-trimmed, white-plumed cap. "I thought that was you, Nellie."

Nell laughed as she twitched at her best red skirts. "Why, lovey, you're a true white knight today, ain't you? I'd have thought you'd be at the queen's palace yourself." He wasn't the first one she wanted to see today, not the one she secretly dreamed of running into. Even whores had their favorites, after all. But Rob was surely working today, and this man was nice enough.

Especially when he helped her to such a vantage point.

"There's a better view here," he said, waving his vel-vet-clad arm over the gray ribbon of the river. "And the company is merrier. Here, have a ginger cake."

"Don't mind if I do." Nell watched as he tossed a coin to one of the vendors hawking his cider and spiced wine, and took the warm cake he bought. As she nibbled at the rare treat, he slipped his arm around her waist and she studied the river flowing in front of them.

Even the Thames seemed different today, clearer, calmer. The boiled heads were removed from the pikes above London Bridge, and the cold air was free from the miasma of the Smithfield fires that were lit all too fre-quently in Queen Mary's day. Instead of the thick stick-iness of fear, there was laughter. It was as if the summer sun came out again after a rainy, chilly night.

Except that it was *still* cold. A damp breeze swept up from the river and curled around Nell, even through her best woolen sleeves and heaviest shawl.

"Cold, Nell?" her companion said, his arm tightening around her. "I can warm you later."

Nell turned to smile up at him. Suddenly a movement on the opposite bank caught her attention, a flash of golden hair among the crowd. Against her will, her heart beat a little faster. She went up on tiptoe, struggling to see across the water and through the shifting knots of people. But the glimpse was gone.

Nell leaned back on her companion's arm, some of the sparkle of the day sputtering and dim. It probably was never him, anyway. He hadn't been to see her in such a long time.

Suddenly a loud trumpet blast split the air, and it was as if lightning suddenly danced over the crowd again.

"She comes, she comes!" the cry went up. Everyone surged forward in one great heave, and Nell stumbled.

Her friend's hand held her steady, and she clung to him as she tried to see the river. It was indeed the queen's procession, slowly floating into view.

The queen's great barge, all golden and white, sparkled like it was a living thing. A Tudor rose, white within red, was painted on the prow, surmounted by a crown and the gilded initials *ER*. Green and white silk hangings draped at its sides and hung from the golden canopy.

Smaller barges followed in its wake, the lord mayor in his dark robes, and all the guilds, decked and trimmed with their finely embroidered banners. But everyone only watched the figure that stood above that painted Tudor rose, her arm raised to wave as she bowed to the crowds.

Nell watched, spellbound. Queen Elizabeth was not

overly tall, and was very slender and young-seeming, her red-gold hair waving loose over her shoulders. Her heart-shaped, pointed-chinned face was milky white against the gold satin, violet velvet, and ermine of her robes. But her girlish figure radiated heat like a summer's day itself, heat and confidence and joy that was infectious to all around her.

For an instant, the roaring crowd went silent at her appearance. Then a cheer rose up, gathering and growing as it swelled along the riverbank and over the whole city.

"God bless Your Grace!" came the cry, flowers raining down on the water.

"And God bless all of you, my good people," could be heard her reply, faint but clear. The queen bowed and waved, smiling brilliantly even though tears could be seen sparkling on her pale cheeks. All around her on the barge were her ladies and her leading courtiers, clad in rich satins and velvets, sparkling jewels, bright swords. But no one could see anyone except the beautiful new queen.

It was just as Nell's grandmother had said of Queen Anne. She knew how to put on a show.

Even Nell, who had thought she was long past being caught by such sparkle, found herself with a tear in her eye. Aye. *That* was a queen, to be sure, and Nell was glad to have seen one at last.

But a girl still had to earn her bread.

"God's teeth, but it's amazing, Nell," her companion said.

Nell shook out her mended red silk skirts and tried to compose herself. To bring herself back to the real moment, real life. "What's amazing, lovey?"

"Why, that she looks like *you*, of course." He laughed, and gestured to the figure in the barge as it drifted away toward the menacing hulk of the Tower.

Nell frowned doubtfully. But then she looked closer at the barge, casting off the magic spell of the crown to try to see the woman beneath. "Bodkins," she breathed, for he was right. Nell saw just such red hair, just such a longish nose and small, high bosom, in her cracked glass every night.

"Maybe I should start charging more," she said, trying to joke despite the unsettled feelings of such a realization. "The royal experience, eh?"

And if only she could find a fine velvet gown and pearl necklace like that . . .

"Shall I come by later, Nell?" he said, as the queen's barge sailed onward and the crowd started to drift after it. "I could use a bit of the, er, royal experience myself."

Nell fondly patted his cheek. "Come early, lovey, and you can be the first."

She swirled around and made her way through the crowd, sauntering easier now that she didn't have to elbow her way through. Everyone was going the other direction now, trying to follow the queen, but Nell had to get home and make sure the house was ready. It was sure to be a busy night.

She left the river behind to plunge back into the twisting, narrow lanes of Southwark, where the meager light of the winter's day was obliterated by the leaning, peaked roofs and overhanging windows nearly touching above the paths.

It was strangely quiet for an afternoon. Usually Nell only found such rare peace when she made her way home in the mornings after a night out looking for customers. The district, shut off from the city gates and beyond the touch of the royal law, made its living in dubious pleasures like bear pits, theaters, brothels, and taverns, and couldn't often rouse itself before noon. But today was different. Today almost everyone was gone to see the queen, and doors and windows were still shuttered.

Except for Old Madge, sweeping the dirty doorway of her tavern, and a flea-ridden cat streaking across the muddy lane, Nell was alone with her thoughts. A strange experience. She couldn't quite get the queen's face out of her mind, or the strangeness that she looked a bit like Nell herself. Who would have thought it? She wagered that whores all over the place would be dyeing their hair now, but Nell's was all natural.

She laughed as she made her way past the midden heap at the back door of the bawdy house, where the pigs rooted, and climbed the rickety steps at the side of the building that led to her room. She and her sister, Bess, paid a bit extra for that privacy, but it was nice for their regulars not to have to make their way through the front doors of the house and past the other bawds.

At the top of the stairs, her door was slightly ajar, but she scarcely noticed as she pushed it open. She was still caught up in thinking about the red-haired queen.

The small room was dim, the shutters still drawn over the cracked window, the fire died down in the grate. Her meager furnishings, the rickety washstand, the stool, the narrow bed with its threadbare hangings, cast shadows on the plastered walls.

Suddenly, one of those shadows shifted. A silent figure rose from her bed.

"Oh!" Nell gasped, startled by the unexpected movement. But then she saw who it was, and she smiled. "So you came back. I'm glad. I've missed you, I have."

She turned to shut the door behind her, letting her shawl fall from her bare shoulders. There was a rustle of movement, a hard hand on her arm.

"No need to be impatient . . . ," Nell said with a laugh.

A blinding pain struck the back of her neck, a flash of brilliant light, a sticky rush. She screamed as she fell forward, hitting the door hard face-first, convulsed by the hot, horrible pain. Her fingers closed on something small and cold, like metal, and she pulled at it as she tumbled down.

Then there was only cold blackness.

CHAPTER 1

Whitehall Palace, earlier that same day

"Hurry, Kate! We mustn't be late."

"I am coming!" Kate Haywood called after her friend Lady Mary Everley as she dashed down the palace corridor outside Kate's chamber. It would be a terrible thing indeed to be tardy taking their places in Queen Elizabeth's procession to the Tower, where all new monarchs spent the nights before their coronations. Kate was meant to play with the queen's musicians on the royal barge.

The queen. How very new and strange those words seemed, and how very wonderful. Queen Elizabeth. It seemed only a moment ago that she was mere Princess Elizabeth, and they were living quietly in the countryside. Now they were in the midst of London itself, stepping into the color and whirl of a real royal court. Into life itself.

Kate's head was spinning with the excitement and urgency of it all. Part of her, most of her, wanted to run out and embrace it all. And part of her . . .

Part of her felt like she was standing tiptoe at the edge of a precipice, about to leap into something dark and unknown. Something that would catch her up like a whirlwind and toss her around until she didn't know herself any longer.

As she took up her lute from where it lay on its stand by the fire in her small sitting room, her father leaned forward from his chair and caught her hand in his. She felt the familiar roughness of his fingertips, callused from long years on the lute strings, and it steadied her pounding heart.

She smiled up at him. Matthew Haywood had served at royal courts since he was a child, first old King Henry, then as chief musician to Queen Catherine Parr, then Elizabeth in her years of exile and danger. But though he had written much of the new celebratory madrigals and pavanes for the coronation festivities, he couldn't play at the processions and banquets himself. His days in the cold, damp gaol before Queen Mary died had weakened him, and he had to stay close to the fire, wrapped in warm robes and with his rheumatic leg bandaged and propped on a stool.

Kate looked into his watery eyes, at the beard that was nearly all white now, and had to force herself to smile brightly. She would not worry her father with her own uncertainties, not for the world. He was all her family, and she his, and it had been thus since her mother, Eleanor, died when Kate was born nineteen years ago.

"I wish you could come today, Father," she said. "It will be so glorious! You've been working so hard to make the music just right. . . ."

"And so don't I deserve my rest? Christmas was *too* merry. It has all worn me out. And it is too cold out there for an old man like me. I will do well enough here at Whitehall, with Peg to look after me. You can tell me every detail when you return."

Kate held up the thick sheaf of vellum in her hand. "But this is *your* music."

"I can think of no safer care for it than you, my Kate. You will make the notes come to true life."

"Kate!" Lady Mary called out again from the corridor. Kate could hear her friend's footsteps pattering closer.

"Go now," Matthew said. "You cannot keep Her Majesty waiting. You did wonderfully well at all the Christmas festivities. Even Sir Robert Dudley himself praised your music. Today will be no different. There must always be a Haywood in the monarch's musical consort."

Kate gave a rueful laugh. The days of Christmas had indeed been a whirl, a gala month of banquets, dances, plays, and masques, all organized to the most lavish degree by the queen's handsome childhood friend and new Master of the Horse, Sir Robert Dudley. Kate had played and sung until her voice grew hoarse and she felt giddy with it all. Not since she was a child at Queen Catherine's court had she seen so many people, heard such fascinating conversation, and eaten such grand food. Only now it was a hundred times more intense, more merry.

The new queen was like the sun, brilliant and hot to a world too long in chilly darkness. All were drawn into her orbit. And Kate was lucky enough not only to see it all, but to be given glimpses of the extraordinary woman behind the royal mask.

"You're quite right, Father," she said. "It will all be grand indeed. I will do your music its justice, I promise."

"And don't forget—your mother is always with you, too." Matthew stroked a gentle touch over the polished wood of Kate's lute. The lute that had once belonged to her mother, Eleanor.

Kate felt the prickle of tears behind her eyes and blinked them away. "I won't forget, Father. Ever."

"Kate!" Lady Mary's head popped around the door.

The gray-yellow rays of sunlight from the window caught on her pale red hair, twined with pearls, and the jeweled trim of her red satin bodice. The daughter of a Protestant family, neighbors of the Grey family at Bradgate Manor who had lived quietly in the country under Queen Mary's reign, Mary Everley was a bright, vivacious spirit who seemed to burst from her exiled cocoon into the whirl of court. At a Twelfth Night banquet, she had sat next to Kate and insisted on learning how to play a new song—one of Kate's own compositions. In return, she taught Kate the new Italian dance, the volta, which was the queen's current favorite. "We must go."

With a last kiss to her father's cheek, Kate hurried out of the room after her friend. Their rooms were at the back of the vast corridors and courtyards of Whitehall, and they ran down and up staircases, circling around servants and courtiers intent on their own important errands on this momentous day. It seemed there couldn't possibly be anyone left on the streets of London; they were surely all packed into the palace.

Lady Mary grabbed Kate's free hand and pulled her along, so eager and joyful that Kate had to laugh with her. As well as helping navigate the maze of court, Mary was just a lot of fun to be around. And Kate's father was right. This was a day for celebration, not worries. All their desperate hopes and prayers had come true at last, and the future was young and bright, opening up before them with endless promise. Elizabeth was queen now.

It was good to have a friend again, Kate thought as Mary pulled her onward through a picture gallery. The portraits hung there—of young King Edward all puffed up in his padded satin doublet; old, bluff King Henry with his red beard and redder face; and the queen's various stepmothers and cousins—seemed to glare down at their laughter. After—well, after she lost her last female friend at Hatfield House, and after the handsome Anthony Elias disappeared into his world of studying the law and making his future, Kate felt a bit lonely. But Mary banished all that. The first day they met, Mary had helped Kate retrieve precious sheets of music lost in the cold wind, and then had made herself something of Kate's protector, sharing all the court gossip and helping her navigate the rocky shoals of a new, complicated life. Even though she had the feeling Mary did not tell her everything, they had fun together.

Just before Kate and Mary spun around the corner and went down the steps to the long gallery, they stopped and peeked into a large Venetian looking glass that hung on the dark wood-paneled wall. Next to Mary's sunset hair and red-and-white gown, her fashionably pointed face and pearl necklace with its jeweled *E* pendant, Kate's dark blue gown and her brown hair and dark gray-green eyes seemed like night to day.

But she meant to be unobtrusive, letting her music be at the forefront, while she observed all that happened around her.

Kate ruefully tucked a loose wave of hair beneath her black velvet hood. At least her hair was behaving for once, not waving wildly out of its confines. And her garnet earrings, a Christmas gift from her father, shimmered against the dark background. She would not disgrace the court.

"Mary! Whatever are you about, girl? The procession is forming."

Some of the sparkle of Mary's smile dimmed as she turned to face her father. Edward, the Earl Everley, strode through the milling crowd, followed by his son,

Lord Henry, and their cousin Richard St. Long. Though they were all handsome, with the earl and Henry sharing Mary's red-gold hair and Master St. Long dark and brooding as any hero in a masque, Kate could not quite like any of them. Or rather, Master St. Long always seemed courteous enough, but the Everley men saw no need to be.

And maybe she did not care for them because whenever the earl or Henry was near, Mary's smile faded. But Mary herself never spoke against them; she rarely spoke of her family at all.

"I had to fetch Her Majesty's pomander," Mary said. She held up the pierced silver ball on its velvet cord, swinging it to send waves of lavender and rose scent into the air.

"Well, hurry now," the earl said, frowning behind his gray-streaked red beard. "You are only a maid of honor, you can't afford to anger the queen."

"*We* can't afford it," Henry muttered. "Imagine us, Everleys, bowing to the arrogant Boleyn. . . ."

"Hush, cous," Master St. Long interrupted. "You daren't say anything against the Boleyns. And Mary is doing her task excellent well. She will do us all proud."

Mary and her cousin smiled at each other, while the earl spun around and strode back the way he came, the crowd making way for him. Richard offered Mary his arm, and Kate followed them down the length of the great gallery. The long, narrow space was crowded, but a wall of windows looked down to the river, letting in the cold light of day and giving the impression of infinite space and sky.

As Kate rushed along, she glimpsed the barges assembling on the water, brilliant with silken banners and the swirl of bright velvets and satins, lush furs, and the glint of jewels, long packed away and now brought out in triumph. She went down a set of water-washed stone steps to the long, covered but open dock and found herself in the very midst of the pageant.

The lord mayor's barge, and the vessels of all the aldermen and guilds, the leading aristocratic families, that were to accompany the queen to the Tower, were already boarded and arrayed on the river, while the queen's barge waited at the dock. The queen herself stood just within the palace doors, her arms held out as her Mistress of the Robes, Kat Ashley, fussed with Elizabeth's fur-trimmed purple velvet mantle.

Other ladies-in-waiting fluttered around the queen like a flock of bright birds, their scarlet and green and blue skirts twirling as they smoothed Elizabeth's loose fall of red-gold hair and her cloth-of-gold train. One of them straightened the jeweled princess's coronet on Elizabeth's head while another hurried away at Mistress Ashley's snapped command to fetch a needle and thread.

Elizabeth herself was still as a statue under all the motion, a glittering figure of red, gold, and white. The only sign of her growing impatience was the twitch of her long, pale, heavily beringed fingers, the tap of her scarlet velvet shoe under her hem.

"We must be gone before the tides are against us," Elizabeth muttered. Her dark eyes, so striking in her white, pointed face, sparkled.

"Now, my dove, no need for such haste. You must look perfect, today of all days," Mistress Ashley *tsk*ed. The small gray-haired lady had been with Elizabeth since she was a toddler, and was practically a second mother to the little princess. She had faced imprisonment for Elizabeth, and the two of them had only just been reunited after being kept apart so long by Queen Mary.

Kate was quite certain only Mistress Ashley could ever call the queen "dove."

"Even the tides will surely wait for you today," Mistress Ashley said.

"As they did not when I was taken there as a prisoner," Elizabeth said. "If I must go to that cursed place, 'tis best I go swiftly. The rest of you, go aboard now. Quickly! You will drive me mad with your flutterings and fussing."

The ladies all bobbed hasty curtsies and scurried onto the barge, followed by the gentlemen of the queen's household. Sir Robert Dudley, the new Master of the Horse, was the last to go. He swept his jeweled cap from his handsome dark head and gave it a great flourish as he bowed low to Elizabeth. She gave a reluctant-sounding laugh and held out her hand for him to kiss.

As he took his departure, Frances Grey, Duchess of Suffolk, led her two daughters forward to make their curtsies. She had lost her eldest, the studious Lady Jane, and Kate had doubts that the two left could ever replace their intellectual sister. Lady Catherine was assuredly beautiful, tall and delicately formed, with golden hair and sky blue eyes in an oval face. It was said she looked like her grandmother, the famously glorious Mary Tudor, Dowager Queen of France. But Catherine loved dancing above books, and couldn't seem to hold a thought in her head for more than a moment.

And Lady Mary, the younger sister—Kate had heard some of the crueler courtiers call her "crouchback Mary." Barely half her sister's height, with a crooked spine, she also suffered from a skin condition. Yet there was a sharpness to her gaze missing from Lady Catherine's, a quickness of observation. Kate was sure Lady Mary should never be discounted.

Lady Frances hoped to find her way back to royal favor through her daughters, mayhap even have Lady Catherine named as Elizabeth's successor, or so it was whispered. After all, the Greys were the queen's cousins, and Protestant. They should be preferred to Catholic, French Mary of Scotland. Yet so far Elizabeth had shown them little favor. Lady Catherine, a Lady of the Bedchamber to Queen Mary, was now made a mere maid of honor, and Lady Mary Grey had no official place at all. Their assigned seats were at the back of the royal barge today.

Elizabeth waved them away, and Lady Frances's face was frozen as she shepherded her daughters through the crowd.

The Count de Feria, the Spanish ambassador, stopped the Grey ladies to bow over their hands. Some of Lady Frances's hauteur melted before his dark-eyed charm, charm Kate remembered well from a visit to Brocket Hall before Elizabeth became queen. Lady Catherine giggled behind her feathered fan at whatever he said to her. Only Lady Mary frowned up at him, twitching her furred cloak over her crooked shoulder.

Elizabeth seemed to notice none of her family's doings. She glimpsed Kate and Lady Mary Everley over Mistress Ashley's head, and beckoned them forward.

"There you are, Kate," the queen said, her voice distracted. "You are needed with the musicians at once. God's teeth, but you would think none of them had ever deciphered a page of music in their lives!"

"Of course, Your Majesty," Kate said with a hasty curtsy. The queen gave her a short nod.

In their days at Whitehall, there had been none of the strange intimacy that grew between the queen and Kate in their last, dark days at Hatfield House. With Christmas and the coronation to be planned, the queen was always closeted away at work with Sir William Cecil and her other counselors, or dancing at one of the revels organized by Robert Dudley. Kate spent nearly every moment lost in her music, helping her father plan the programs for all the events and instructing all the other musicians on their parts.

When their paths did cross, Elizabeth would nod and ask after the new songs, but her dark eyes were always full of shifting distraction. Kate knew it could be no other way.

But knowing she could help the queen once made her eager to do more. Eager to help make sure the rare promise of this day lasted and was protected. The new queen had many enemies, and most of them hid their dark thoughts behind brilliant smiles.

Clutching her lute, Kate hurried aboard the queen's barge. The large vessel, which had long ago belonged to the queen's mother, Queen Anne Boleyn, had been re-painted and refurbished in creamy shades of gold and white. Rich silk and taffeta hangings in the Tudor green and white fluttered from the railings, and the queen's great, thronelike chair was set at the prow. All her most favored courtiers were taking their stools and cushions arrayed behind her, wrapping their furred cloaks against the cold wind off the river.

The musicians were to sit behind the queen and around the railing, where the merry sound of their lutes, tambours, and flutes could be heard by the crowds along the riverbanks and on the bridges. Kate quickly took her low stool and laid her lute on her knees.

They were ready to launch into the first planned song when the queen finally boarded the barge and made her way to her throne. Robert Dudley led the way while

Lady Mary Everley and Mistress Ashley carried her golden train. The oarsmen in their shirtsleeves took up their oars and the barge slid into the slate gray waters of the river.

Over the polished wood of her lute, Kate glimpsed a group of lawyers from the Inns of Court aboard their own barge. For just an instant, she thought she saw a familiar handsome face among the black robes.

Anthony, she thought with a surge of pleasure. Could it truly be him, after all these long weeks with no word at all from her friend?

But then whoever it was turned away and was lost to sight. The other barges fell into place behind the queen's, two hundred of them in all, and Kate could think of nothing else but her music and the cheers of pure, burning joy that greeted the new monarch on every side.

The glory of the day was palpable, a feeling that hung on the air like a sweet perfume drifting over the whole city. Surely it truly was a new day. And nothing could mar the bright perfection of it.

CHAPTER 2

"Kate! Kate, wake up."

Kate gasped, abruptly startled from the tangle of her dreams by a hand on her shoulder and a whisper in the darkness. For an instant, she couldn't remember where she was. It wasn't her bed in the small chamber at Hatfield, where the roof leaked and the fire smoked, for she could hear the stirrings and sighs of people all around her.

Then she remembered. She was in the Tower, lodged with the junior ladies-in-waiting in a large chamber below the royal suite in the Queen's House. But the remembrance didn't calm her, for the chilly stone walls of the room that had seen too much seemed to press in close around her. Ever since the queen's barge docked at the gate of the Queen's Stairs and they processed between the high watchtowers, a cold beyond the winter wind seemed to seep into her very bones.

Even the lavish banquet in the great hall hadn't banished the sensation of being stared at by unseen eyes.

Kate wasn't one to believe in ghosts, but here in this place it felt as if the real, bustling, everyday world ended at the thick stone walls, and her dreams were full of blood and screams.

She shivered and pulled the blankets closer around

her shoulders. Those dreams still had their skeletal arms wrapped around her, making her mind a blur. Slowly, she saw the chalky ray of moonlight from the high, narrow window falling over the sleeping figures all around her. Lady Mary Everley shared her cot, but it wasn't she whose voice woke Kate. Mary still slumbered under her counterpane, her red hair spilling from her lace cap.

"Kate!" the whisper came again, and a hand on her shoulder turned her around.

Kate blinked her eyes hard, scarcely daring to believe what she saw. It was Queen Elizabeth herself, kneeling beside Kate's bed.

"Your Majesty?" Kate whispered. The queen wore a fur-trimmed bed robe of pale satin, her hair falling in a thick red-gold braid down her back. The moonlight turned her face a stark blue-white, her eyes fathomless dark pools.

"I am sorry to wake you, Kate," Elizabeth said softly. "But there is something I must do tonight, and I can ask no one else to help me."

"Of course I will help you, Your Majesty, in any way I can," Kate answered, confused. Elizabeth was always surrounded by courtiers, ladies, and servants ready to leap at her smallest sigh. The evening had been full of ceremony, ritual, and lavish food and music, merely a preamble to so much more to come. What could Elizabeth have to do tonight? And with the help of Kate, of all people?

Kate thought again of Hatfield, and all that had happened there in the last days of Queen Mary's dark rule. Things that could never be spoken of, but were never forgotten.

"Come with me." Elizabeth helped Kate up from the low cot, waiting with a tap of her silk-slippered foot as

Kate wrapped a shawl over her linen smock and found her shoes. They tiptoed past the slumbering ladies into the hall beyond.

Elizabeth had left a lantern burning on a table outside the door, and its amber glow showed that the remains of the feast were only half cleared away. Silver plates gleamed dully under torn hunks of bread and streaks of spiced sauces. Goblets tipped on their sides, dripping the dregs of fine Rhenish wine onto white damask cloths, scenting the cool air with fruity sweetness blended with melted wax candles and the lingering remains of expensive perfumes.

Only the queen's greyhounds breathed in there, an elegant new pack gifted from the King of France that she had insisted on bringing with her. They slept under the tables, replete with scraps from the feast. But the lantern light glowed on the gold-tinged figures of the tapestries on the walls, Diana and her acolytes at the hunt, making them seem to run and move.

Those rooms had once been refurbished for the coronation of Elizabeth's mother, the walls painted and paneled, Tudor roses carved on the cornices with entwined Hs and As along with Queen Anne's falcon badge and her motto—The Most Happy. Most of those had been hastily removed long ago, but a few ghostly As still lingered, overlooked. She was the last queen the rooms had sheltered on the day before a coronation, until now.

And those rooms had also housed Queen Anne on the eve of her death.

Kate had tried not to think of that as she listened to the tributary speeches, as she played for the dancing. Tried not to think of how it must feel to have such glorious triumph turn to bitter ashes. Today was a new day.

But surely the queen tried not to think of that as well.

Perhaps that was why she could not sleep, tonight of all nights.

Elizabeth led Kate down the short flight of stone steps and pulled open the door to the outside. Guards were stationed there, their pikes at the ready, their new red and gold livery stiff and shining. But they moved not at all when they saw who hurried past them.

Kate wrapped her shawl tighter around her shoulders as she followed Elizabeth onto Tower Green. The night was very cold, as clear and sharp as a diamond as it bit into her lungs, but the snowflakes had ceased to fall. Everything was perfectly still, as if all London held its breath. The sky beyond the crenellated Tower walls stretched out an endless soft, velvet black, scattered with tiny pearl stars, and the frosting of snow lay over the grass and paving stones underfoot.

The buildings around them—the Bell Tower, where once Elizabeth had been a prisoner; Beauchamp Tower, where Robert Dudley and his brothers once languished; and the sturdy, square White Tower in the center of it all—crouched close, their small windows blank and dark, and Kate again had that sensation of being watched.

But strangely she felt no fear now, only the tingling touch of excitement dancing along her fingertips and toes. This was an adventure indeed, just as she had dreamed of in those long, quiet days at Hatfield. And adventures always started with a blind leap into the unknown.

Elizabeth led her across the dark, grassy stretch of the green, her robe swirling behind her. The queen seemed very sure of what she was doing, just as she always did. Even in the most dangerous days, when her sister Queen Mary hated her and sought her downfall, Elizabeth's confidence never wavered and she always sailed forward into life, serenely, surely. But suddenly she went still, her head tilted back as if she scented something on the cold breeze.

Kate shivered as she looked at Elizabeth's still, white face. "Perhaps we should go back inside, Your Majesty," Kate ventured. "It is quite cold, and you haven't slept. There is much to be done tomorrow." The queen was to create new Knights of the Bath before one more night in the Tower, a long, complicated ritual that couldn't be done if the monarch had caught a chill. "Surely whatever errand can be done in the morning."

Elizabeth gave her head a sharp, impatient shake. Her hair, the famous Tudor red-gold, rippled over her shoulders. "I can only do this tonight. Now. Don't you feel it, Kate?"

"Feel what, Your Majesty?" Kate whispered, wondering at the madness of the night. It seemed to have affected even the unflappable queen.

"They are here with us." Without a word of explanation, Elizabeth hurried onward. Her steps slowed as they skirted around the stone courtyard where once scaffolds had been built, where Queen Anne, Queen Catherine Howard, and Lady Jane Grey had ended their lives under the sword and the ax. But she lifted the furred hem of her robe and rushed on.

Kate realized where the queen was going. The long, low church of St. Peter ad Vincula, which lay just beyond the execution site. The clear, bright moonlight caught and glowed on the windows, and for an instant it looked as if a light flashed from inside the church, but that illusion was quickly lost once more in darkness.

There were no guards there, and Kate wondered if the queen had sent them away. Elizabeth pulled hard on the door, and it creaked open just enough for them to slip inside. The door clanged shut behind them, closing the two of them in stuffy, stone gloom. The wind was abruptly cut off, leaving the scent of dust, wax candles, and old flowers.

Kate looked around at the carved monuments along the walls, the engraved letters only half-illuminated by the light from the tall, wide mullioned windows and the flicker of Elizabeth's lantern.

Elizabeth took Kate's hand and drew her down the aisle. The click of their shoes on the marble floor echoed to the beams of the ceiling. The queen's clasp was tight, her jeweled rings pressing into Kate's fingers, but Kate could say nothing. She felt as if she had dropped into another world altogether, one of echoing silence and shadows.

"He said it was here," Elizabeth murmured as they reached the altar against the far stone wall, below a faded image of Christ in judgment. Like churches all over London in the mere weeks since Elizabeth had become queen, the elaborately carved altar and screen here were replaced by an altar table draped in white cloth. A plain silver cross sat there, gleaming in the darkness.

" 'He,' Your Majesty?" Kate asked, whispering as if she could be overheard. Indeed, she wondered if she still lay in her borrowed cot, trapped in more dreams.

"One of the old guards I found this afternoon," Elizabeth answered. She set the lantern down on the altar steps and her dark eyes scanned along the stone floor beneath her feet. "He has worked at the White Tower for decades, since he was a boy, and he was here when it happened. He told me he saw them carry her to—here."

Kate watched in astonishment as Elizabeth knelt down on the cold floor, her furred skirts fanning around her. She bent her head and her braid of hair slid forward to half conceal her face. The queen pressed her hands flat to the marble.

"My mother is here," she said, so softly Kate could barely hear her.

"Oh, Your Majesty." Kate choked out the words, so overcome by her own shocking, sudden flood of emotion that she knew not what to say or think. She knelt down beside Elizabeth on the cold floor. She should have realized that was why they came here to this silent place in the dark of night, so secretly.

Elizabeth had brought her mother's family back from their exile, raised her Boleyn cousins to places at court, but she never spoke aloud of her mother or the old, scandalous doubts about what happened to Queen Anne over twenty years ago. To the English crowds who cheered her now, she was all old King Henry's spawn, the lion's cub, "mere English." There were those who would still call her mother the Great Whore, still have doubts about the legitimacy of the marriage. But never here.

Elizabeth still held her hands to that thin line in the stone floor that indicated a hollow crypt beneath. "He said they used an elm box once used to bring bowstaves from Ireland. No coffin had been prepared, but she was so slender that her wrapped body fit just so. Her ladies placed her thus, and she was lowered here, beside my uncle, her brother."

"Your Majesty," Kate said carefully, her voice thick with the tears she held back. "It was such a very long time ago." And yet here, in the closeness of that haunted place, it seemed only a moment ago. "Surely the fact that you are here now brings her soul peace."

"Does it? Do I vindicate her now, being here beside her as queen?" Elizabeth suddenly looked up at Kate, her dark Boleyn eyes burning in her white face. "Do you remember *your* mother, Kate?"

Surprised, Kate shook her head. "Nay, not at all. She died the day I was born."

"But surely your father talks about her. It has always been obvious that he misses her."

"Aye, he says he could never have married another after her," Kate answered, thinking of the few tales her father would tell her about Eleanor, the beautiful, gentle, brilliant woman he had loved and lost. "When he talks about her, I do feel like I can see her. Know her."

"And you play her lute. Your father says you are a great musician, as she was. That you look like her."

Kate was surprised that the queen remembered all that. "So he does. I am no beauty as he says she was, and no great musician. But I hope that my love of the song comes from her."

Elizabeth looked back down at the blank floor. "No one ever spoke my mother's name to me, not even Kat. Everything I learned of her I heard in secret whispers. Until I met my Boleyn cousins, Henry and Catherine Carey, and they told me of their own mother's stories."

"They do say Queen Anne was most extraordinary," Kate said carefully.

A proud smile touched the edge of Elizabeth's lips. "She knew many languages, you know, Kate. She went to Austria and France when she was only a girl, and dazzled everyone there. Margaret of Austria herself told my grandfather Thomas Boleyn that she was more beholden to him for sending her such a jewel of a girl than he was to her for accepting her. My mother could dance and ride and sing better and longer than anyone else. . . ." Elizabeth's smile faded. "I am sure she was not frightened here in this place. She had a stout heart, as brave as any man, no matter what anyone says. I know it to be true."

Kate was silent for a long, heavy moment, thoughts of the past and the tangled-up present racing around in her mind. "Do you remember her at all, Your Majesty?"

"Sometimes I think I do. She smelled of roses, and her voice was soft and low, full of laughter." Elizabeth shook her head. "I have a dream that comes to me sometimes at night, where I see her leaning over my bed. There are tears in her eyes, and she sings a French song to me as she touches my hair and tells me not to be afraid. Perhaps it is a memory. Or perhaps it is only a dream."

"I wish I had such a vision of my own mother."

"Perhaps our mothers knew each other!" Elizabeth said with the sudden sunburst of another smile. "Perhaps they played music together. Did your parents not meet at court?"

Kate realized that, for all her father's tales of her mother, she knew little of their courtship. Little of where her mother came from before she was Mistress Haywood. "I believe so."

"Then I am sure they met. And that they see us here now, thinking of them." Elizabeth was silent for a moment longer, looking down at the floor. Finally she smoothed one last touch over it and pushed herself to her feet. "Come, Kate, I have kept you from your bed too long. It will soon be dawn, and there is much to be done."

"Aye, Your Majesty." Kate hurried after the queen as they slipped out of the silent church and back into the cold night. The sky was indeed growing lighter, the palest of pearl grays at the edges, casting some of the mysteries of the Tower back into their hidden corners for one more day.

Elizabeth was walking briskly back toward the Queen's House, without a backward glance at the haunted church.

But Kate couldn't help the feeling that something had changed, something very deep and strange. Emotions she had never realized she even possessed stirred inside of her, feelings of loss and memory.

She parted with Elizabeth on the stairs, the queen to go on up to her grand chamber, where she would slip past Mistress Ashley and into her curtained bed, and Kate back to the crowded ladies' dormitory.

Shivering, Kate took off her shoes and slipped back between the chilly bedclothes next to Mary Everley. Everyone still snored and stirred in their dreams, buried deep in the night as if nothing at all had changed.

But Kate knew she could never sleep again that night.

Mary suddenly rolled over and seized Kate's hand. Startled, Kate tensed. But when Mary laughed, Kate was glad her friend was awake too, that she didn't have to be alone in that quietest part of the night.

"Where did you go off to so secretly, Kate?" Mary whispered.

"To the jakes, of course," Kate whispered back.

"Indeed? But there is a chamber pot right under our bed. And you were gone a passing long time." Mary's fingers tightened excitedly on Kate's hand. "Are you sure you were not meeting someone? You can tell me."

Kate laughed. "Who would I be meeting?" She could never tell Mary, or anyone, what had actually happened that night. None would believe her anyway. She could scarcely believe it herself.

"A handsome suitor, of course."

"When would I have time to meet a suitor, handsome or otherwise? We have had only a few weeks to prepare for the coronation, and I have been working every waking moment. Unless you think I have a passion for Master Cawarden?"

Cawarden was the old Master of the Revels, a little, bandy-legged, paunchy man with a short temper who possessed an equally moody wife.

"Nay, not him," Mary scoffed. "But I am sure you must have had a sweeting in Hertfordshire that you left behind. Mayhap you have found him again here in London."

Kate bit her lip as she remembered that glimpse she had on the barge. Of a tall man in a lawyer's black robe, with dark hair and strong shoulders. But she was sure now she had just imagined it was Anthony.

"Nay, there was no one," Kate said. "It was most quiet at Hatfield. Queen Mary would allow few visitors."

"There are many men Queen Mary would not have known. Men who aren't courtiers," Mary said.

Something in her musing tone caught Kate's attention. "Do *you* have a sweetheart, Mary?"

For a long moment, Mary was silent, her face turned away. But then she laughed. "I shall not settle yet for one where there are so many to fancy at court. Tell me, Kate. Which do you think the handsomer? Robert Dudley or Lord Hertford? I daresay the queen would say Sir Robert, for all that he has a sickly wife buried in the country somewhere. But I hear tell Lady Catherine Grey would declare for the other. . . ."

CHAPTER 3

"**A** maid of honor! When we were Ladies of the Bed-chamber to Queen Mary. How is such a humiliation to be borne?" Lady Catherine Grey muttered as she paced before the window of their small sitting room in the Tower. The winter sun was creeping over the high stone walls as the long night ended, and attendants hurried along the gravel walkways to prepare for the ceremony appointing new Knights of the Bath in the White Tower.

But no Greys were to be appointed that day, and Catherine and her mother and sister had been sent word that their attendance was not needed on the queen that day, either.

"As all such things are borne, my dearest," Lady Frances Grey, Dowager Duchess of Suffolk, said as she carefully lowered herself into her cushioned chair. Her handsome young husband, Adrian Stokes, offered her a plate of sweetmeats, but she waved it away. As her illness advanced, her appetite receded. "With a smile and silence."

"How can we be silent!" Catherine cried. "We are of royal blood, and she treats us as mere servants. Queen Mary made us Ladies of the Bedchamber. She gave you the precedence you were due at court, even above Princess Elizabeth. . . ."

"And perhaps we pay for that now that she is *Queen*

Elizabeth." Frances sighed and watched Catherine's pacing with her tired, faded blue eyes. "Queen Mary was of a rare merciful temper. After your father's foolishness in rebelling against her not once but twice, we were fortunate not to be tossed in a dungeon."

"If even Queen Mary could give us our due, why must this new queen cast us down? We are of legitimate Tudor blood. She is a mere Boleyn bast—"

"Catherine!" Frances snapped. In a rare burst of her old fiery temper, she slammed her fist down on the table, making the plates rattle. Adrian hurried to take her hand as her labored breath wheezed in her throat. "You must have a care or you will land us all in trouble—again. And I have not the strength to drag us out as I once did."

Something in her mother's desperate tone pierced through Catherine's anger, and she spun around to face the table. Frances had indeed grown much thinner in the last few months, her fine gowns hanging on her tall frame, her heart-shaped face sharp-boned and gray-white. Her once-abundant golden hair was thin and brittle, streaked with silver.

Knowing that her daughters were honored, given their due as great-granddaughters of King Henry VII, would surely have eased her, Catherine thought. But Elizabeth made it heartily clear that she disliked the Grey women, Catherine in particular, and that the rightful favor they were shown by Queen Mary was a thing of the past. This demotion to mere maid of honor was only the latest humiliation, and Catherine was sure it would not be the last.

"I am sorry, Mother," Catherine said softly. She hurried over to kneel beside Frances and took her mother's hand in her own, summoning the copious charm she was known for. Frances's fingers were cold, her jeweled rings loose. "You are ill today, I shouldn't give you more worries than you already have. It is just that . . ."

"That injustices stir your Tudor temper," Frances said with a hoarse laugh. She gently patted Catherine's cheek. "It was thus with your grandmother when she saw her brother King Henry dishonor his throne by chasing after Anne Boleyn. And then with me, too, when I was young and stouthearted."

"And still now at times, my love," Adrian said, gesturing at the tumbled plates.

Frances gave him a fond smile. "And sometimes now. We are Tudors, my dearest Catherine, and our fires will never go out entirely. But you must tread most carefully. Being so near to the throne can be a curse as well as a blessing. Remember your poor sister, your father."

"Jane. Yes," Catherine sighed. Jane, who had been a queen for little more than a sennight. But Jane had no "Tudor fire." Jane did as she was told, and then scurried back to her books. Jane would not have fought for rights, nor for true love. Not as Catherine would.

"My dearest," Frances said, drawing Catherine up to sit beside her. "You are my beautiful angel. But I fear I have given you too much of my own pride. You must learn to govern your feelings. Elizabeth is queen now, and warring with her will avail you nothing."

Aye, and that was the gall of it all! That a bastard like Elizabeth should be raised to the throne, while Catherine had naught. "If she would name you her heir, as she should by rights, I would not war with her."

"I married beneath me," Frances said with another smile at her young husband, who had once been her Master of the Horse. A love match it might have been, but a brilliant one, too, for it removed Frances and her family to a place of safety after her husband's rebellion and traitor's death. "I can be no royal heir."

"Then it should be me," Catherine insisted. "We are her nearest family, but for Mary of Scotland, and *she* can never be heir here, not now that she is dauphine of France." Indeed Queen Mary Tudor had once seemed near to naming Catherine as her heir. If only Mary had lived longer . . .

"Hush," Frances hissed. She pinched Catherine's arm hard with a flash of that old temper. "There are eyes and ears everywhere. You must be careful."

Catherine slumped back in her chair, feeling as sullen and resentful as she had when denied a sweet as a child. But this was a thousand times worse, a thousand times more unjust. "I only speak the truth, Mother, and you know it is so. If I have no position at court, what else is there for me?"

"I should have seen to your marriage long ago, after Pembroke left and annulled your marriage," Frances said. "Queen Mary would have given permission readily enough, if a suitable gentleman had been found. She may have even let you remarry Pembroke! They say Elizabeth does not wish her ladies to wed."

"I am not truly one of her ladies, though, am I?" Catherine said. She snatched up a linen napkin, twisting the fine fabric between her fingers. But the mention of marriage was like a touch of fire under the ice of her discontent. Not marriage to that milksop Pembroke, though. He hadn't been able to consummate things when he had the chance.

She thought instead of sweet, beautiful Edward Seymour, Earl of Hertford, her darling Ned. Those golden days at his estate at Hanworth, the touch of his hand, his secret kisses . . .

Catherine sighed to remember it all, and the too-quick glimpses she'd had of him at court over Christmas. They hadn't been able to dance together, not yet. Her mother was right. Eyes were always watching.

But, aye. Marriage, the right marriage, could be a fine thing indeed. A step toward her rightful place.

There was a knock at the chamber door, and Catherine tossed away the napkin as a page stepped inside with a bow. "The Spanish ambassador has arrived, my lady."

"Ah, the Count de Feria," Frances said with a smile. "Show him in at once."

"Feria?" Catherine said with a spark of interest. In a new court that seemed to turn against her family, only King Philip's ambassador gave them their due. Feria visited often, bringing news of Spain, gossip about courtiers, and small gifts. And he was handsome and charming, all that a royal emissary should be.

"My fairest duchess! And Lady Catherine," the count said as he swept into the room in a swirl of pearl-embroidered black velvet cloak and bowed over their hands. "I trust you are well today? My wife hopes that her jars of comfits have brought you some respite from the chill."

"The countess is ever kind," Frances answered. Lady Jane Dormer, now the Countess de Feria, was still their staunchest friend from Queen Mary's old court. "We fare well enough. Better for your company today."

"I also bear greetings from my master King Philip," Feria said, producing a letter closed with the royal Spanish seal. "He is most anxious to hear of your health after his dear wife Queen Mary's death."

"We are most gratified by the king's attentions," Frances said as Catherine hurried to find a cushioned chair and goblet of wine for the count. "It was fair days indeed when he was among us."

"His Majesty will always be most careful of your futures,

senora la duchess," the count said, taking the goblet from Catherine with a smile. "He always remembers his friends."

"We have received many moving messages of late," Frances said. Catherine carefully studied her mother's smile, and saw the echo there of the old, courtly, dashing Frances, before misfortune and ill health overtook her. The beautiful Frances Grey, who could save her family even from the consequences of treason merely with her charm. "Just yesterday we had a letter from King Henri in Paris."

"King Henri?" Feria's dark eyes flashed, but his smile never faltered. "Surely you must know my master's friendship will always surpass that of the French king. Henri will look to the interests of his own daughter-in-law Mary of Scotland above all."

Frances sighed. "My poor girls. I fear they shall be alone and abandoned in the world very soon. Quite forgotten." The bells of the Tower rang outside their window, calling for the beginning of the day's ceremonies. "Their rightful place but a memory."

"My master will never abandon them, senora," Feria said solemnly, his gloved hand over his heart. "As you will see if you read his letter. He has a proposition for you, and for the beautiful Lady Catherine. If you would be willing to hear it."

Catherine's gaze met her mother's wary one, her heart suddenly lurching with excitement. Surely it was as she had hoped! King Philip was so much more powerful than an upstart like Elizabeth could ever be. Surely if he stood as their friend . . .

Anything could be possible. Even a marriage grander than that to any earl.

"We are always happy to talk to our *true* friends, my dearest count," Frances said carefully. "Do have some more wine while I read the king's letter. . . ."

CHAPTER 4

Kate tiptoed to the back of the crowd gathered in the lord lieutenant's hall, freed of her musical duties for the night. The queen didn't dance that evening, but instead chose to watch a play before she retired to her bed for one last night in the Tower. Tomorrow she would process through London to her palace at Westminster, close to the Abbey, where she would stay for a few days after the coronation.

After weeks of dancing and dining until the small hours, tonight was quieter. Elizabeth sat in her high-backed, velvet-cushioned chair set on a small dais where she had a good view of the stage. The tale appeared to be a pastoral romance, Kate thought as she studied the painted scenery of trees and green, summery grass. A story of a lost princess, disguised as a shepherdess, courted by two lovers, one truehearted and one not.

Elizabeth's attention seldom wavered from the players. Her usual lightning energy was stilled for the moment. Her jeweled hands rested on the lap of her green satin gown, and she only occasionally reached out to take a sweetmeat proffered by Mistress Ashley.

Behind her sat her chief counselors, Sir William Cecil in his usual solemn dark robes, a frown creasing his brow as he studied Robert Dudley a few seats away, just to the

right of the queen. There was nothing at all solemn about
Sir Robert in his purple and green doublet sewn with
pearls. He murmured and laughed with his friends, all of
them equally richly clad, all of them merry and entirely
at their wine-soaked ease, as if all the pageantry was only
for their amusement.

One would never know Sir Robert was in charge of
moving hundreds of people, their horses and carriages,
through the city tomorrow. He leaned forward with an
easy, careless grace to offer Elizabeth a goblet of wine.
She smiled down at him from her higher chair as she
took it, their fingers brushing and lingering.

Sir William's scowl deepened and Mistress Ashley
plucked at Elizabeth's diamond-strewn sleeve to turn
the queen's attention back to the stage. Surely if Sir Robert weren't already married to his country-mouse wife,
Cecil would truly have something to worry about. Kate
knew it was said he favored a foreign royal marriage,
perhaps to an Austrian archduke.

Kate went up on tiptoe to see above the heads of the
people seated in front of her on their rows of benches.
Everyone had their places in strictest order of precedence, the grandest of the great families, such as the Howards, the Sheffields, and the Vavasours, and the queen's
Boleyn cousins Lord Hunsdon and his sister Catherine
Carey and their many children at the front, a sea of shining silks and velvets. The lower families stood along the
tapestried walls, shifting on their heeled shoes amid the
soft rustles of fine fabrics.

The young maids of honor were arrayed on cushions
in front of the queen's dais, their silver skirts spread
around them. Kate glimpsed Lady Catherine Grey there,
her golden hair twined with pearls, but her mother, Lady
Frances, was nowhere to be seen. It was said her health

was failing, and the queen seemed to feel no pangs in excusing her presence. Lady Catherine fidgeted with a ribbon on her sleeve, her gaze restlessly scanning the crowd much as Kate's did.

But where Kate studied the gathering to see what she could read in unguarded moments, Lady Catherine seemed to seek one face in particular. And when she didn't find it, a pout touched her rosebud mouth and she spun back to face the stage.

Lady Catherine, in her turn, was being watched. Kate saw the Spanish ambassador, the unfailingly correct Count de Feria, sitting with his delegation at the far side of the room. Kate well remembered him from their dinner at Brocket Hall months ago, when Elizabeth was not yet queen and her brother-in-law, King Philip, wanted to secure her future friendship. Feria had lived a life of diplomacy for many years, serving his king in England and the Low Countries, his charming, pleasant smile never wavering, no matter what his thoughts might be.

It was said King Philip himself intended to propose to Elizabeth soon, and that was why Feria lingered in England. But right now he did not watch the queen, instead eyeing Lady Catherine. For the merest instant, his smile flickered and his dark eyes narrowed in calculation. The unguarded second was quickly gone. He smiled again, and whispered a word to one of his companions. The rest of the Spanish, who still wore deepest black mourning for Queen Mary, did not seem to be enjoying the romantic play at all.

Unlike their French counterparts across the room. It was said that King Henri, in the privacy of his own court in Paris, declared Elizabeth to be a bastard pretender, and his own daughter-in-law, Mary of Scotland, was the true Queen of England. But his ambassador, Monsieur de Castelnau, had been full of compliments and declarations of affection for Elizabeth from Mary, and he and his fellows seemed to enjoy themselves wherever they went—dancing, hunting, drinking freely of the queen's wine, spreading lavish gifts in every direction.

The French also knew a great deal about music, which Kate appreciated. But their merriment was no more trustworthy than the Spanish solemnity, and they sought allies only for their own master's benefit.

Kate's gaze darted around the crowd as she wondered who chose alliances where. The Duke of Norfolk, the queen's cousin and the highest noble in the land, the leader of the Howard family, sat near the queen with his pretty young wife, Margaret Audley, who was Lady Catherine Grey's friend. The duke glared at Robert Dudley, whom everyone knew the old families considered the merest upstart, but the duchess seemed to be enjoying herself in her new high position.

Kate tried to find Mary Everley, yet she could catch no glimpse of her friend. Mary had vanished after dinner and not yet reappeared. Her father and brother sat near the French ambassador, with Lady Frances Grey's young husband, Adrian Stokes. Kate remembered Mary mentioned her family had once been neighbors of the Greys, and friends with the Seymours. Once the Seymours had been the most powerful family in England, the Duke of Somerset Lord Protector to his nephew King Edward VI, and Lord Thomas married to Dowager Queen Catherine Parr. Then they lost it all in scandal and executions for treason. Now they were trying to rise again with the Protector's son Edward, Lord Hertford.

Kate turned her attention to the stage, where the shepherdess princess was dancing with one of her suitors. Kate hadn't looked too closely at the players yet, being too intent on the audience, but one of them caught her study. He looked rather familiar, the princess's suitor, even beneath his wig and stage paint, the fluttering ribbons of his doublet.

Kate strained on her toes to see closer. Could it be one of Rob Cartman's players, who had come to Hatfield so fatefully before Elizabeth became queen? Her breath caught as she realized that the shepherd was indeed one of Rob's players, and she glanced around quickly seeking a glimpse of Rob himself, his blond hair or teasing smile. He and his players had gone away after his uncle's death and Elizabeth's accession, and she'd heard naught from him since. If he was here, if his troupe had been commissioned to play before the queen . . .

Surely he must be faring well.

Keeping to the edges of the hall, behind the thick of the crowd, Kate made her way closer to the stage. As the princess and her suitor clasped hands, she saw they were indeed actors in Rob's troupe, the former Lord Ambrose's Men. Yet she didn't see Rob, even when more of the players twirled onstage to join the dance.

The actor-princess caught sight of her as she carefully lifted her hand, and his eyes widened. He gave her a quick nod before he was spun away.

Once the scene changed and a painted castle was rolled onstage, Kate only had to wait for a few more minutes. A small boy, one of the actors playing a minor role, slipped out from behind the stage and rushed to her side to tug at her skirt.

Kate knelt down to hear his whisper. "Be you Mistress Haywood?"

"I am."

"Harry said to tell you we are most glad to see you here, as Rob begged him to get you a message if he could," the boy said, mentioning one of the actors of Lord Ambrose's Men that Kate remembered from Hatfield.

Rob had wanted to talk to her? Then where was he? Kate had the sinking feeling that the handsome actor just might be in some trouble again. She looked to the stage, where Harry, an attractive youth in his lady's costume, nodded to her. "What sort of message? Where is Master Cartman?"

"He wants to see you. Harry says he needs your help. He's at the sign of the Cardinal's Hat in Southwark, and he dares not leave to come here."

"Southwark?" That did not sound like good news at all, if Rob felt he couldn't leave the lawless district of theaters and brothels beyond the city gates. She herself never ventured there. She almost sighed at the unfortunate knowledge that her instincts had been right. Rob Cartman was too handsome and too impulsive for his own good, or the good of any lady's heart.

But if he was indeed in bad trouble, she knew she had to try to help him. He had saved her life once, carrying her to Hatfield House when she was shot with an arrow and almost bled to death.

"What has happened?" she asked.

The boy shrugged. "Harry says either he or I can take you there, mistress, if you meet us later by the Cradle Tower gate. He'll tell you all then."

Kate glanced over the boy's head to meet Harry's stare. Harry was truly a handsome young lad, still pretty enough to play a princess, with a guileless smile. But in that one instant she saw the flash of stark panic in his eyes. She realized Rob must truly be in trouble.

The brave, reckless, dashing fool.

Kate nodded, and Harry nodded back before he danced away.

"Tell him I will meet him there," she said. As the boy dashed off, she straightened and turned to study the queen.

Elizabeth was whispering something in Robert Dudley's ear as he leaned closer to her. The two of them laughed together, and Mistress Ashley tugged at Elizabeth's sleeve again as if to draw her away.

Kate knew she wouldn't be needed again that night. The queen would be surrounded by fussing attendants at every moment. Kate slipped out of a side door into the night to make her way back to the ladies' lodgings. She had preparations to make before the play was over.

The evening was quiet, for everyone was gathered for the play. Only a few guards made their rounds, their boots scuffing on the gravel walkways, their breath silvery on the cold air. Their voices as they talked together were low and muffled, interrupted only by an occasional, heart-startling shriek from one of the Tower's ravens.

They paid Kate no mind as she rushed past them. She went up the steep stone steps to the parapet that wound its way around the Tower walls. From there she could see the river, a half-frozen gray ribbon lined with bobbing lanterns from the wherrymen's boats. Beyond the strange, static quiet of the fortress, the city was still alive as people already sought out vantage points to watch the queen's procession. Kate could hear the pulsing echo of their mingled voices.

And somewhere out there, on the other side of the river, was Rob Cartman. In trouble. And she couldn't just leave him to it.

Kate hurried around a corner on the walkway, and her feet suddenly scudded to a stop, startled to find she wasn't quite all alone after all. A couple stood in the thick shadows against the dark stone wall, entwined in each other's arms, oblivious to everyone else.

The moonlight caught on Mary Everley's red hair, bound with a distinctive gold laurel-leaf bandeau Kate had helped her fasten before the banquet. Mary clung to the man as they kissed frantically, but he wore plain dark clothes and his face was hidden by his cap. He glanced up for an instant, giving Kate a glimpse of strange, almost golden brown eyes before he kissed Mary again.

"Walter," Mary whispered, the one word carried lightly on the wind.

Kate backed away and hurried in the opposite direction before they could see her. If Mary was involved in a secret romance with no desire to confide in Kate about it, then Kate had no desire to interfere. Surely there was trouble enough to be had at court without running at it headlong.

She only hoped that Mary knew what she was about, and that none of that trouble would attach to her now. . . .

CHAPTER 5

"This way," the boy called as he led Kate across London Bridge. Harry had not been able to escape the queen's revels and had sent the messenger lad in his place to meet her. The boy moved in and out of the knots of people, bobbing and weaving so that she could hardly see his head.

She hurried to keep up with him, moving faster in her borrowed doublet and breeches than she ever could in skirts. She'd learned after last year's adventures at Leighton Abbey that a male disguise could help her blend in almost anywhere, and she was glad she remembered to pack the boy's clothes for their London journey.

She tugged her cap lower over her forehead and moved as fast as she could with people pressed all around. Even so late at night, the bridge pulsed with life. The excitement over the new queen's coronation crackled in the air, and no one seemed to want to miss a moment of it in sleep. Most of the shops on either side of the bridge were open, their front windows thrown ajar to display ribbons, books, and trinkets, all sparkling in the lantern light.

The air smelled of sweet ginger cakes and sugared almonds, spiced apple cider dipped out of deep barrels, the richness of roasting meats, and the tang of woodsmoke curling into the chilly wind. It almost covered the sour scent from the river swirling below, the pong of chamber pots tossed from the upper windows into the water.

Just like laughter and music covered any quarrels or shouts. This wasn't a time for real life, for real worries or the everyday struggles of illness, hunger, and fear. This was a night for pleasure, for forgetting, and every face around Kate shone with smiles. Smiles—and probably wine flowing from the public fountains.

Ordinarily, Kate would have highly enjoyed being among them, singing with them, enjoying a mug of cider. But Rob was waiting out there, in some sort of trouble, and that was all she could think of.

"Come on!" the boy called, his grubby hand reaching up to wave at her through the crowd.

A cup-shot group stumbled in front of her, leaning heavily against one another as they laughed. One of them fell into an icy puddle, making his friends laugh even more uproariously. Kate dodged around them, even as they called out to her.

One of them reached for her sleeve, but she spun away.

"Come have a drink with us, friend," the man called, his voice full of drunken mirth. "'Tis a night to meet new people, is it not?"

Kate shook her head. She had no time to be waylaid by affable drunkards, who were no doubt thinking of some scheme to make mock of someone who appeared to be a young country lad. She knew to avoid conycatchers. But something about his voice seemed familiar, and she glanced back at him over her shoulder as she hurried away.

A beam of torchlight fell over his face, and Kate saw it was Mary Everley's cousin, Richard St. Long. His dark, tawny-streaked hair tumbled in tangled waves over his brow, and there was a smudge of mud on his lean, clean-shaven face, setting off his pale blue-gray eyes. His fine doublet was unfastened to show a dirt-smeared linen shirt, and he had a pottery jug in his hand.

She remembered he was not at the play with Mary's father and brother, and now she knew why. He had more amusing things to do.

She quickly scanned the faces of his companions, trying to see if she knew them, but most of them were unfamiliar. There were so many new and old families flooding the court after years in exile, scrambling for favor. So many fresh, eager faces. But she did recognize Edward Seymour, the young Lord Hertford, as Master St. Long pulled him up out of the puddle. His fine doublet and pretty face were dirtied, but he only laughed.

"Come on!" the boy shouted impatiently, and Kate rushed on, leaving the drunken courtiers behind.

They passed under the tall arch of the bridge. The severed heads of traitors had been removed from the spikes high overhead, and only living eyes were there to watch them. But no one seemed to care what they did; everyone was too intent on seeking their own illicit joys in Southwark.

For a while they followed the path along the river, and Kate could see the stone hulk of the Tower across the water, lit only by rows of torches on the walls. Then the boy grabbed her hand and dragged her down a narrow walkway between two close-pressed buildings by the water stairs. They emerged into the teeming nighttime swirl of Southwark itself.

The laughter here was even louder than on the bridge, punctuated with shrieks and shrill cries. Two women with red and white painted faces and frizzed hair, their stained yellow satin gowns drooping from their shoulders, stumbled past with a stout old man between them. From behind the walls of a bear pit were enraged roars

and barks, shouted curses. Two men tumbled out of a
tavern door and fell into the muck of the lane, seemingly
intent on strangling each other.

It was only across the river from where the queen sat
watching her play, but Kate felt as if a whirlwind had
swept her up and dropped her into a different world altogether.

She stepped over a squawking chicken that strayed
from the tavern yard, evaded a grasping old woman in
tattered gray homespun, and ran after the boy.

He took her to the end of Carter Lane, where a cluster
of leaning buildings looked out over a small strip of garden. It was slightly quieter there, away from the bear pit.
These were a bit above the lower grade of bawdy house,
places with window glass and the midden heaps tucked
behind, out of sight if not out of smell. Once the pits were
closed, it would be louder there, but for the moment only
two girls peered down from one of the open windows,
their faces ghostly white in the night.

The boy led Kate to the farthest building, a half-timbered structure with a steep tiled roof and smoke twining out of the chimneys. A sign painted with the distinctly
phallic image of a red cardinal's hat swung from above
the street door. It was closed, and a guard stood before
it with his ham-sized arms crossed over his leather jerkin. He was quite the most gigantic person Kate had
ever seen, with a bald, shaved head and blank eyes.

But the fearsome giant let the boy run past him and
pull open the door. He drew Kate after him into a long,
empty corridor and the door clanged shut behind them.

The corridor was dim and quiet, and for an instant
Kate felt the icy touch of doubt. Why would Rob send
for *her* now, when they hadn't seen each other in many
weeks? Why would he bring her to such a place? She had

been too trusting of people she considered friends before, and it nearly got her killed. She had vowed to be done with that piercing curiosity.

But she had already come too far to go back now. She slid her right hand over her left wrist, feeling the cold metal weight of the hilt of the dagger strapped under her doublet sleeve.

In between hours of practicing music, she had persuaded one of the queen's sergeants at arms to teach her some swordplay. She wasn't exactly ready for the queen's army, but at least she didn't feel entirely helpless.

She was glad of its hard touch on her skin as she followed the boy up a steep flight of stairs. At the landing was an open door, spilling out light and laughter, the smell of wine and heady jasmine perfume, but they kept going up the steps until they came to another long corridor at the top.

The doors there were all closed, emitting only faint sounds of giggles, grunts, and the rustle of straw mattresses. The boy knocked at the last door, which was immediately flung open.

A woman stood there, tall but delicate-boned in a fine but faded bright green gown with no sleeves or partlet. Her hair, an improbable deep red color, fell down her back, and she stared out at them with brown eyes heavily rimmed in kohl.

"You took your time, didn't you?" she said, reaching out to cuff the boy across his ear. "Where's Harry?"

The boy ducked away. "Couldn't come, could he? Not when he was doing a play for Her bleeding Majesty. He told me to bring *her* instead."

"Her?" The woman looked past him, her eyes narrowing when she saw Kate standing there. "Don't look like no woman to me."

At least her disguise was working, Kate thought with a faintly hysterical desire to laugh. "I'm Kate," she said softly. "Where is Rob?"

A dour smile touched the woman's painted mouth. "Ah, so *you're* Kate. Rob said you would help if you could. I said he was daft, no court lady would come here to the Cardinal's Hat."

"I'm not a court lady," Kate answered.

The woman's gaze flickered over Kate's doublet and hose, her scuffed borrowed boots. "So I see. You'd best come in, then."

The boy ran off, disappearing back down the stairs, and Kate followed the woman through the door.

"I'm Bess," she said, lighting a candle on the table to add to the crackling flames in the fireplace. As the light filled the space, Kate saw it was a small chamber, nearly entirely occupied by a washstand, a stool, and a narrow bed drawn around with faded hangings. Shutters were pulled tight over the one window, and the air was warm and stuffy, close with the smells of smoke, unwashed garments, and Bess's rosewater perfume.

And next to the fire huddled Rob Cartman. He turned to watch as Kate came into the room, blinking against the light that washed over him.

But he wasn't quite the man she remembered from Hatfield, the dashing, golden-bright player with his handsome face and nimble acrobatics who could charm his way into any house. The man who had caught her up in his strong arms when the arrow pierced her body on that country road.

His bright hair was tangled and limply matted, his jaw covered with stubble, and his eyes were rimmed in purple as if he had not slept in days. His shirt was unlaced and his boots muddy.

Kate glimpsed a blanket on the rush-strewn floor behind him, as if someone had wrapped it around him and he shrugged it away. An untouched plate of bread and cheese sat nearby.

"Bodkins, Rob, but what has happened?" Kate gasped.

Bess rushed over to him in a flurry of mended green silk skirts and knelt beside him to reach for the blanket. "He never did do it!"

A faint glimmer of the old Rob kindled in his blue eyes and he pushed himself to his feet. "You did come, then, Kate."

"Of course I did," Kate answered, bewildered at the change in him and wondering what on earth was going on. "When the boy said you needed my help—well, you helped me once, didn't you? I won't turn away a friend."

He smiled again, a real grin like the ones she remembered. "Even when that friend asks you to come to the stews?"

"I didn't know that was where you were when I left the Tower," Kate said truthfully. "But now that I'm here, you had best tell me what has happened. Why are you hiding here instead of performing with your troupe for the queen?"

Before Rob could answer, Bess cried, "Because he daren't show his face until they find who really did it! He'd be hanged for sure. He said you solved some murder at Hatfield House last year, that you would surely know what to do. How to find who did this."

Hanged? Kate was even more confused, and a touch frightened. "Did what?"

Rob shook his head ruefully. "Killed my mistress, of course. Her name was Nell; she was Bess's sister. And I found her right in the room next door yesterday, after the queen's barge passed by. . . ."

CHAPTER 6

"When was the last time you saw Nell?" Kate asked once Rob had told her some of his tale. Bess had opened the window to let in the fresh, cold air, and had fetched some ale to make the cramped room more comfortable.

But most of the time the girl hovered close to Rob, watching him carefully.

"'Twas more than a fortnight ago," Rob answered. He had combed his hair and splashed his face with cold water, and was now looking more like the man she remembered. "We've been busy ever since we heard from the Master of the Revels that the queen wanted us to play for her at the Tower. I only had the chance to come yesterday."

"And you found her dead," Kate murmured, remembering his earlier words. He'd run up the outside stairs to her room, laden with gifts, to find his mistress sprawled dead on the floor.

"What happened to her body?" Kate asked, her mind racing with questions. Doubts.

"I got Mad Henry, the guard at the door, to carry her away," Bess said. "The landlady, Mistress Celine, don't want no trouble, does she? And no one would ask questions about someone like Nell. They would just haul one of us away and say we did it."

There was a hard kernel of deep bitterness in Bess's voice, very different from the softness in her eyes when she looked at Rob.

"We worked here together, Nell and me," Bess added, "but I was off with a friend that day. Didn't know what happened till it was too late."

"And you found Rob here with her?"

"Nay, I hid when I heard someone coming up the stairs," Bess said. "I didn't know who it was, could've been the killer coming back for more. Then I heard Robbie here cry out. . . ."

Rob's face went white under the sun brown of his skin, and his long, elegant actor's fingers tightened into fists. "If the foul murderer had been here when I found poor Nell, I vow I would have torn him from limb to limb."

Kate studied him carefully. She knew he was an actor, and a good one, practicing all his life to embody rage, pain, love, joy. But she believed him now, that he was caught in anger and grief. That whatever else he might be, a shepherd or a prince, he was no killer of women. He had proved himself to her at Hatfield.

"Then I am glad you were not here," Kate said gently. "Or you might be dead, too."

For one flickering moment, some of Bess's fierceness faded. She laid her hand gently on Rob's trembling shoulder. "'Tis exactly what I said. Poor Nell, she was torn apart. Her head was that much crushed. Whoever did it was an animal, worse than those dogs at a bear pit."

Kate still watched Rob, the distance in his eyes. "But you cared for her, Rob?"

He shrugged, but Kate could see the stark grief in the harsh lines of his face. "She was a merry girl, always full of good words and kind deeds."

"Aye, Nell never met a stranger," Bess said. "She always wanted to talk to people, hear about their doings. That's why she went off to see the queen yesterday when it was her day off. She was always going on about our grandmother's tale of Queen Anne's coronation."

Kate's mind turned over Bess's words. "So she had no jealous lovers? Mayhap some angry wife who followed her husband here and caught them together?"

Bess shrugged. "There were jealous ones, true enough, but none who ever attacked Nell. She was too good at jollying anyone out of a temper. And she never gave anyone the French pox or anything of the like. And wives . . ."

Rob gave a wry laugh. "You're probably the first lady to ever come to the Cardinal's Hat, Kate."

"Fine ladies don't want to know their menfolk come here to get what they can't in their grand chambers in the Strand," Bess scoffed.

"Well, I am not a fine lady," Kate said. "I'm only a musician."

"A woman who works for the queen's court," Rob said. He reached for Kate's hand and held it tightly between both of his, and Kate understood Bess's tender looks for him. "That is why I need your help. You can move about in court easily, find him if he's some fine courtier."

"I do owe you much, Rob, for what happened at Hatfield," she said. "But how can I help you?"

Rob's face hardened. "I wasn't here to save Nell, but I must do what I can for her now. As you said, I—I cared for her. I would find who did this. But I must beg for your help, Kate."

Surprised by his words, Kate slid her hands from his and sat back on her stool. "*My* help?"

"I told him not to be a fool," Bess snapped. "If he

starts asking questions around, waving his dagger about, they'll say he did it for sure. Everyone in Southwark knew he was one of Nell's regulars."

"I'm not such a cabbagehead as all that, Bess, my beauty," Rob said with a flicker of a smile. "I know where I can go freely and where I can't. And I cannot go to the queen's court."

"But I can," Kate said quietly. She studied the two of them in the firelight, Rob looking sad and desperate, Bess doubtful and fierce. She knew she should be sensible and stay far away from such matters. Court was full of dangers and pitfalls aplenty without the muck of Southwark, the blood of a Winchester goose. She had much work to do, a place to establish for herself and her father in the new royal court. And yet . . .

Yet had Nell not been a person, too? A woman of "merry" nature, an enemy to none, if what her sister said was true. And still she had been horribly murdered. And Rob, who had once proved himself to be Kate's own friend, had cared about Nell. Cared enough to risk his neck to find her murderer. Even if the girl had secrets, she deserved for the truth to be known.

And the curiosity that had nearly been Kate's downfall—that need to discover and see and know—was taking hold of her again. Nell surely deserved justice in this new, bright England that Queen Elizabeth was building. If Kate could help with that, even in a small way . . .

"Tell me more about Nell," Kate said. "Who were her friends? Which gentlemen from court visited her the most often? What did she look like?"

Rob smiled in a sudden burst of relief. "Thank you, Kate. You are a true friend."

"Do not thank me yet," Kate warned. "I might be able

to discover nothing at all. It's not easy to get people such as the queen's courtiers to give up secrets. They are too good at being guarded."

"At least you will try," Bess said grudgingly. "Most would not, not for the likes of us. But I can tell you whatever I've learned of Nell's gentlemen. Some of them we shared. And as for how she looked . . ."

"She looked like Bess here," Rob said. "Red hair and snow-white skin, with a delicate neck like a swan and a pointed chin like a kitten."

"Like the bleedin' queen, we are," Bess said with a humorless laugh. She took a tiny object from the purse at her belt and tossed it into the air before catching it. "Should be very fashionable now to have hair like this."

"You are called, er, Henry, are you not?" Kate asked the bald giant of a man who guarded the door of the Cardinal's Hat. She was waiting for the errand boy to escort her back to the Tower, and in the meantime had decided to see what she could find out from the house's residents about Nell.

The bawds were forthcoming enough, once Bess told them Kate was a friend, but were able to tell her little. Most of them had been gone the day of the procession, wanting to see the queen themselves and drum up a little business from the crowds. They hadn't seen anything out of the ordinary, and when asked about Nell's regular visitors, their comments became mostly laughing comparisons of the gentlemen's—assets.

And none of them had red hair like Nell and Bess, though they admitted some men did prefer such a hair color.

This was probably not useful, Kate thought wryly, especially the information about various men's codpieces.

Unless she asked the men of the court to drop their breeches for comparisons. But she did make some interesting notes for future reference.

Henry, though, might be different. Bess said he was almost always at his post, and surely saw everything. She had to swallow a nervous knot in her throat at the sheer size of the man, and the number of his fearsome scars, to approach him.

"I'm called Mad Henry," he said shortly.

"Er—aye. Of course," Kate answered. "Bess said you might be of some very valuable assistance."

Mad Henry scowled doubtfully as he stared down at her from his great height. "Assistance with what?"

"Finding who did this to Nell."

A spasm of emotion passed over his face, gone as quickly as a flash of sun on a winter's day, but it was enough to show that he was not quite as stolidly unemotional as he wanted to appear. "Poor Nellie. Bess thinks you can help?"

"I am going to try."

"How did she send for you, then? You don't seem the sort who would know the girls here."

"I am friends with Master Cartman. We witnessed a murder in Hertfordshire last year, and I never wish to see another villain go unpunished."

"Even a whore like Nellie? Most would say it scarcely matters."

So "most" would, Kate thought sadly. They would shrug and say there were plenty of whores where that one came from. But Kate would not. "I would not be one of those 'most.' Everyone deserves justice. Nell was a person, was she not? A living, feeling woman, and from what Bess and Rob say, a nice one as well."

Mad Henry's fearsome face softened. "Aye, that she

was. Always one for a laugh. She never deserved what happened."

"Then you will help me?"

His gaze flickered over Kate's small, slender figure, over her boy's doublet to her muddied boots. She stood still beneath his regard, unflinching, and something he saw seemed to reassure him. He nodded.

"I'll help ye, if I can," he said. He paused to let two cup-shot young men through the door. "What d'ye want to know?"

"Nell must have had some regular visitors," Kate said. "Did any of them seem especially—jealous of her attentions?"

Henry thought hard, frowning so fiercely she almost feared his mind would burst from the effort. "None in particular, I'd say. We pulled a villain with a knife off one girl last week, but Nell didn't seem to attract the bloody-minded ones. She was a friendly sort, able to make anyone laugh. But drink and lust, they don't mix well, if you know what I mean."

Kate feared she did know what he meant. She had seen the free flow of wine lead to many screaming arguments and violent endings at court, though seldom in death. "I do indeed, Mad Henry. I am a musician's daughter. I have seen many different sorts of men in my life."

"There are quarrels sometimes, but I break 'em up right quick. None of the bawds have ever been hurt here at the Cardinal's Hat while I was on watch. Mistress Celine wouldn't let it."

"But you weren't on watch that day?"

Henry shook his head regretfully. "There weren't very many here, were there? They all went to look at the queen. Afternoons are usually quiet, anyway. Nell was the last to leave, and she told me to go have an ale at the Rose and Crown. But I should have stayed!"

His ham hock of a fist suddenly shot out and pounded into the doorframe. Splinters went flying, and Kate instinctively ducked.

"You—you could not have known what would happen," she said gently. "So Nell had no especially ardent suitors of late? No one who came often?"

"She had ones that came here regular, aye," Mad Henry said, with a visible, heaving effort to calm himself.

"Do you know any of their names? Were many of them from the court?"

"Aye, some of them dressed fine indeed, but they don't often give their names," Henry said. "Even the bawds don't know their real names ofttimes, or at least they pretend they don't."

"Could you describe some of them?"

Henry thought very hard again, but none of his descriptions could be very helpful. They sounded like every man at court, Kate thought. Handsome, plain, tall, some bearded, some clean-shaven, some dark, some blond. Some with those fashionable pearl earrings that Sir Robert Dudley favored and thus every young blade emulated. She tucked away every detail she could to go over later, along with the nicknames Mad Henry knew and bits of gossip he had heard from the women.

"Thank you, Henry, you have been very helpful," Kate said when it seemed he had told her all he could remember.

"I'll help in any way I can."

The errand boy came running out of the house to tug at Kate's doublet sleeve. "Rob says you have to get back to the Tower, miss, afore sunrise!"

Kate nodded, and turned to follow him back the way

they had come. Suddenly she remembered a very important question indeed, and looked over her shoulder to Mad Henry.

"What happened to her body, Henry? Bess said you, er, took care of it."

Henry blinked hard, his eyes suddenly shining as if he would cry. "Aye, I took her to a church I know. St. Botolph's. They don't ask many questions there, and they buried her right quick in the churchyard. I made sure she was wrapped up decent."

"Very good of you," Kate said. It was better than what Bess seemed to suggest, that Henry had tossed Nell into the river. But Kate still couldn't examine the body herself. Even if it was still there, she was not a coroner. She was a musician, a woman. No one would let her, surely, and it would only bring suspicion on her and her friends. "Did you notice anything—not right when you wrapped up her body?"

Henry hesitated for a long moment. Then he reached inside his jerkin and took out a grimy handkerchief. He stepped closer to Kate and held it out to display a silver button.

It was finely made, smooth and polished, with a distinctive braided edge, but there were no identifying initials or crests.

"This was clutched in Nellie's hand," Henry said. "As if she had ripped it off when she tried to fight him away, poor mite. I kept it, thinking I might see someone come by wearing the same buttons."

Kate studied the object carefully. It was an expensive bauble, surely off a gentleman's doublet or a lady's sleeve. A tiny smudge of dried blood marred the decorative edge. "I doubt whoever did this will come back, or if he did, he would surely repair his garments first. That braid work *is* unusual, though."

"You take it, then. See if it matches to any of those preening peacocks at court."

"Thank you, Henry." Kate tucked the button away carefully. "If you think of anything else, send me word through Bess."

"Mistress! We have to go now," the boy called.

Kate nodded once more to Henry and hurried away. It had been a strange night indeed, she thought. And sure to get even stranger before it was all over, and she could escape into her music again.

CHAPTER 7

"The cushion! Oh, where is it? It cannot be lost!"

Blanche Parry, the queen's Second Lady of the Bedchamber and her attendant since she was a child, scurried through the crowd gathering in the forecourt of the Cradle Tower gate of the Tower, waiting to form the procession into London. Her graying hair straggled from its fine velvet and lace cap, and her eyes were as wide and wild as if she had lost the crown jewels. Everyone around her shook their heads, preoccupied with their own last-minute arrangements to their finery.

Kate stood near the back of the brightly colored flock, feeling strangely as if she watched everything in a dream. The sky arching over their heads and beyond the high walls was a low, leaden gray. Tiny, bitingly icy snowflakes drifted down to dust the earth. It seemed that the famous astrologer Dr. Dee, who had drawn up the queen's horoscope and proclaimed this to be the most fortunate date for her coronation, had not predicted the weather.

But all around were as many colors and as much movement as if it were high summer. Hundreds of ladies and knights, bishops in their gold-embroidered cassocks, city aldermen and foreign ambassadors, all rushed to find their places in line, a tangle of satin and jewels and banners. Laughter and shouts startled the ravens into the gray sky.

Kate had no official duties that day. A lady could not play music in public, only at the queen's private revels. She was to ride in one of the ladies' chariots behind the queen, along with Mary Everley. But Kate couldn't resist going to talk to the trumpeters who were to walk before the queen's litter, making sure everyone was there and knew the order of the music her father had so carefully planned.

Now she couldn't find Mary, and was fascinated by all that was happening around her.

"Blanche!" Queen Elizabeth shouted, her voice ringing out above everything else. She stood beside her white and gold litter as footmen harnessed it to four white mules draped in gold brocade, standing still as some of her ladies straightened her skirts and smoothed her loose hair. "Blanche, I pray you, stop fussing about the cushion. There are quite enough of the benighted things in the litter already, and you are driving me to madness."

Elizabeth swatted away one of the ladies and twitched her gold-edged ruff into place herself. She gleamed like the sun that had failed to make an appearance, robed in twenty-three yards of cloth of gold and fine ermine. A scarlet velvet cap, ringed with her gold princess's crown, sat atop her rippling hair. She looked every bit the goddess-queen, the center of the world.

Except for the frantic pink color high in her pale cheeks.

"No time for madness, Your Grace," Robert Dudley said, with one of his flashing white pirate's grins, the smile that made ladies giggle and swoon everywhere he went. His purple and silver doublet sparkled with diamond and pearl embroidery, and he wore a pearl earring in one ear. "All is nearly in readiness."

"We shall be late," Elizabeth grumbled, but she smiled at him in return.

"England is yours," Robert answered. "It waits only for *you*, from now forward."

"Then let us begin. Blanche! Where is my special cushion?"

Blanche Parry ran past Kate, sending her stumbling under the stone arches of the forecourt. That was when she finally glimpsed Mary Everley, who stood with her friend Lady Catherine Grey. They were both talking to the Count de Feria, their three heads bent close as they whispered, seemingly oblivious to the chaos around them. Mary and Catherine giggled and gave each other a secret little glance.

How very strange, Kate mused as she watched them, that someone as friendly and sweet as Mary should seem to have so many secrets. First the golden-eyed man on the walkway, and now . . . what? Was the queen's lady not allowed to talk to her ambassador? But to be so intimate with someone as suspect as Feria seemed odd.

And there was something strange in the closeness of the moment for someone as seemingly low in courtly rank as Mary. Also there were all the whispers that Lady Catherine was not at all content with her new place. . . .

"Everyone must now be ready!" Cawarden, the Master of the Revels, called as his horse trotted down the disorderly line of people. "Quickly!"

Before Kate could call out to Mary, Feria and Lady Catherine hurried away and Mary's brother, Lord Henry Everley, broke out of the crowd to grab her arm. His short velvet cloak swirled around them, and for an instant they were both concealed from Kate's sight. When she saw them again, she glimpsed the dark red color flushing Henry Everley's handsome, bearded face. He gave Mary's arm a hard shake, his fingers crumpling her fine silk sleeve, and she tried to push him away.

Mary, who always seemed to be laughing, looked just as furious as her brother. She shook her head, pulling again at her arm. They were much too far away from Kate for her to hear their quarrel, but something like a cold flash of stark fear broke through Mary's anger.

Moved to help her, Kate started toward them, but a sudden shout pulled her back.

"Kate Haywood!" the queen called. "To me."

Kate spun around to see Queen Elizabeth waving her forward with an imperious gesture. Kate glanced back at Mary. She and her brother had disappeared and the place under the shadow of the arches was empty. Kate had no choice but to go to the queen, yet that flash of fear on her friend's face lingered in her mind.

"Yes, Your Majesty?" she said, as she hurried toward the queen. She carefully held the hem of her new black-trimmed white satin gown above the frosty ground and darted around the frozen droppings of the waiting horses.

"One of those trumpeters is completely out of tune," Elizabeth said testily. "He is giving me a headache. You must speak to him at once."

"Of course, Your Majesty," Kate said, though she feared she could never decipher which of the dozens of trumpeters in their scarlet and gold tabards was the offensive one.

By the time she had organized the musicians and found her place in one of the ladies' chariots, it was nearly time to depart. Mary Everley already sat on one of the fat red pillows among the other ladies, and she slid over to make room for Kate. Mary offered Kate the other end of a fur-edged lap robe, but she wouldn't meet Kate's eyes and had a most distracted air about her.

Far ahead of them in the line of chariots and palfreys, Elizabeth raised her bejeweled hands and everything fell silent.

"Oh, Almighty God," she cried. "I give Thee most hearty thanks that Thine hast been so merciful to spare me to behold this most joyful day."

Then she let Robert Dudley help her onto the white satin cushions of her waiting litter. He took his own mount just behind, where he was to lead the queen's white mare, and the chosen noblemen raised the scarlet canopy of state above Elizabeth's head.

With a blast of trumpets and sackbuts, the gates were flung open and the church bells of London rang out. Crowds immediately surged close amid cries of "God save Your Grace!" and "God bless Queen Elizabeth!"

The noise of such great joy was too loud at first for Kate to say anything to Mary. Eventually the celebration made even Mary smile, and she waved to Catherine Grey, who rode with her sickly mother, Lady Frances, and her tiny sister, Lady Mary, in the chariot just ahead.

The queen often called the long, snaking procession to a halt as they made their slow way down the Strand, past the grand houses of the nobility, so she could take flowers and greet the people who pressed close on all sides.

Tall railings draped with silk hangings and guarded by men from the guilds could not keep them back. Flowers were tossed from the crowded windows of every house, and children were held up high on their parents' shoulders to throw the new queen their tokens. Even the hidden sun peeked out from behind the clouds.

"Oh, Kate!" Mary gasped, clutching at Kate's hand. "Isn't it all so beautiful? How blessed we are to see such a day."

"Blessed indeed," Kate murmured. It was indeed a glorious thing to see Elizabeth take her rightful throne, to know the Haywoods and all the queen's friends no longer had to fear. That the future held such promise. Yet Mary had only an hour ago been quarreling with her brother, and Henry Everley would no doubt be waiting for her when they reached Westminster Palace.

Kate thought of poor, dead Nell, and her grieving sister, Bess, of how women always had so much to fear and no place to turn for shelter. She stared out at the vast sea of faces, the swirl of people from every walk of life, rich and poor all together, and she feared it would be a hopeless thing to find Nell justice in such a clamor.

The procession wound to a halt at Fenchurch Street for the first of the city's pageants for its new queen. A tiny, golden-haired child clad all in white stepped out onto a high, velvet-draped dais and began to speak. Even from a great distance, Kate could see that the poor child looked terrified, and his carefully rehearsed words couldn't even be heard above the roar of the crowd.

"Good people, I pray you silence," the queen called. "So I may hear the words of this angel."

The child blinked hard and began his speech of welcome again, as the queen listened attentively.

Kate leaned closer to Mary and whispered, "Are you quite well?"

Mary turned to her with her red-gold eyebrows raised. "I am always well! Have you known me to be ill, Kate?"

No, Mary was never ill. Yet Kate couldn't help but remember that flash of fear on Mary's face. Mary had been such a good friend to her, helping Kate when she was so new to courtly ways. If Mary was in trouble now . . . "Your brother . . ."

Mary abruptly turned away, her hand falling to her side. "My brother knows not of what he speaks. Men never do. At least most men. Have you ever known a man to be sensible?"

Kate thought of Anthony Elias, of her friend's steady manner and smiling green eyes. "Perhaps one."

"Only one? Then you see my meaning. Oh, look! 'Tis Gracechurch Street. What do you suppose will be the meaning of this pageant?"

Kate wasn't distracted by Mary's words, but she knew this was not the place to press for secrets. She nodded and peered ahead to see that the queen's litter had lurched to a halt again, and was in fact backing up through a garland-bedecked arch.

"What is happening?" Mary asked, as all the ladies in their chariot leaned to the side, struggling for a glimpse amid the shouts and chaos, the showers of flowers and ribbons.

Kate also strained to see, trying to remember every vivid detail so she could tell her father about it later. "It is a platform of three tiers with an arch to pass underneath . . . ," she said. It was so large she could see only parts of it at one time. Stretching from one side of the street to the other, the arch was surmounted by a painted and gilded Tudor rose, white within red. Two statues, labeled *Unity* and *Concord*, held the whole elaborate affair up. At the bottom, Kate recognized a robed man's figure in a flat cap and a woman in an old-fashioned gabled hood and high-waisted gown.

"I think it is King Henry VII and Elizabeth of York, the queen's grandparents," Kate said. "And . . ."

She strained to see, and glimpsed a young woman at the top of the platform, her flowing red hair showing she was Queen Elizabeth herself. In the center was old King Henry VIII, as portly and bejeweled as he ever was in real life, before illness and girth overtook him. He seemed to stand astride all the world, beefy fists on his hips. Next to him . . .

Next to him was a lady in black velvet, her dark hair falling over her shoulders. A pearl and gold *B* pendant hung from her neck.

"Oh." Kate fell back to her seat, stunned and saddened by the sight.

"What is it?" Mary demanded, her own view blocked by the canopy of the chariot.

"It is Queen Anne Boleyn," Kate answered. She instinctively looked toward the queen, far ahead in her white and gold litter, remembering how Elizabeth had knelt on the cold floor of St. Peter's, searching for her mother. Now her mother was *there*, receiving her due honor as queen before all of London. Kate could see the tears sparkling on Elizabeth's pinkened cheeks as she looked up at that dark figure.

But Kate's own mother still seemed a world away.

Kate longed to go to Elizabeth, to cheer Queen Anne with her, but it was too far to go and she would be lost in the long procession. The crowd surged again against the railings, close enough to jostle even Kate's chariot. She and Mary held on to each other to keep from being tipped out.

"Kate! Kate Haywood!"

Startled by the sound of her name amid the wordless, joyful cacophony, Kate studied the heaving mass of people. A bright green plumed cap waved in the air, and she glimpsed Rob Cartman. He was taller than most of the people around him, and Bess hung on to his arm. Her red hair and green gown glowed, and she was frantically gesturing to someone behind Kate in the procession.

She glanced back over her shoulder, but she could see nothing except more of Elizabeth's lords and ladies on their gold-draped horses.

"What is it?" Kate shouted back. The procession had already lurched onward, and Rob and Bess were lost to her sight. She longed to know what they were trying to tell her.

"Who are you talking to, Kate?" Mary asked. She, too, looked behind them, and she suddenly smiled as if she saw something that pleased her.

It was probably *not* Henry Everley, then, Kate thought.

"No one," Kate said. "I just imagined I saw someone I knew."

"The queen is right," Mary said, still smiling that soft, secret smile. "This seems a most blessed day to see."

CHAPTER 8

"**I**s that not Matthew Haywood's daughter?"

Anthony Elias's attention was suddenly caught by Master Hardy's words from across the room. Master Hardy, the lawyer who had been Anthony's employer and mentor ever since he decided to apprentice in the law himself, stood beside the open window of his new town house with Mistress Hardy, watching the new queen's joyful procession go by.

"Matthew Haywood?" Anthony said, as he made his way through the crowd of the Hardys' guests to join them. He tried not to betray too much interest at hearing Kate's name. It had been many weeks since they last met, and his new work in London kept him very busy indeed.

Yet too often, late at night while he studied thick legal volumes by candlelight, he would remember how Kate's laughter sounded, like a beam of sudden sunlight on a gray day. Or how it felt to hold her hand to help her out of a boat or over a puddle in the road. It had taken all his strength to let go of her slender fingers then.

Anthony was still a long way from setting up his own practice of the law, and his widowed mother in their country village relied on him alone. He had raised himself from the son of a blacksmith to nearly establishing a law practice of his own through hard work and dedication. Master Hardy often said a young man in such a position should wait to begin a family. That the right wife with the right connections could be beneficial—at the right time. Anthony knew such advice was only sensible.

Yet Kate Haywood was not like anyone else he had ever known. She was so intelligent, so interested in the world around her. So—so alive. Their friendship in the long, dangerous days in Hertfordshire had been all that sustained him sometimes.

And he was as excited as a young pup at the thought of even glimpsing her again—even though he was meant to be so serious in his new black robes, solemn and somber. He had to laugh at himself, yet he couldn't stop from joining the Hardys at the window.

"You remember the Haywoods, I am sure, Anthony," Master Hardy said. He held his wife's hand as they watched the sparkling array of lords and ladies halt below their Gracechurch Street house, only recently purchased. "Matthew Haywood served the Tudors for many years; he was especially a favorite of Queen Catherine Parr, I think. But they suffered much under Queen Mary."

"As did we all," Mistress Hardy said, squeezing her husband's hand. No doubt she was remembering, Anthony thought, those days not so long ago when Master Hardy was arrested and his offices in Hertfordshire ransacked.

"Very true, my dear," Master Hardy said. "But Matthew Haywood was ill, and his daughter little more than a child when they had to flee after Princess Elizabeth was taken to the Tower after Wyatt's Rebellion. I am happy to see them find royal favor now."

Anthony peered down at the crowd, but he couldn't

see Kate in the bejeweled throng. Ahead, it looked as if the queen's litter had halted for a pageant workmen had been building for days, giving him time to study the faces closer.

Mistress Hardy sighed, her faded blue eyes turning misty. "Matthew Haywood was the most divinely talented lute player, I remember from our own courtly days when my father was lawyer to noble families. Matthew always played for the dancing."

"And all the ladies sighed with love for him," Master Hardy teased.

His wife laughed. "Not I, for I could only see *you*, young jackanapes that you were. And Master Haywood only had eyes for his wife. Such a beauty Eleanor was. Do you think he will play for the coronation feast?"

"Since his daughter is now in the queen's train, perhaps so," Master Hardy answered. "I have heard nothing of them since that sad business in Hertfordshire."

"I cannot see Mistress Haywood," Anthony said, too eager to see Kate to fully conceal it any longer.

"Is that not her, in the black-and-white gown with the new high ruff there?" Mistress Hardy said. "She does look like her mother, does she not?"

"Anthony is a young man, my dear, and surely cannot tell one style of ruff or gown from another," Master Hardy said.

But Anthony had at last glimpsed Kate. She leaned out of one of the chariots crowded with the queen's ladies, trying to see ahead to the pageant. Her black-and-white gown, though finely made of a lustrous satin (Anthony did know *something* of gowns, thanks to Mistress Hardy's conversation on nights he dined with the older couple), was simple compared with the jewel-trimmed velvets of the others. Her dark hair was twisted and pinned atop her head, leaving her graceful white neck bared above the delicate lace ruff.

She wore no pearls or diamond necklaces, but she had no need of them. She looked like a swan among crows, and Anthony had to make himself look away from her. He did not deserve her, not yet.

"She does look like her mother," Mistress Hardy said. "Eleanor Haywood was most extraordinary. Perhaps you will see the Haywoods, dearest, when next you call on Anne Somerset at court."

The Dowager Duchess of Somerset, the mother of the young Edward Seymour, the Earl of Hertford, and the widow of King Edward VI's uncle and executed Lord Protector, was Master Hardy's greatest noble client. Anthony suddenly felt a reluctant touch of hope thinking he might have a way to see Kate again.

"Perhaps I shall," Master Hardy said. "The Seymours are in great need of much legal counsel these days. I shall look for Matthew Haywood and his daughter."

Mistress Hardy slid a sly glance at Anthony. "And perhaps Anthony would care to accompany you there? He must find the company of only old sticks such as us dull indeed."

Anthony feared he could feel his face turn hot at her teasing words. He looked back to the street.

"Perhaps so," Master Hardy said distractedly. "And speaking of old sticks, I must speak to our guests and be sure there is enough wine. It has been a long time indeed since we entertained in such a fashion. . . ."

On the street below, the procession lurched again into motion, on its way to the next pageant. Kate sat back in her chariot, whispering with the red-haired lady next to her, and she was lost from his sight. But at least he knew she was really out there, safe and whole and prospering.

As Master Hardy moved away, his wife took Anthony's arm and sighed. "Yes, indeed," she said, seemingly as if to herself. "Eleanor Haywood was most extraordinary. I am sure her daughter is also very interesting. Were you not friends with her, Anthony, when you and my husband were in Hertfordshire?"

Friends? Aye, Anthony thought. They had been that, and only that. "I did know her there. She lived with the queen's household at Hatfield. Though I saw her very seldom."

"Such pretty dark-haired children she would have someday," Mistress Hardy said whimsically with another sigh. "I am sure she will look for a musician, though. . . ."

She drifted away into the midst of their guests, leaving Anthony to stare down at the street. A line of trumpeters were just marching past, blasting their salute into the winter air. Was one of them a suitor to Kate?

Aye, he thought. He should most assuredly accompany Master Hardy the next time he had Seymour business at court. Perhaps Kate would be happy to see an old friend.

CHAPTER 9

There were thirty-nine ladies arrayed behind Queen Elizabeth at Westminster Palace, arranging their long scarlet velvet trains and their gold coronets as they waited to begin the walk to the coronation at the Abbey. But Lady Mary Everley was not among them.

Kate hadn't seen her since very late the night before, when all the ladies had fallen into their makeshift beds at Westminster, exhausted from the procession and the long banquet after. There had been no time to ask Mary about her tryst on the Tower ramparts, or about her brother and his fit of temper, and Mary had been quiet and remote. That morning Mary was gone when Kate awoke, and even Lady Catherine Grey hadn't seen her.

Kate stepped back from her task of arranging the line of trumpeters and drummers who were to lead the procession to the Abbey, scanning the ladies' faces again. Still no Mary.

Even the queen seemed to have noticed her absence. Elizabeth turned away from Blanche Parry adjusting her sleeve to study the scarlet flock arranged behind her. Despite the glories of the day, Elizabeth's face was very white, her dark eyes frantically sparkling, the tip of her nose slightly red as if with a cold. Her hand, arrayed in jeweled rings, fluttered over the crowd.

"Where is that blasted Everley girl?" Elizabeth muttered. "She is never where she is meant to be, and after I gave her this place as a favor, too. She is meant to carry my gloves. Kate! Kate Haywood!"

Startled by the sound of her name, Kate hurried to the queen and dropped a low curtsy. "Your Majesty?"

"You are friends with Mary Everley, are you not?" Elizabeth said impatiently. She yanked her arm away from Mistress Parry to smooth her gold satin sleeve herself.

"I do know her, Your Majesty," Kate answered. "But I fear I have not seen her since last night." She remembered Bess's description of her sister Nell's murder, and a shiver danced over her skin. It was a long way from a Southwark brothel to the queen's palace, but surely it could not be safe for Mary to wander alone.

Unless she wasn't alone at all.

"Go and seek her now," Elizabeth said with a fierce sneeze. Ten ladies leaped forward with handkerchiefs. She snatched up one and waved the rest away. "We must depart anon. If she isn't here within five minutes, I will give the gloves to someone else and Lady Mary can go rot in the countryside."

"Yes, Your Majesty." As Kate backed away, she saw the young Duchess of Norfolk standing behind the queen, waiting to carry the royal train. With her was one of the many elderly Howard aunts, Lady Gertrude. She was stooped, leaning on a cane, swathed in black velvet and an old-fashioned headdress, but her eyes were bright and alert in her raisinlike face.

She suddenly stood up straighter as Kate's gaze caught hers, and her rusty cry made Kate freeze for an instant. "Eleanor! Is it you?"

Eleanor. Could old Lady Gertrude mean Kate's mother? "I—I am Kate Haywood, Lady Gertrude."

Lady Gertrude shook her head, a doubtful frown flickering over her wizened face. "But you look like *him*, just as she did. Why has she not come to see me for so long?"

"Kate!" the queen shouted, and Kate abruptly remembered her errand. There was no time to ask Lady Gertrude about her strange words, and the duchess was taking the old lady's arm to lead her to a chair.

Kate ran down one of the narrow corridors of the medieval palace, toward the queen's chambers. She had no idea where Mary could be, but that seemed a good place to start. The rooms and halls were full of bishops and lords readying themselves for the procession, of pages scurrying around with last-minute messages, and maidservants on errands. But there was no Mary.

At last Kate glimpsed Mary's cousin Richard St. Long. She well remembered the last time she saw him, reeling drunkenly through Southwark with Edward Seymour, grabbing for the sleeve of her boy's disguise. But maybe he could help her today.

The rumpled hair and dust-streaked, half-fastened garments of Southwark were gone, and Master St. Long was as handsome as a courtier should be in the torchlight. His sun-streaked brown hair was brushed back from his thin, clean-shaven face, and he wore a black velvet doublet and gold-lined short cloak. Like so many of the young men who sought to emulate Robert Dudley, he wore a pearl drop earring in his left ear. But there was something not quite correctly fitting about his fine clothes, a strange pulling across his broad shoulders, as if he couldn't afford clothes quite as closely tailored as Henry Everley's.

He was laughing with Edward Seymour, the two of them handsome and glowing with robust health and manly, courtly charm. Anyone looking at them now would never know only two nights ago they had been falling down in Southwark mud puddles. She wondered if they had known Nell.

"I beg your pardon, Master St. Long," Kate said as she hurried toward him. "I am bid by the queen to find Lady Mary. Have you seen her?"

Richard smiled at her, but Edward Seymour fidgeted with an impatient frown on his angelically handsome face.

"I haven't seen her since last night, I fear, Mistress Haywood," Richard said. "But it's a fearful thing for her to keep the queen waiting. Shall I help you look?"

He seemed everything open and friendly, worried about his cousin, yet Kate felt a touch of disquiet as she looked up into his eyes. Eyes that were blue, not a strange gold color. But there was no need to go on an extensive search.

"Here I am!" Mary called.

Kate turned to find Mary weaving between the bejeweled throngs, her scarlet train looped over her arm. She smiled, but her pretty face was taut, her eyes sparkling frantically like the queen's. Her red hair straggled from beneath her cap.

Several steps behind trailed her brother, scowling above his red-blond beard.

"The queen is looking for you," Kate said.

"I mislaid my earrings, so stupid of me," Mary said with a shrill laugh. She grabbed Kate's arm and hurried toward where the queen waited.

Kate glanced back to see Henry Everley and Richard St. Long muttering together. Henry's fist was tight around the hilt of the jeweled dagger at his belt, but Richard looked after Mary with a thoughtful tilt of his head.

"Mary, what is wrong?" Kate said quickly, knowing there was not much time for them to talk but worried about her friend.

"My brother is a foolish hedgepig, that is all," Mary said with a laugh. "He usually lets out his temper in Southwark, but the queen has kept him too busy lately. He will come around soon. He *must*. Everything depends on that."

There was not a moment to say anything else. The queen impatiently waved Mary into place, and a footman handed her the velvet cushion holding the queen's embroidered gloves. Kate went to find her own place in line, behind the musicians.

Lady Gertrude Howard was watching her again, she saw as she smoothed her hair. Lady Gertrude frowned fiercely, and her words rang in Kate's head. *You look like her. Eleanor.*

Her head whirled with the frantic, lightning energy of the day, with all that had happened in only a few moments. She knew she would have to consider and absorb it all later, next to her own fire. But now the doors of the palace were thrown open, letting in the cold gray day, and the tumbling outpouring of the joy of an entire city.

A blue carpet was laid out from the palace to the Abbey, and to the accompaniment of the trumpets and drums, a choir singing the "Salve Festa Dies," and all the pealing church bells of London, the court made its stately journey.

The scarlet-robed bishops in their gold miters went first, then knights and pages, noblemen bearing the heavy crown of Edward the Confessor, the scepter and orb, the spurs and sword, without which no monarch could be crowned.

Then the Duchess of Norfolk took up the queen's

train, and the canopy of state was raised over her head by the Barons of the Cinque Ports. The Earls of Pembroke and Shrewsbury walked beside her, but none could outshine the gold and white queen, in her cloth of gold and ermine robes sewn with pearls, her glorious hair falling free down her back.

Held back by railings to either side, the crowds that had waited so long in the cold night to see her burst forth with deafening cheers and surged forward.

Elizabeth's impatience and fit of temper inside the palace seemed forgotten as she beamed out over the crowds.

"God have mercy on you all, my good people!" she called as she walked past them. Once she was gone, they fell on the fine carpet, tearing it to pieces for remembrances and nearly knocking over the Duchess of Norfolk in the process.

Once inside the hush of the Abbey, Kate's eyes were so dazzled for an instant she could hardly see. After the gray glare of the day, the cavernous church glowed with the soft golden light of hundreds of candles and torches, which scented the cool air with their waxy smoke. More nobles sat on the tiers of benches set up along the long aisle, watched by the stone eyes of the funerary monuments.

The lords and ladies rose as one in a rustle of velvet and brocade when the queen appeared in a fanfare of trumpets. The music could not have been arranged better, Kate thought with a glow of pride. It soared into the vast church, as if it came from the heavens itself to greet the bright new day.

Queen Elizabeth herself seemed to float down the aisle on a cloud of that music, poised and assured, as glorious as if she had always been a queen, and had never been a bastardized exile who had to fight for her very life and those of her friends. She glided toward her crown with a serene smile, and a beam of light fell through the jewellike window to gild her red Tudor hair.

Kate was astonished that she herself was there to see such a glorious moment, such a queen, and she knew she would do anything to serve Queen Elizabeth. That this was truly the beginning of a new day, for all of them.

Elizabeth reached the dais where the bishop of Carlisle waited to crown her.

"Do you, good people of the realm of England, desire this royal person Elizabeth Tudor for your lawful, God-given queen?"

"Yay! Yay!" the shout poured out. "God save Queen Elizabeth. . . ."

CHAPTER 10

"Walter? Are you there?" Mary Everley tiptoed into the silent darkness of the abandoned Abbey. She held her stiff velvet and brocade skirts tightly to keep them from rustling, but her heart was pounding so loudly in her ears she feared it could be heard all the way back to the queen's banquet at Westminster Palace.

The banquet where she was meant to be right now, waiting on Queen Elizabeth. How angry her father would be if he saw she wasn't there! Mary almost laughed to imagine the glaring light in his eyes, the way his jowly face flamed red whenever he was unhappy about anything. And that seemed to be all the time of late.

"I have bribed and begged our way back to court, and I won't let an ungrateful chit like you ruin it all!" he had thundered just that morning, when Henry told him what he had discovered. Henry was a rat of a brother, but she had always known that. That was why she knew she could rely only on herself to get what she wanted. That was why she went to the Spanish for help.

"Elizabeth might be just an upstart Boleyn bastard, but she's better than Queen Mary. This is our one chance. . . ."

Mary frowned at the memory of those shouted words, of her father's hand slapping smartly across her face. It was *his* chance, mayhap, his and Henry's and Richard's.

They had schemed for it during all those long years of country exile while Mary Tudor was queen. But they hadn't counted on their own quiet Mary not going along as their contented pawn.

She had her own plans. And they were so close to coming true, she could almost reach out and touch them.

Mary stumbled on a crack in the floor, pain shooting up from her slippered toes as she pitched forward. Her hand clutched not at her dreams but at a cold stone pillar, and she leaned against it to catch her breath.

The church felt cold, so empty after all the crowds of the coronation. Empty and full of twisting shadows. Mary shivered as she studied the carved effigies all around her, their stone eyes watching her blankly in the dim light of her lantern. Perhaps this had not been the best place to ask Walter to meet her, but she could think of nothing else so sure to be deserted at such an hour. Everyone else would be feasting and dancing until dawn.

Mary glanced back over her shoulder. She had left the side door ajar, as she told Walter she would, and now she only had to wait for him.

Surely he would come soon. She knew he couldn't bear to stay away from her, just as she longed for him. Soon, very soon, they would never be parted again at all.

Mary took a careful step and found the pain in her foot was fading. She hurried on, past the ghostly, empty throne in front of the high altar, and into the burial chapel of King Henry VII and Elizabeth of York. Their gilded figures, forever staring up into the heavens side by side, glowed as the lantern light flickered over them.

Mary carefully put down her lantern on a stone ledge. Her hands trembled too much to hold it. Where *was* Walter? Surely he should be here by now! She dared not stay away too long for fear her father or brother would notice her gone. She could bear no more of their slaps or their orders.

Yet neither could she bear not to see Walter. Only her stolen moments with him seemed real to her now. They were all she wanted, all she longed for. And even those instants had seemed like a dream, until she'd drunk too much port one night and whispered confidences to Catherine Grey.

Catherine was a true friend, and Mary was sure she would keep the secret, as she harbored more than one of her own. Just saying the words aloud—*Walter kissed me, Walter loves me*—made them seem real.

Once or twice, Mary considered telling Kate Haywood as well. Surely any lady who could write such beautiful songs would know the pain and the soaring joy of love! Yet something had always held back Mary's words from her new friend. She had to be very, very careful now if her plans were to come to fruition.

The vast church, so cold only a moment before, now seemed like a desert. Mary swept off her velvet cap and shook her hair free, letting the red waves fall over her shoulders. Once she had hated its strange color, longing to be blond like Catherine Grey. Now, thanks to Queen Elizabeth, it was fashionable to have red hair. And Walter did seem to like it so....

A sudden noise split the silence, a heavy footfall on the stone floor. Mary spun around, her heart soaring with happiness. Walter! Surely it had to be. A tall, slim figure in a plumed cap strode out of the shadows and reached for her.

"You whore!" the person shouted. Mary realized with a cold bolt of fear that she had been terribly wrong.

But it was all much too late.

CHAPTER 11

" 'The sighs that come from my heart, they grieve me passing sore! Sith I must from my love depart, farewell my joy forever more . . . ,' " the chorus sang, their sad-sweet words ringing out over the great feast.

Kate leaned over the railing of the musicians' gallery to watch as Sir Edward Dymoke, the Queen's Champion, rode into Westminster Hall in full armor to challenge any who dared dispute her title, just as the Royal Champion had for centuries. None made challenge, of course, but there was much laughter and applause as the queen's health was drunk once more. She had the best of views from up so high; she could see everyone arrayed below.

It was now after eleven at night, and the banquet began at three in the afternoon, so the noise grew louder and more abandoned as the hours flew by. Remove after remove was brought to the long rows of white damask-draped tables set up under the rafters of the old hall. Leeks in almond sauce, chicken amorosa, fish stuffed with lemon and spices, veal in rosemary, fresh white loaves of manchet bread, sugar subtleties in the shapes of castles and rivers. The wine flowed freely into the gold and silver goblets, a steady stream of ruby red that fueled the merriment.

And no one looked merrier than Queen Elizabeth,

now crowned and anointed. She sat on a raised dais at the high table beneath her canopy of estate, her dark purple velvet gown lustrous in the torchlight. On her head was a jeweled crown, said to have been worn once by Queen Anne Boleyn at her own coronation banquet, and two of the highest noblemen, Lord William Howard and the Earl of Sussex, served her sweetmeats on bended knees.

Elizabeth held out her hand to thank her gallant champion, her face radiant against the curtain of her loose red hair. It gladdened Kate's heart to see it, for the queen's life until that night had held little gaiety, little grandeur. It was a glorious night indeed, before work to rebuild an England left in ruins by Queen Mary would have to begin again in the morning.

But not just yet. As Elizabeth laughed, the crown atop her bright hair sparkled, and Kate remembered what Bess said about Nell. That she had longed to see a queen's coronation after their grandmother's tales of Queen Anne's procession. But now poor Nell was gone, after her glimpse of the new queen, and someone in this vast city had killed her.

Mayhap someone in that very hall. Kate studied the rows of faces, all of them laughing and bright with drink beneath their jeweled coronets. Had one of them, in a fit of fury, bashed in a woman's head and left her for dead?

Kate feared she could well believe it of some. She'd seen fits of temper aplenty at court, had heard bitter whispers from men resentful of being denied what they saw as their rightful glories by the new queen. Feria the Spaniard hated her; the Seymours and the Howards thought she passed them over for upstarts like Robert Dudley and William Cecil.

Men such as that were accustomed to holding the power tightly in their own hands, not wielded by the delicate white fingers of a woman like Elizabeth. A woman who would not give way to their bullying, and whom they could no longer control. What violence were such men capable of when thwarted?

Kate suddenly sat up straight as a terrible thought struck her of a man of power and strength who imagined his rightful place was being denied him by the queen. What depths of fury would fill him? Such white-hot anger could not be taken out on the queen herself. But a helpless Southwark bawd . . .

Like the bleedin' queen, we are . . . , Bess had said.

Kate's gaze swept over the crowd again. Edward Seymour was laughing raucously with his young friends, many of them the same drunken boors Kate saw in Southwark the night she went to see Rob. They looked as if they never thought of anything but their wine and their jokes, but she had seen just such careless young courtiers turn from indolent laughter to duel-worthy fury in an instant.

The Seymours had long hated the Boleyns, ever since Jane Seymour supplanted Queen Anne. Young Edward had seen his father, the Lord Protector Somerset, and his uncle Thomas Seymour killed on the block by the Tudors. Now Elizabeth's Boleyn relatives, like Baron Hunsdon and his sister Catherine Carey, took high places at court while the Seymours were ignored.

Kate saw Lady Catherine Grey seated at one of the lower tables with the other maids of honor, watching Edward Seymour with her wide blue eyes. Her elegant hands were twisted painfully in the lap of her silver silk gown, and hectic, angry red stained her high cheekbones. Not *only* men could feel angry, of course, or displaced from their rightful positions. Catherine and her mother were said to be furious at their treatment.

Yet surely only a man would have had the strength to

batter Nell bloody. Catherine Grey, despite her anger and wounded pride, was a slight woman. She had friends, though. Such as Feria and his Spanish cohorts. Mayhap even King Philip himself?

Kate studied the black-clad Spaniards at their table. Unlike most of the other revelers, they hadn't taken much of the fine wine, and they watched the ever increasing abandon around them with pinched faces and disapproving eyes. Kate remembered Catherine Grey and Mary Everley whispering with them.

Mary—where was she? Kate's attention flashed past the blur of laughing faces to find Lord Everley, Mary's father, at his place in the middle of the hall. Her view was half-blocked by a tall silver saltcellar, but she saw the earl's bearded face and gold coronet as he talked to the lady who sat next to him. The earl had long been a widower, and he smiled as he made the women giggle. It was the first time Kate ever saw him look anything but stern or disapproving.

He gave his more accustomed frown as he glared at the empty places on his other side. Henry Everley and Richard St. Long were not there, though Kate was sure she had seen them take their seats before she was distracted by the banquet music. They were not seated there now, though many of the younger lords had gone wandering as the night went on, seeking their friends and flirtations.

But Mary wasn't at her place among the maids, either. Kate knew there were many places she could be, but the image flashed through her mind of Henry Everley grabbing Mary's arm. A shiver of cold disquiet seemed to slide over her.

"Mistress Haywood," one of the musicians called. "Shall we do 'The Princess's Madrigal' now?"

Startled out of the ever more oppressive world of her

thoughts of violence and missing courtiers, Kate glanced over to find the other lute players watching her. She had forgotten her purpose for being there, which was to play the new songs she wrote for the night.

"Yes, of course," she said quickly, and took up her lute again.

The instrument had once been her mother's, and it was a thing of great beauty with its lustrous Italian wood and mother-of-pearl insets. On the back of the neck was the flowering initial *E*, with a smaller *K* beneath it that her father had carved when he gave it to Kate. It sounded exquisite, too, light and delicate, responsive to Kate's slightest touch, always following where she led when the flood of notes and moods overcame her.

She liked to imagine that her mother watched her when she played, helped her. Music could always take her out of herself, out of the dark world around her, and into a different realm entirely. One where there was only sound.

Kate had worked hard to finish those songs in only a few weeks for the coronation. But tonight she couldn't lose herself in them as she usually did. Too many things kept flying through her mind to let the notes take full hold. Nell and Bess. The glories of the day just finished, and the dangers the new queen would face even in the wake of such joy.

She had practiced the tune over and over, though, and the strings of her lute brought it forth readily enough. When they built, built, to a crashing crescendo, there was a ripple of applause from below, and the other musicians smiled. They had been most reluctant to work with her, a mere woman, even though she had the authority of her father. But they came round somewhat when they heard her play.

Kate glanced down to the royal table, and was startled to see the queen looking up at the musicians' gallery. Elizabeth caught her eyes and gestured to her to come down.

Whatever could the queen want in the midst of her banquet? "I shall return anon," Kate quickly told the others. She carefully tucked the precious lute beneath her stool.

She heard them begin "Pastime with Good Company" as she hurried down the stairs to the banquet hall. It was a song written decades ago by the queen's own father, an old tune that needed little guidance.

Kate made her way carefully down the narrow, winding stairs to the main gallery and along the corridor that led to the kitchens. Servants were rushing past, carrying platters of more delicacies, sweat trickling down their faces despite the winter's night outside. The smells of beef in cinnamon sauce and stewed salmon mingled with the tang of woodsmoke from the cavernous fireplaces, and the rose and jasmine perfumes of the courtiers.

The noise, which was a low, indistinct roar from the musicians' gallery, hit Kate like a wave of sheer sound when she stepped out into the hall. The night had begun decorously enough, with everyone seated in their proper places to watch the peacocks roasted and redressed in their own feathers and the pretty sugar subtleties paraded past. But now the wine and spiced ale, the merry music, had done their work, and everyone was in a great tumble of loud merriment.

Kate threaded her way past the tables, neatly sidestepping a pack of the queen's greyhounds fighting over a leg of lamb, and made her way to Elizabeth's dais.

The queen was whispering with Robert Dudley, leaning close to whisper in his ear. He laughed, and she tapped at his hand with her feathered fan.

"Ah, Kate, there you are," Elizabeth called. "You have a good vantage from your gallery, I think. Have you seen your friend Lady Mary Everley?"

Was that why the queen had summoned her? Kate wondered as she dropped a quick curtsy and hurried toward the dais. Surely Elizabeth *did* have supernatural powers of observation, as some people claimed! Otherwise, how would she see one maid of honor was missing in such a throng?

"Nay, Your Majesty," Kate said. "I have not seen her since the banquet began."

"And she was late to the procession as well," Elizabeth said with an impatient sigh. "I shall have to speak to her father. I feared she was not best pleased with her new position, and there are plenty of young ladies eager to have her place."

Was Mary to be tossed out of court, then? Kate started to shake her head, afraid that would make Mary's brother even more furious. Surely there had to be a good reason for her absence now.

"Nay, my queen, don't be so hasty to judge the lady," Robert Dudley said. "This is a night for revelry, not duty."

He kissed her hand, making her laugh again. "Aye, for tomorrow is soon enough to deal with our troubles. Still, I would know where she is. Will you look for her, Kate, and quickly? We shall want more music for dancing soon."

"Of course, Your Majesty." Kate backed away from the dais, where Elizabeth and Dudley were whispering again. She glimpsed Sir William Cecil, the queen's new chief secretary, frowning at their closeness, but she had no time to ponder the quarrels of the queen's two highest courtiers. She had to look for Mary, and swiftly.

Mary was nowhere to be seen at any of the tables. Lady Catherine Grey said she had not set eyes on her all evening, though Kate was sure Catherine hadn't turned her gaze from Edward Seymour the entire night and would have seen nothing else anyway. Mary's brother and cousin were still not in their seats, and her father looked as if he would burst into a temper at any instant. She thought it best not to speak to him.

She remembered the strange man with the golden eyes who was with Mary at the Tower, and she wondered if they were together now. Mary had been so secretive of late; it would surely be just like her to slip away for a tryst while everyone was distracted by the feast. Perhaps she would soon reappear, laughing at her own secrets.

Yet Kate had a troubled feeling that would not be quieted.

She left the hall to peek in at the ladies' lodgings, which were empty. As she came down the back stairs, she noticed a door ajar and pushed it open to let in a rush of cold, snowflake-dotted wind.

It looked out over a small garden, and just beyond was the great Abbey. Its dark walls were silent now after all the celebrations of the day just past, its windows blank and its spires almost skeletal against the starry sky. The silvery moon seemed to hang, ghostly, on one of the bell towers.

From the city beyond, Kate could hear the echoes of more revelry, shouts and laughter, songs. Wine would flow from the fountains all night, and the red-gold glare of bonfires flickered like banners in the black night.

Kate started to pull the door closed, but then she glimpsed a tiny dot of light where there should be none. It came from within the Abbey itself. She peered closer and saw that one of the side doors, almost hidden within the church's elaborate stonework, stood open and that was where the light shone.

She quickly snatched up a blue cloak from a hook nearby, where it seemed the kitchen staff left their wraps, and swung it around herself before she launched into the chilly night.

She hurried through the garden and to the open doorway, her heart pounding. Pressing her palm to the cold stone, she peered into the church.

The light was not as near as she thought. It burned somewhere deeper within the deserted Abbey, and it flickered as if it would soon go out. Kate carefully stepped over the threshold, and the wind that tugged at her cloak instantly stilled. The soaring, silent stone seemed to close around her.

She stood still for a moment, letting her eyes adjust to the gloom. The cathedral was like an ancient cave, the fan vaulting soaring over her head, the stone monuments of lords and ladies looming to either side. Their ghosts seemed to peer out at her, waiting to see what she would do.

The smell of candle smoke and incense lingered in the air like the spirits of those ancient knights. The memories of past glories, lost in the extinguished flames. Kate tiptoed past them.

"Mary?" she called softly. "Are you there?"

There was no answer. Only the distorted echo of her own voice.

But she saw the fluttering light of that candle coming from Henry VII's chapel. She ran toward it, eager to be gone from that haunted place but unable to leave Mary behind if she was indeed there.

Henry and Elizabeth of York stared up at the vaulted ceiling, unperturbed by earthly doings, their relatives arrayed around them in stone repose. A lantern sat on a shallow stone step, guttering low, fluttering like a dying moth.

Kate leaned her trembling hand on a stone pillar and blinked hard in the dim light. All was still and silent, the peaceful rest of decades except for the freshly closed vault that held Queen Mary.

Then a small flutter, like that of a real ghost, made her gasp. Kate whirled around, her heart thundering, to see the tiniest movement of a scarlet velvet hem along the ground.

For an instant, she was tossed back to the horrible events at Hatfield House. Dead bodies and blood, complete stillness. Her head swam and she feared she would faint. She took a deep breath and curled her fingers tight around the cold strength of the pillar until she felt steady again.

She turned toward that tiny movement and saw a crumple of scarlet cloth, a spill of bright red hair that made her think of the queen's, against the pale stone floor. As if in a dream, she dashed toward the heap of color and stumbled to her knees.

It was Mary Everley, but scarcely recognizable as the pretty, vivacious young lady who had befriended Kate and waited on the queen. Mary lay on the floor next to one of the stolid, pitiless pillars, facedown, her arms outflung and her hands curled into claws. Her nails were torn away at the tips. Dark red blood clotted the hair at her temple.

Kate felt a scream crawling up her throat, threatening to strangle her, and she forced it back down. Screaming and panicking wouldn't help Mary now. She quickly glanced around, half-fearful that the villain might still be lurking nearby. The church seemed empty, silent. Not even ghosts dared linger nearby.

She reached out to touch Mary's wrist to see if a pulse yet beat there. Mary was quite still, her skin already turning cold. Kate tried frantically to remember when last she saw Mary at the banquet. Surely she couldn't have been dead for long?

But the banquet had been such a whirl of faces and sound that Kate couldn't remember when she first saw Mary was gone.

"I'm so sorry, Mary," Kate whispered. She carefully laid Mary's hand back down at her side. Where her head was turned to the side, Kate saw that Mary's eyes were half-open, glazed and glassy as she stared sightlessly into the darkness of the chapel. Her lips were parted as if frozen in a startled cry. One sleeve was torn from its gold ribbon ties, but other than that, her clothes were unruffled.

There was only the wound at her temple, the red mat of blood staining her white skin and seeping into her loosened hair. And clutched in her hand was a silver button with a braided edge. Kate quickly slid it out of her grasp, to compare it with the one Nell had held. She choked back a sob as she did so.

Who would do such a thing to Mary? A young lady who, despite the fact that she seemed to hold secrets, was of such a friendly, sunny temperament? Kate felt a wave of mingled anger and sadness wash over her.

She slowly stood up, knowing she had to fetch help but reluctant to leave Mary alone in such a cold place.

"I will return," she whispered, and spun around to run back the way she had come.

The loud laughter of the hall seemed twice as raucous as before when she dashed inside, and almost nauseatingly incongruous to the absolute silence and the coppery tang of blood she had just left. Kate swallowed down her feelings, knowing she had to stay calm now. Panic would have helped nothing when she found those bodies at Hatfield, and it wouldn't help Mary now.

She instinctively looked toward the table where the Everleys sat. Mary's father was still there, watching the celebrations with a pinched expression on his face that even the giggling lady at his side could not erase. But his son and nephew were gone.

"Mistress Haywood, what is amiss?" someone said behind her.

She whirled around to find Robert Dudley watching her. For once, he was alone, with none of his train of admirers behind him. His dark eyes were solemn, his mask of merriment dropped, and for an instant he looked older and harder than usual. Here was a man who had faced battle and imprisonment, the deaths of his father and brothers as traitors, and come out a court leader again.

Was he someone she could really trust? Kate had her doubts. But she did need his help now.

"The queen feared you had been gone too long and sent me to find you," he said. There was careful gentleness in his voice, a touch of worry. No condescension toward a mere musician's daughter. "You do look very pale."

Kate realized then she had no choice *but* to trust Robert Dudley now. He had the queen's trust, after all. Mary had to be seen to, and the queen's Master of the Horse was best positioned to do that.

He could also help her find Henry Everley and Richard St. Long.

"I—I found Lady Mary, in the Abbey," she said hoarsely. "I fear she is dead."

Something flickered in his eyes, and his hand reached for her trembling arm. But he was too well versed in courtly concealment to show his surprise any further. "Dead? Are you sure, Mistress Haywood?"

Kate nodded. "I fear she appears to have been murdered. Lord Everley must be told, I think."

Sir Robert nodded grimly. "The queen first. Can you come with me now? Do you feel strong enough?"

Surprised by his thoughtfulness, Kate nodded. "I am well enough."

A footman in his scarlet and gold and livery was hurrying past with a heavy tray of goblets. Sir Robert snatched one and handed it to her. "Drink this quickly, it will steady you. You feel very cold."

Kate gulped down the strong, sweet wine, and found that it did stop the trembling she'd scarcely felt in the shock of the moment. Over the silver rim of her cup, she saw Queen Elizabeth watching them, a worried frown on her white brow.

"You are right, Sir Robert," Kate said. "The queen must be told."

CHAPTER 12

"The dirty varlets! And at my very coronation, too. When they are found, I will rip them apart with my own hands. . . ." Queen Elizabeth's shouted words were interrupted by a violent sneeze.

Kat Ashley ran forward to give Elizabeth a fresh handkerchief and plumped the bolsters piled high on the grand royal bed. The reddened nose of the day before had turned to a full-blown cold, and the queen was confined to her chamber with herbed possets and fur blankets. The celebratory joust was canceled, leaving the court to play cards and mill about the palace corridors in snowbound idleness.

Thus far no official word had been given of Lady Mary's death, though surely rumors were circulating like the tides of the river under London Bridge. Kate knew a small, insular world like a royal court could never long hold secrets.

Lady Mary's father had been told, and was supposedly confined to his chambers with his family, though Kate had not seen them since last night's banquet. There was no sign of the man with the strange golden eyes. Sir Robert had summoned the Coroner of the Royal Household, who was responsible for any deaths within a twelve-mile radius of the queen, and they had seen to Lady Mary's body.

Kate had spent a sleepless few hours in her bed, her thoughts spinning over and over the scene where she had found Mary. The blood, the torn fingernails that had tried to fight off her attacker, the red hair against the stone floor. The silver button in her hand. Surely poor Nell of the Cardinal's Hat had looked much the same.

It seemed unlikely that the deaths of a court lady and a Winchester goose could be related. Yet some of the same men frequented both Whitehall and Southwark. Men like Henry Everley, mayhap?

She had been able to organize little of her jumbled thoughts, so she rose early and dressed to wait to be summoned, playing her lute softly to distract herself. She held the lute now, cradled in her hands like a protective talisman.

Elizabeth sneezed again, and impatiently waved away Mistress Ashley when the lady tried to press on her a bowl of broth.

"You were friends with Lady Mary, were you not, Kate?" Elizabeth said, her voice rough.

"We sometimes talked, Your Majesty. She was a most friendly lady, very welcoming to me when I came to London."

"Too friendly, mayhap?" Elizabeth mused. "Did she have any romances? Any jealousies?"

Kate thought of the man who had embraced Mary on the Tower ramparts, but something held her back from talking about that yet. "Not that she ever spoke of. I don't think she yet had any thoughts of marriage; she seemed most happy to be here at court."

"To be away from the close quarters of her family in the country?" Elizabeth's long, white fingers plucked at the velvet counterpane tucked around her. "I am sure her father would have arranged an advantageous match for her in time—the man has been constantly pleading poverty ever since he came to court."

"Poverty, Your Majesty?" Kate asked in surprise. The Everleys seemed as lavishly attired and accompanied by retainers as anyone else at court.

"My sister was not always very generous to her Protestant, or formerly Protestant, subjects as she was to our Grey cousins," Elizabeth said. "And Lord Everley's son and heir does not seem the prudent, self-denying sort. Did Mary say nothing of them to you, Kate?"

"Very little." Kate remembered Henry Everley shaking his sister's arm, his face a mask of fury. "I think they may have had a disagreement, though."

"A disagreement? How so?" Elizabeth said. Kate told her the little of what she had seen, and the queen frowned as she went on plucking at her blanket. "I must visit Lord Everley myself, as soon as I can rise from this blasted bed. Do you know the other Everleys at all?"

"Nay, Your Majesty. Lord Everley and his son take no interest in music. Master St. Long has been friendly enough."

"Ah, yes—the cousin. I know little about him, I fear. Perhaps you could find the time to speak to him, then. Find out more about him."

"Yes, Your Majesty. Mary seldom spoke of him, except to say he came to live with them when he was young and his parents died." Kate suddenly realized how very little she *did* know about Master St. Long, except that he was considered handsome by the court ladies. Where had his family lived before they died? Where was he educated?

"What of her other friends? She was often whispering and giggling with my cousin Lady Catherine Grey."

"They did seem to enjoy each other's company." Kate had never been around them when they were together. The Greys tended to keep to themselves, except among those they considered their equals. And there were not many of those; Lady Frances was always very aware she was the niece of Henry VIII.

Elizabeth shook her head. "My cousin bears close watch, I think. She has some foolish friendships indeed. She is coming later to see me with her mother. I will see if she can recall anything of interest about Lady Mary's secrets. Since you live among the other ladies, Kate, mayhap you can find out more. Gossip is a silly way to pass the hours, but there can be useful kernels plucked from idle words."

"I will do my best, Your Majesty," Kate said, softly but fiercely. "I want to help in any way I can to find out who did this wicked thing."

Elizabeth studied her in silence for a long moment, her dark eyes narrowed. The only sound was the crackle of the flames leaping high in the grate, and the whispers of the other ladies gathered across the room, too far away to be understood. Kate curled her hands tighter around her lute to keep from fidgeting under that steady, all-seeing gaze.

Finally, the queen nodded. "You were most helpful in those terrible events at Hatfield, Kate. You have a sharp sense of justice, I think, and a willingness to seek it that is most rare. Together we will find who did this to Lady Mary, and why. No one mars my coronation and escapes my justice, I vow it!"

Another sneezing fit followed, and Kate handed Elizabeth a clean cloth as the queen sank back down onto her bolsters. Her cheeks were a hectic, fevered red.

"I can do little until I feel well enough to leave this

cursed bed," Elizabeth said. "You must tell me what you find outside this chamber, Kate."

Kate nodded. She was eager to start seeking Mary's killer, but also nervous she might fail. Might disappoint the queen, and herself. "I fear I did discover something else, Your Majesty. Something that is very probably not connected to Lady Mary, but 'tis hard to know yet."

Elizabeth frowned. "Something else?"

Kate told her of Nell in Southwark, and her sister, Bess, who needed help to find the murderer.

Elizabeth's scowl deepened. "A red-haired Winchester goose, you say? And killed in the same manner as Lady Mary?"

"I did not see Nell's body, but Bess and the guard at the bawdy house told me her head was—wounded." Kate stopped to think about that for a moment. Aye, both women had died from a blow to the head, it seemed. But Bess and the guard had said there was a great deal of blood in Nell's case. Mary had only the one wound on her temple.

Elizabeth sighed. "'Tis true that there might be a connection, but I cannot see where Lady Mary would have the same false friends as this Nell. Men are ever villainous, though, with no care for the women around them. We females are always in danger, especially ones who are foolishly romantic."

The queen looked away, and she seemed to retreat somewhere deep inside of herself. To see things in her mind no one else could share. She bit her lip, and for a moment she looked both younger and far, far older than her twenty-five years.

"Your Majesty?" Kate said gently, fearful lest the queen drift too far away into the horrors of the past.

Elizabeth turned back to her, her eyes wide as if she

was startled to find herself in her own palace chamber. "Do you remember Lord Thomas Seymour, Kate? Nay, you would not. You were but a child when his wife, my stepmother Queen Catherine Parr, died."

"I do remember him a little," Kate said. Though she had indeed been very young when her father was chief musician to Henry VIII's last wife, Queen Catherine, and then later at the widowed queen's house at Chelsea, she could remember Lord Thomas Seymour, the younger uncle of King Edward. He would be very hard to forget, a large, loud, handsome man, always lavishly dressed and planning equally lavish parties.

Everyone had been most surprised when Queen Catherine, only a few months a widow, married him. Princess Mary had departed her household amid the scandal, but Princess Elizabeth, barely fifteen, stayed. Yet life at Chelsea, and at Lord Thomas's estate at Sudeley, had been very merry for a time. Queen Catherine, usually so solemn and studious, learned to laugh, and Kate's father was kept very busy with his music.

It all ended much too soon. Kate remembered Princess Elizabeth leaving the queen's household amid tears. Queen Catherine took to her chamber, pregnant and ill by then, and died when the child was born. Kate's father then wandered from noble house to noble house with his music, until Elizabeth summoned him to serve her in her exile. Kate remembered those short days as golden ones in her childish memory.

But then, when she was a child she knew naught of why Elizabeth left Queen Catherine's house so suddenly. It was when she grew older that she heard snatches of the scandalous, scurrilous gossip. Lord Thomas had pursued the young princess, had flirted with her, kissed her, even entered her bedchamber in the mornings before she was dressed. Possibly he even schemed to marry her, without the permission of her brother—the king—and his council. It led to his execution in the end.

And Elizabeth never spoke of him.

"You are young, Kate," Elizabeth said sadly, twisting her handkerchief between her fingers. "Just as your friend Lady Mary was. And youthful hearts are the most vulnerable. They have yet to learn prudence. I hope you will be cautious."

Kate was confused. Cautious about what? Was it love that had led to Mary's downfall? She had yet to find out. "I—I have no thoughts of marriage, Your Majesty," she said carefully. She forced away a sudden flashing thought of Anthony Elias and his green eyes.

Elizabeth gave a hoarse laugh. "I know. You care only for your music, and that is a fine thing. For I will never easily let talent such as yours slip away from my court. But I fear your friend Lady Mary would have nothing like that to distract *her*. A handsome man, wise to the ways of the world—what young lady can resist his blandishments?"

Blandishments like those of the doomed Lord Thomas? The Seymours had been too much mixed up in matters of late, and Kate couldn't yet decipher how they fit into everything. "You think Lady Mary did have a lover, then, an older man leading her astray?"

Elizabeth shrugged. "Who can say? I know much about my court, but not yet everything. Nay, not yet. I am disturbed, though, by what you tell me about this bawd with the red hair."

Before she could say more, Mistress Ashley rushed over. "Your Majesty, Lady Frances and Lady Catherine Grey are on their way!"

"God's teeth, but I had forgotten about them," Elizabeth muttered. "It is difficult enough to talk to my cousins when I am well. I am in no humor for them now. Ah, well, I suppose I must have it done with."

"Shall I go, Your Majesty?" Kate said.

"Nay, nay," Elizabeth said with an impatient wave of her handkerchief. "You should stay and listen, Kate, if you are to help me discover what happened to Lady Mary. Lady Catherine was her friend, was she not? She may have something useful to say, but she will be too careful in talking to me."

And she would never notice someone like Kate. "Of course."

"The Count de Feria also begs an audience with you, lovey," Mistress Ashley said as she fussed with the queen's bedcovers. "He has sent several messages today already."

Elizabeth sighed deeply. "A plague on all ambassadors! He and his master, King Philip, have nothing to say I want to hear. They are all pretty words and false smiles."

Kate thought of Catherine Grey and the Spanish ambassador whispering together. And Mary with them. "Your Majesty—is Lady Catherine not acquainted with Senor de Feria? They are often seen talking, and only yesterday I glimpsed Lady Mary with them."

Was it truly only a couple of days ago she saw Mary laughing with Catherine Grey and the Spanish ambassador? It seemed a decade ago.

Elizabeth's eyes narrowed. "Aye, indeed. Very clever, Kate. Feria does seem to think he can gain from Lady Catherine's friendship, and my silly cousin is all too easily flattered. Perhaps they can be useful after all."

A footman in the queen's scarlet and gold livery announced, "Lady Frances and Lady Catherine Grey, to see the queen."

"Go and seat yourself at my new virginals over there, Kate," Elizabeth said, letting Mistress Ashley smooth her hair and her fur-trimmed brocade robe. "Play a quiet song, and listen to what my dear cousins have to say. No doubt they will importune me about their position at court again, or try to convince me to send my Boleyn relations away."

Kate nodded, and quickly went to sit down at the instrument that rested near the bed, half-hidden by the velvet bed-curtains. As she waited for the Greys to be admitted, she carefully ran her fingertips over the cool keys. Despite her nerves at being pulled suddenly into such terrible events, she had to admit she took pleasure in such a beautiful instrument. It was not new, but handsomely restored of polished, burnished wood, inlaid with Queen Anne Boleyn's falcon badge and newly tuned. Perhaps it had once belonged to the queen's mother, but now it sounded like new.

At last Elizabeth was ready, and she gestured to Mistress Ashley to let her cousins into the chamber. Lady Frances and Lady Catherine made properly low curtsies before Elizabeth impatiently waved them closer. Kate carefully studied them under the guise of her song.

Lady Frances had once been beautiful, tall and slim with her Tudor mother Princess Mary's red-gold hair and blue eyes. But long years of political turmoil, watching her family torn apart and her eldest daughter, Lady Jane, and husband Lord Suffolk executed, along with ill health, had made her pale and thin, her cheeks hollow. Her fine purple brocade gown hung on her figure, as if she had lost weight since having it made for the coronation festivities.

But her gaze on the queen was steady and determined enough, her fingers curled tightly around her daughter's hand.

Lady Catherine, on the other hand, was in the full bloom of youth and beauty. Her cheeks glowed pink, and the soft curls of her blond hair bounced under her embroidered cap. Her large blue eyes were wide, studying everything around her in the royal bedchamber. Kate remembered that Lady Catherine had been demoted from her place as Lady of the Bedchamber to Queen Mary, and was now merely a maid of honor.

"How do you fare today, Cousin Frances?" Elizabeth said lightly, stifling another sneeze.

"We are well enough, Your Majesty," Lady Frances answered. She smiled, but her voice was tight. "But we were most distressed to hear that you are ill."

Elizabeth smiled sweetly, which Kate knew was never a good sign. Sweetness meant she was about to spew fire. "And you came rushing forthwith to assure yourselves about my state of health. Most kind of you, Cousin, to take such an eager interest."

"We are cousins, Your Majesty. My mother was your own father's sister," Frances said. "Nearest of kin. Naturally we are concerned. If only my Catherine could be closer to you in your household, we could be of more immediate assistance."

Frances tapped hard on Catherine's hand. The young lady ceased looking around the room to hastily curtsy. "Indeed, Your Majesty," Catherine chirped. "We wish only to serve you, as family should."

"I am suddenly peculiarly rich in family," Elizabeth said. "'Tis most gratifying."

Lady Frances's gaunt face hardened. "Lord Hunsdon and his offspring, I suppose, Your Majesty. But as your *Tudor* kin . . ."

Yet Kate had heard whispers that Baron Hunsdon *was* "Tudor kin," the son of Henry VIII and Mary Boleyn, though he himself always claimed otherwise. Of course the Greys would not like that.

"I will let all my relations know how best they can serve me, cousin," Elizabeth snapped. "Have I not been generous? Have I not gifted you with the Sheen charter-house to be your London home, though surely you cannot need so very much room? Have I not given your daughters places at my court where they can prove themselves?"

Catherine's pretty face hardened just like her mother's, a sudden flicker of tightening bitterness that aged her a decade. But it was quickly gone, hidden behind her vacant smile. Hurt pride could be a dangerous thing, Kate thought.

"Your Majesty has been very generous," Lady Frances said. "We wish only to serve you as our rank demands, and be rewarded however you see fit. Just as your siblings and your father did."

"So you shall be," Elizabeth agreed. But even Kate knew it was doubtful the Greys would be rewarded as they really wished—with the naming of Lady Catherine as Elizabeth's heir. "In good time. Today, I fear, I must be the bearer of some sad news. You were friends with Lady Mary Everley, I think, Lady Catherine."

That did catch Catherine's floating attention. The lady went very still, watching the queen closely. "I am, Your Majesty, though I have not seen her since last night."

"I fear that is because Lady Mary has suddenly died," Elizabeth said. Her voice was soft and kindly, but Kate saw that her dark eyes watched Catherine very closely. "She was discovered in the Abbey late last night. Did you know nothing of this?"

Lady Catherine might be a court lady from birth, Kate thought, but she was no stage player. Her large blue eyes grew even wider, and her face turned a stark stone white. She opened her mouth, but nothing came out except a tiny squeak. She swayed back as if suddenly pushed, and Lady Frances had to catch her arm to keep her from falling.

Kate would wager Lady Catherine had known naught of Mary's death until that moment.

"Dead?" Catherine whispered.

"Was it a fever, Your Majesty?" Lady Frances cried. "Is there a plague loosed upon us, even now in winter? Should we leave the city?"

Elizabeth tapped her fingers thoughtfully on her velvet-covered lap. "There is no danger of contagion, Cousin. Lady Mary met her death by misadventure."

"Misadventure?" Catherine gasped. "But how—who . . ."

"That we do not know yet, but be assured we will soon discover everything," Elizabeth said. "Perhaps you could be of help, Catherine, since you were her friend."

Lady Frances looked up from her sobbing daughter with burning eyes. "Your Majesty cannot think that my daughter had anything to do with such villainy! Catherine has only been attending on her duties. . . ."

"Lady Mary confided things in you, did she not, Lady Catherine?" Elizabeth said, ignoring Lady Frances. "You had friends in common as well, such as young Lord Hertford, and the Count de Feria, I think."

"I—I talk to many people, Your Majesty," Catherine choked out. "Mary also knew some of them. But it was only to talk of—of music and cards, fashion. Nothing that could h-hurt her."

Kate saw how even in the midst of stunned grief, Lady Catherine neatly sidestepped the mention of Feria.

"Did she have any romances? Any quarrels?" Elizabeth persisted.

Lady Catherine frantically shook her head. "Nay, Your Majesty, none at all! She wished only to be of service to you here at court, as we all do. She wished no one ill."

"Well, it seems someone wished *her* ill, and we had all best beware," Elizabeth said. She studied Lady Catherine in silence for a long, tense moment before she finally nodded. "You are shocked, Cousin Catherine, and will surely remember more later, which you can then tell us. Go and rest now."

Lady Frances helped her daughter to her feet and led her slowly from the chamber. Elizabeth watched them go, her fingers tapping again.

"Frances and her cohorts certainly bear watching now," she muttered. "'Tis bad enough I must bide such foreign vipers in my court, but among my own family, too . . ."

Kate let her song wind to a halt and rested her wrists on the edge of the keyboard, considering all she had just seen. Catherine, silly as she seemed, was indeed hiding something. But what? And what had Mary known of it? "They do say Senor de Feria is fond of music, Your Majesty."

"So he is, Kate. And you know many Spanish songs."

"They are always fashionable."

Elizabeth nodded. "I have heard that the count is hosting a gathering for cards and music tomorrow evening at Durham House. I am sure he would appreciate hearing some of our new English songs. You shall go to the Spanish embassy, and see what they know of Lady Mary's doings. In the meantime"—Elizabeth broke off on another loud sneeze—"see if you can find that blasted brother of hers. The Everleys seem like the Greys in their constant dissembling."

Kate nodded, eager to go someplace where she could find real answers. Of course the lion's den of the Spanish embassy would conceal many secrets. "I will, Your Majesty. And if I could, I would like to visit Mary's body before it is buried."

Elizabeth frowned. "Are you quite sure, Kate?"

Kate was not *sure* about that at all. It would surely be best to remember Mary as alive and laughing, not cold in her coffin. But she had to help Mary however she could now. "Aye, I am sure. I have seen dead bodies before, you know."

"So you have. Very well, speak to Robert Dudley, he will know where the coroner had her taken. Then send Sir Robert to me. I am perishing of boredom in here."

"Yes, Your Majesty." Kate curtsied and turned to leave the chamber. She glanced back when Elizabeth softly called her name.

"True friends are rare in this world, Kate," the queen said. "I am sorry you have lost another in such a terrible way."

Kate remembered Hatfield House and all that had happened there. True friends were indeed rare, and all too often proved false. Mary had helped Kate find her way at court when she was new and a bit confused, a bit lonely. She had made things seem brighter. Even if Mary had embroiled herself in some trouble that led to her death, she had been kind, and she deserved justice. Just as Nell did.

"Thank you, Your Majesty," Kate answered. "I will do what I can for Lady Mary now, though I fear it will be all too little."

"You will never be without friends, Kate. I do take care of my own, no matter what my good cousin Lady Frances says."

Kate nodded, puzzled by the queen's words. Took care of her own? Kate and her father had always worked for

Elizabeth and her family, and God willing, they always would. They were the queen's "own," as all her household was. Yet Elizabeth watched her with a still, silent intensity, as if she tried to say more.

But in the end Elizabeth just nodded and waved Kate away. As she made her way down the crowded corridors, she scarcely saw the richly dressed, now idle courtiers as the packs of dogs ran past. She had much to prepare for. She had to find Henry Everley and his cousin Master St. Long, and discover where they were when Mary died. She had to find out who the man with the strange gold eyes was. She had to visit the lion's den of the Spanish embassy. She had to—horrors!—try to wriggle secrets out of Lady Catherine Grey.

Perhaps in one of those places she could learn more about poor Nell, as well as about Mary. She had to step very carefully, and never let her mask slip. She shivered, feeling scared and exhilarated all at the same time.

But first, she had to visit Mary herself.

CHAPTER 13

"This way, Mistress Haywood," Robert Dudley called over his shoulder as he led Kate down a narrow lane toward the small chapel that waited for them at the end of Catte Alley.

Kate had been most surprised when Sir Robert himself offered to take her to see Mary. After all, he was the queen's Master of the Horse, her favorite courtier, and surely had a great many claims on his time. She'd fully expected never to even see him in person when she delivered the queen's message, but only to find one of his servants to direct her. Yet Sir Robert had left behind his retinue to help her himself.

Kate studied him carefully as she hurried behind him through the ancient, winding streets around Westminster. He was very handsome, there was no doubt about it, tall and lean, dark as a pirate, but adroit at concealing his thoughts and emotions. Surely imprisonment and war would do that to a man. What would ambition do now?

Could he have known Lady Mary better than was believed? Was that why he took such concern about this terrible event now? Sir Robert was married, of course, to a sickly lady who never came to court, and much of his time was spent in attendance on the queen. But he was charming to almost everyone who did not arouse his short temper, with a quick smile to hide his granite-hard shrewdness.

Certainly ladies enjoyed his company, and he didn't seem the sort to deny himself his pleasures, now that all the dangers he had lived through were past and he had Queen Elizabeth's favor.

Kate held the heavy hem of her cloak above the mud of the lane and rushed after him. Sir Robert's long, powerful legs could make time far more hastily than she could.

"You are most kind to assist me so, Sir Robert," she said. "I am sure you have many duties."

He smiled down at her, but it was not the dazzling, deflecting grin he wore most of the time. It seemed strangely sad to Kate, crooked, not quite meeting his wary-looking dark eyes.

"None more important than helping the queen, Mistress Haywood," he said. "She has told me of your bravery at Hatfield last year, when I regret I was not there to protect her myself. We all owe you much gratitude."

"Not at all, Sir Robert," Kate said, surprised he had heard of any of that. Or that he would remember. "Like you, I wish only to serve the queen. We have all waited so long to see this day. To have it thus marred . . ."

"It was a wicked deed," he said tightly.

Kate gathered up her courage and asked, "Did you mayhap know Lady Mary or her family, Sir Robert?"

If he suspected her intentions in asking, he gave no indication. She could read only weary sadness on his sun-lined face as he shook his head. "Not well. I was once friends of a sort with her brother, Lord Henry Everley, when we were boys. We were both fostered for a time with one of the branches of the Seymour family."

Ah yes, the tangled web of kinship, friendship, and loyalties among the Protestant nobility. How often had they had shifted in those days, the Greys, the Seymours, the Dudleys. Where did that loyalty stand now? Where did Sir Robert's lie?

"But you are not friends now?" Kate asked cautiously.

"Our paths diverged after those boyhood days, Mistress Haywood. I fought in France for King Philip, to secure my release from the Tower, and Henry Everley lived quietly at Everley Court, near the Seymours, from what I remember. There was talk that the Everleys meant to go abroad, as many Protestant families did then, but they stayed in the end."

"Do you remember Lady Mary from that time? Or the Everleys' cousin Richard St. Long?"

"Lady Mary I do remember a little. She was a pretty girl, but she seldom came near us." Sir Robert frowned as if he was trying to remember. "Master St. Long I do not much recall. Perhaps he was a poor relation taken in by the Everleys and then fostered elsewhere. I never knew him until they arrived at court for Christmas and Henry Everley sought to renew our acquaintance."

"And has he asked you to look into the matter of his sister's death now?"

"Nay, I have not seen Henry or his father today. I am concerned about this matter, Mistress Haywood, because—" Sir Robert suddenly halted, almost making Kate bump into him. "Tell me, have you noticed Lady Mary's resemblance to Eliz—to the queen?"

Kate swallowed hard and nodded. "It would be hard to miss, I fear. Do you suspect someone was trying to kill the queen and mistook Lady Mary for her?"

Sir Robert rubbed his hand over his bearded jaw. "'Tis far-fetched, I know. Anyone with sense would surely know Queen Elizabeth would never leave her own coronation banquet to go wandering alone in the Abbey."

"But not everyone is in their right wits. If someone with an angry grudge saw a slender young woman with red hair and a fine velvet gown by herself. And there in the darkness . . ." But what if Mary *had* been mistaken for the queen? Or if the killer knew very well who it was, mayhap he thought to send the queen a message by killing a lady close to her, one who resembled her.

Sir Robert's eyes narrowed as he looked down at her. "You have thought about this, Mistress Haywood."

Kate nodded. For a moment she wondered if she should tell him about red-haired Nell from Southwark, but she decided to keep that to herself for now. She had promised Rob Cartman she would protect him if she could. She had told the queen of it already, and had to be careful of others.

Everyone at court had so many secrets, so many complex plans and ambitions they kept hidden. She couldn't afford to trust too easily any longer.

"Of course I have thought about it," she said. "Lady Mary was my friend, and finding her thus so horribly haunts me. I want to help if I can, and so must think of everything."

Sir Robert nodded, and turned to continue on their way. The few people out and about on such a cold day, and on such a back lane, dreary after the queen's wine-soaked celebrations, instinctively made room for him.

"I am sure it will turn out to be the usual sad sort of tale," he said. "A lovers' quarrel, or a family disagreement that grew out of control."

"Hopefully we can find the truth very soon," Kate said. She remembered the man with the strange eyes at the Tower. She had to discover who he was. And she had to find out if Sir Robert knew anything about the Everleys' past he was withholding.

As they stepped into the dim, stuffy warmth of the small church, a short, rotund man in dark robes with a horn tablet attached to his belt hurried toward them.

"Master Simpson," Sir Robert whispered to Kate. "Clerk to the coroner."

"The jury has gone, Sir Robert," Master Simpson said, in a hasty, breathy, nervous little voice. He put Kate in mind of a mouse. "They have returned a verdict of foul murder by persons unknown, unlikely to be discovered so long after the fact. The coroner has departed."

Sir Robert gave a brusque nod, and the clerk scurried away.

"Everything is concluded so quickly?" Kate asked, startled.

Sir Robert laughed wryly. "The coroner is not a man to linger at his task. Not when there is not a clear culprit. He is only paid from the estates of convicted murderers."

Kate was appalled to know Mary's murderer could get away so quickly, simply because whoever the villain was had the good sense not to stay standing over her body with blood on his hands for the coroner to see. "Of course the man will never be found if he is not sought! Were there any witnesses found, perhaps on the street outside the church? Was anyone even asked?"

"Everyone was at the banquet, and could have heard nothing," Sir Robert said, his voice full of resigned sadness. Surely he of all people knew about selective knowledge.

"Not even Henry Everley? Where is he now?"

"With his father, sequestered in their mourning. Perhaps we should visit to condole with them this evening, Mistress Haywood."

Kate suddenly realized that Sir Robert Dudley could be of help in places where she could not. He could get people to talk to him where they would not to her. But, on the other hand, people would unconsciously reveal things to a young musician they would be too on their guards to say to the queen's favorite. Most interesting. "That would be the polite thing to do."

Sir Robert nodded, and his expression turned solemn when a priest in his black-and-white robes stepped out of a doorway and bowed to them. The tonsure he wore under Queen Mary's reign was growing out. "All is in readiness within, Sir Robert."

"Are you sure you wish to do this, Mistress Haywood?" Sir Robert asked her quietly. "To see a friend thus . . ."

Kate nodded. They said Robert Dudley had watched from his Tower cell window as his brother's beheaded body was carted past from Tower Hill. This could be no worse than that. "I have seen death before, Sir Robert. I must see her now. I will not faint."

He took her arm and led her into the church. It was an old space, austere and dark, with a short aisle leading to an altar made plain by the return of the reformed religion. The queen had stated she would make no changes yet, but some had anticipated her wishes. A makeshift bier was set up in front of the communion table, holding up a plain wooden coffin surrounded by candles.

"I will leave you for the moment," Sir Robert said.

Kate barely sensed him move away as she hurried down the aisle of the empty church. She knew she had to be done with this unpleasant task, and quickly.

The figure that rested in the coffin was Lady Mary, and yet not. Something that had struck Kate deeply after the events at Hatfield was how swiftly life departed a body, leaving nothing but empty blankness behind. But that emptiness could not cancel the claims of friendship or justice.

Lady Mary wore her fine gown from the coronation feast, restored to a semblance of order, and the edges of her winding-sheet were drawn away so Kate could see her. Most of her red hair was covered beneath a white cap, and without its bright frame her face was stark white and slack. Death had softened the features that once held a certain sharp delicacy, like the queen's. Her skin was pale, like the melted wax of a candle. Coins held her eyes closed.

Kate took a deep, steadying breath, inhaling the scent of dust and old incense, of perfumed strewing herbs and the first sickly-sweet hint of decay, to force herself to closely examine the body for any clues. The only wound she could see was the hollow, bruised area on Mary's temple, now cleaned of blood, and an older bruise just below her cheekbone.

Kate studied the hands crossed on Mary's chest. They, too, were waxy white, the tips turning blue, and she saw the nails were still ragged where Mary had tried to fight for her life. Kate remembered the button caught there, like with Nell. They were empty now, and Mary's rings were gone.

In fact, Kate saw, she wore no jewelry at all. But someone had been there and tried to adorn her, for a wilting posy of greenery was tucked into one hand. Rosemary for remembrance, laurel for triumph. And something pink and sweet for love.

"I will find who did this, Mary," Kate whispered. "I promise."

The deep silence of the chapel was suddenly broken by the echo of running footsteps on the stone floor. Startled, Kate leaped away from the coffin and glanced around the hushed space.

Surely it could not be Sir Robert or the priest; they

would have called out to her first. And she'd been so sure she was alone.

"Who is there?" she called. Her only answer was more running footsteps, vanishing down a side aisle.

Kate ran after them. "Wait!" she shouted, but the steps only ran faster.

She stumbled into a tiny chapel that opened to the back of the church just in time to see a man, tall, broad-shouldered, clad all in simple black, pull open a door to the street outside. He looked back at her over his shoulder, and she glimpsed the glow of catlike golden eyes under the brim of his plain cap.

"Walter!" someone shouted from the street. "Over here!"

The man slipped through the door, letting it slam behind him.

Her heart pounding, Kate ran after him. The door was heavy, but she yanked it open and rushed outside.

For an instant, the glare of the gray-yellow sunlight after the darkened church dazzled her and she couldn't see anything. She blinked hard, jostled by the passing crowd, for this lane was busier than the way they arrived.

The black-clad man was at the end of the street, vanishing around a corner. Kate followed, pushing her way past people and stray dogs, but it seemed the man was part cat in truth, for he had completely disappeared.

"Walter!" she cried, but no one answered. She almost cursed in frustration. He had been so close and he had slipped right away from her!

"Mistress Haywood! What is amiss?"

Sir Robert Dudley ran to her side, his hand curled tightly around the hilt of his sword. He studied the crowd around them suspiciously, and once again everyone moved around him to make way.

Kate wondered fleetingly what it would feel like to have such power. But she also now realized that being inconspicuous, fitting into the background, was what allowed her to observe everyone when they thought they weren't being watched.

Not that she had been inconspicuous enough to keep from driving away the mysterious Walter. She cursed at herself for calling out before she could think.

"I saw someone in the chapel," she said. "I thought once I had seen him talking to Lady Mary before, but he fled when I called to him."

"A man?" Sir Robert said. His frown deepened. "Do you know his name?"

Kate shook her head. "I think it might be Walter, but I haven't seen him at court. He was tall, dressed all in black. Good-quality garments, but not rich." She had had many chances to observe fashion in recent days.

"There are many Walters in England, Mistress Haywood, but I cannot think of one associated with the Everleys. 'Tis most suspicious he fled, I vow. You would know him if you saw him again?"

Kate thought of his eyes, the almost unearthly glow of them. "Perhaps."

"We should go, then." He took her arm with his free hand to lead her away, keeping the other on his sword. "It grows late."

As she followed Sir Robert back past the church, she wondered if Walter wore silver buttons on his plain black doublet.

CHAPTER 14

 #One of the first people Kate saw on returning to the palace was Richard St. Long. It was nearly time for the court to sup, and he was striding across the almost empty courtyard. A footman led away a horse, as if Master St. Long had just returned from a ride. His dark gold-streaked hair was rumpled, and his boots were muddy. He wore the same black and tawny doublet from the coronation procession, and Kate was again struck by the way it didn't seem to fit quite right over his strong shoulders. As if he could not afford to be bothered to get the careful tailoring Henry Everley's garments exhibited.

He was scowling down at the cobblestones, as if deeply distracted, but when Kate called out to him, he glanced up and smiled.

"Mistress Haywood," he said. He came to a halt and quickly ran his hand through his hair, as if to bring some semblance of order to the locks. "How do you fare today?"

"I fear I have had better days, Master St. Long," she answered. "I have just been to see Lady Mary before she is to be buried."

His eyes widened, as if he was startled she would do such a thing. She saw that they were quite lovely eyes, pale blue, fringed with dark lashes. "That was most kind of you. You were a good friend to my cousin, I think, Mistress Haywood."

"She was kind to me, when I first came here to court and knew so few people," Kate said. She watched Richard carefully as she spoke, but he only looked politely concerned and perhaps a bit tired, though solicitous of her. He seemed the sort of man she had seen often in her service to Elizabeth, the kind of man who considered women to be weak and delicate. Being the country miss, unsure in the sophisticated ways of a royal court, seemed as fine a guise as any.

"Lady Mary often advised me," she continued. "It is hard to know who to turn to for true friendship."

Richard nodded and smiled patiently. He leaned closer, as if to protect her from the cold wind swirling around the courtyard. He smelled of horse and French cologne. "Mary was a kindhearted lady. She was most warm and welcoming to me when I first came to live at Everley Court, when most would have taken no notice of a bedraggled poor relation."

So he was the "poor relation," was he? Kate had suspected as much from his clothes, and the swaggering, overly merry demeanor that often meant a gentleman was making up for something. She remembered Sir Robert saying he did not remember Master St. Long from his foster days with Henry Everley.

Yet Richard's horse and clothes were fine enough, despite the ill-fitting quality of his doublet, and he wore expensive cologne. He also went carousing in Bankside with men like Edward Seymour, Earl of Hertford. He seemed to be making his way in the world well enough now.

"So you did not always live with the Everleys?" she asked innocently.

His expression did not waver. "Nay. I was orphaned young, and my mother's brother, Lord Everley, was all the family I had left. I was sent to live with him, while my sister went to a foster family in the country somewhere."

"Will your sister come to court now?"

"Nay." His smile at last flickered for a moment, and he glanced away. "She has since died, I fear. I must make my own way in the world."

"I am sorry," Kate said. "I never had any siblings at all, for my mother died when I was born. 'Tis just my father and me."

"And I never knew my father at all. We are a castaway pair, Mistress Haywood."

Castaway, was he? And where was his cousin now? What was happening in this strange Everley family? "But you have your uncle and your cousins."

"So I do. Though Mary was the best of my family, I am afraid. We shall never be the same without her."

"I will miss her, too," Kate said, laying her hand in a brief, confiding gesture on his sleeve. He winced a bit but did not move away. "I hear that your uncle is so grief-stricken he cannot leave his chamber. Does his son stay with him?"

Richard studied her for a moment before he smiled again. "Come with me, Mistress Haywood, so we may talk quietly for a moment. As quietly as one can in a palace."

Master St. Long took Kate's arm and led her to a small stone arbor set in the wall of the courtyard. Kate thought of men lurking in dark churches, but the courtyard was bright enough, bustling with servants. And Richard St. Long was being carefully gentle and gallant. She did wonder what he had to say.

"I must tell you, Mistress Haywood, that what I say

must be in secret." Richard ran his hand through his hair again, pushing it back behind his ears to show his stylish pearl earring. "I should say nothing at all, but I fear the worry may drive me mad if I do not. And you do seem kind, much as Mary herself was. At least, she said you were a good soul."

Secrets? Kate could hardly breathe. "Of course you can confide in me, Master St. Long," she said softly. "If I can be of some help."

"I fear my cousin Henry is not with Lord Everley. We don't know where he has gone, and of a certes I do fear for him."

"Not with your uncle? At such a sad time?" Kate said, confused. Confused—and alarmed. She remembered Henry Everley's anger toward his sister, and cursed herself all over again for not watching him closer. "Could he have gone back to Everley Court? I have heard tell that grief can make people behave most strangely."

"My uncle has sent men to Everley Court, but Henry hasn't been seen there. Nor has he been to any of his usual pleasurable escapes. I have just come from searching across the river."

"At Southwark?" Kate murmured.

"Aye, and at a tavern nearer the palace, the Bull. None have seen him anywhere. I only heard tell of him at one place."

"Where was that?"

"At a goldsmith he has gone to for small loans before, when he didn't want his father to know how much he had lost at the primero tables. A Master Lucas in Cheapside. He saw Henry yesterday, and made him an advance."

"Did Henry know of his sister's death before he visited this Master Lucas, or after?"

Richard's square, stubble-covered jaw tightened. "Oh, aye, before. 'Twas mere hours later he vanished."

Kate's thoughts raced, and she tried to keep her face smooth and expressionless. Henry Everley borrowed money and fled right after his sister was foully murdered. A convenient confession of guilt? Or something else? "As I said, perhaps grief has made him mad. Was he close to his sister?"

"When we were children, perhaps. But since we came to court, I fear my uncle and cousin became set on Mary's betrothal to a wealthy lord of some advanced years. She had some objections."

Kate remembered the man at the Tower, Walter, who ran from her at the church. "I would imagine she would."

A rueful smile touched Richard's pale, drawn face. "Aye. I heard her shouting she would be no Queen Catherine Howard, married to a stinking old lecher. Henry was not best pleased."

"So you think this disappearance has something to do with Mary's sad death?" Kate said bluntly.

He looked startled at her sudden words, but he gave a slow, reluctant nod. "Henry can be an amiable companion, generous in his own way, and ladies do seem fond of him. Yet he does not care to be crossed."

"Especially not by his own sister?"

"As you say, Mistress Haywood. I do fear for my family. They are all I have left now."

Family was indeed important. What would a man like Henry Everley, or his father, do to a mere female who defied them? What would Richard St. Long do, where would his loyalties lie? "I do understand family loyalty, Master St. Long, and you honor me with your confidences. I am not sure how I can be of help to you. I know of little except music."

"And friendship, Mistress Haywood. Mary said you knew much of that, and my cousin and I understood each other." He reached out and gently took her hand between both of his. His fingers were blunt but strong, the tips callused as if he worked at swordplay more than cards, the nails bitten. "Confiding in you has helped me much. I feel much more at peace in my mind."

"Richard!" someone shouted. Kate glanced over her shoulder to see one of the young, brightly dressed courtiers who followed Robert Dudley about. He waved at Richard.

"I will be there anon," Richard called back. He kissed Kate's hand gently and let her go. "If I do hear word from Henry, I will tell you."

"I will help however I can," Kate said again. "Perhaps I should visit your uncle? Try to comfort him with good memories of Lady Mary?"

Richard gave a rueful laugh. "If you dare, Mistress Haywood. I doubt he will even open his door, though. I shall see you again soon."

Kate nodded and watched him hurry away to greet his friend. She was most puzzled as to why Master St. Long would confide in her about so grave a worry concerning his cousin, but his tidbits of information were undoubtedly most interesting. How long could the fact that Henry Everley was no longer at court be concealed? What did Master St. Long and his uncle know that they were *not* saying? Who was the "stinking old lecher" to whom Mary had been betrothed?

And how long would she have to discover the answers before Henry's departure was known to everyone, and a general search destroyed every fragile clue?

Wrapping her cloak tighter around her against the wind, Kate hurried into the palace. She nearly collided with the young Duchess of Norfolk, who was rushing past, dressed as if for riding in a fur-edged velvet doublet and veiled cap. Her ladies and young friends tumbled after her amid laughter.

Except for old Lady Gertrude Howard, who followed slowly, leaning on her walking stick. Though her movements were careful, the dark eyes in her wrinkled face were bright. She caught sight of Kate and raised her hand in a trembling gesture.

"Eleanor!" she called. "Why don't you come to see me any longer?"

Just as it had on the day of the procession, the sound of her mother's name squeezed at Kate's heart. "Nay, I am Kate . . . ," she cried to the old lady, but the duchess was already hurrying her forward.

"Come along, Auntie Gertrude," she said impatiently. "The barge waits, and we cannot miss the tide or it will be too dangerous to brave the river beneath the bridge."

Then Lady Gertrude and the others were gone, but Kate could still hear that word lingering in her ears. *Eleanor.* Had Lady Gertrude really known her mother? What could she tell Kate about her? Kate ached to know, to hear any small tales of Eleanor Haywood. But she feared that would have to wait for another day.

She had to pay a visit to Lord Everley. If he would open his chamber door.

Lord Everley's rooms were not the grandest in a palace crowded with courtiers jostling for every inch of space, but neither were they the meanest. They were at the end of one of the seemingly eternal twists of branching corridors, and Kate was lost more than once before she found them.

The door was ajar, left open by two footmen who ran past Kate bearing boxes. She peered carefully inside the chamber to find a scene of chaos.

With Lord Everley's daughter so newly dead, Kate would have expected silent mourning, black crepe draped over looking glasses, subdued movements. Yet the room was filled with open chests and stacks of papers, clothes scattered about on the floor. One of the carved trunks she recognized as Mary's, brought from the ladies' chamber. A maidservant was sorting through the fine silken gowns, the embroidered smocks and ribbon-tied sleeves.

Lord Everley himself sat by the fire, wrapped in a heavy cloak despite the heat of the flames. He was tossing papers into the grate, muttering to himself as if no one else were there. The servants only scurried about on their errands.

Kate knocked on the open door, but no one paid her any more attention than they did the muttering earl. She strode into the middle of the room and said loudly, "Lord Everley! Her Majesty has bid me speak to you."

That caught Lord Everley's attention. He glanced back at her. She could see that once he must have been handsome, in the healthy, hearty, fair, countryman way Lord Henry was, a man of swagger and loud laughter. Now, though, he seemed to have sunk in on himself overnight. His cheeks were creased, his eyes bloodshot and circled by purple rings. His gray hair was uncombed and greasy, and fell over his heavy brow.

"Her Majesty is rather late with her bidding," he said. "I have no time now. My son has already departed for Everley Court, and I must follow soon. Today."

"Departed?" Kate said. So it was true—he had run already, the cowardly knave, with his own sister not yet cold in her grave! "But, my lord, your daughter has been murdered! Surely you and your son must stay in London until her foul killer is found."

"My daughter!" Lord Everley shouted. His face looked like that of a wild animal, spittle flecked at the corners of his lips. "Mary was no good daughter of mine. I told her that coming to court was our last chance to redeem our rightful place in the world, to make our lost fortune again. I told her that her foolish, romantical fancies had to cease. We spent coin we could ill afford to give her those gowns over there, to make her fit to serve a Boleyn of all things. An Everley should never have to do such things."

"Lord Everley . . . ," Kate began, bewildered by his strange state.

He cut her off, swinging back abruptly to the fire. "Once we would never have had to lower ourselves. But Mary was careless of her honor, of her family! After all I did for them, my children. It got her killed, as I told her all wickedness would be repaid. Now we must make our fortune another way. So I sent Henry home to court an heiress whose estate neighbors ours. He should not have had to do it. Her family are *merchants*, raised too high. But Henry must marry her. This time he will obey me!"

"Master St. Long said he did not know where Lord Henry has gone. But if you know, you must fetch him back to court," Kate argued. "The queen will wish to speak to him at once."

"Must!" Lord Everley roared. He threw something at her head, a small, heavy wooden box, and Kate ducked out of his way. "I must do nothing for such a queen! She could not even protect my own daughter who served her. My family is ruined! And she sends a mere slip of a girl to command me! Richard should know better than to gossip with the likes of you."

Kate felt a small hand grasp her arm and pull her away before Lord Everley could throw something else. She glanced down to see it was the maidservant who had been sorting through Mary's clothes. The girl looked terrified, but Kate felt strangely numb.

"Come, mistress, you should be away," the maid whispered. "When he gets in a temper like this . . ."

Kate saw that Lord Everley had broken into sobs, hunched in his chair, and she knew he would tell her nothing. Perhaps he *could* tell her nothing. His daughter was dead, his son fled, his nephew nowhere to be seen. She would have to find out what had happened for herself.

She nodded and let the maid lead her away. On top of a trunk by the door, she glimpsed a pile of velvet doublets, elaborately embroidered as Lord Henry's garments always were. On top was a small miniature portrait of Lord Henry, the fair young man grinning horribly from the image. On impulse, she scooped it up and tucked it hastily into the pouch at her waist. Maybe someone in Southwark would recognize him, and help her connect him to Nell. And thence to Mary . . .

CHAPTER 15

Durham House was one of the grand mansions built like a string of sparkling jewels along the thoroughfare known as the Strand, marching in an ever more elaborate row behind large gatehouses down to the river. Somerset House and Seymour House, once owned by the executed Seymour brothers; the remains of the old Savoy Palace; Arundel House. But Durham House was one of the most splendid, and one of the oldest.

Most visitors approached the house from the river, landing at the foot of its stone water steps and walking through a maze of lawns and gardens. But Kate rode there on a borrowed horse, her lute strapped behind her as she held nervously to the reins. Despite having lived in the countryside, she'd seldom had the chance to ride and didn't entirely trust horses.

She was distracted from being sure she would fall into the icy gutter at any moment when they passed through Durham House's splendidly carved gatehouse into a cobbled courtyard. Facing her was the wing holding the great hall and the chapel, where it was said many secret Catholics slipped in to hear Mass. The four stories of mullioned windows glittered with fractured golden light, a beacon against the darkening winter sky. The wings to either side, which Kate had been told held the private apartments of the Spanish ambassador and his staff, were dim and silent.

As Kate scrambled down from the horse, thankful for the solid stones under her feet again, she studied the house and remembered the tales she heard of its long, twisting history.

Originally the palace of the powerful bishops of Durham, it was seized by Henry VIII and passed as a plum between his courtiers and relations until it landed with Princess Elizabeth for a time, only to be snatched away by Queen Mary and given back to the bishops. For a while, under King Edward, John Dudley, the Duke of Northumberland, had lived there and had hosted the wedding of his son Guildford to Lady Jane Grey in its great hall. It was said that was one of the most lavish weddings ever seen in England, swathed in acres of cloth of gold and silver, ropes of pearls and diamonds. And a most sad bride.

The bridegroom and many guests were then laid low by a case of food poisoning, which should have been seen as some kind of omen. But Northumberland's power went on for a time.

After those glittering days the house had gone dark for a while. Now it housed the Spanish embassy, since Queen Elizabeth refused to give them lodgings at court. Kate heard it said the Ambassador de Feria complained bitterly about being thus exiled, but it seemed a gilded exile.

Kate took up her lute and followed a footman through the open doors. They made their way through a maze of winding corridors, moving so quickly she could barely take in the tapestries hung on the dark-paneled walls, the gleam of silver and alabaster ornaments in the shadows. Down another corridor she had a quick glimpse of the infamous chapel, a flashing impression of a jeweled crucifix, a gilded remonstrance.

At last they reached the door to the great hall. The murmur of voices and clink of fine plates flowed out to the corridor, much more subdued than the abandoned laughter of the queen's banquets.

A silver-bearded majordomo stepped forward holding his baton of office, scowling down at her from above a stiff, high lace collar.

"Who is this?" he demanded in Spanish. "The servants' door ..."

Before the footman who was her guide could answer, Kate said in her own halting Spanish, "I am a musician to Queen Elizabeth. Her Majesty sent me to entertain the count and his esteemed guests as a special favor."

The man's lips pinched together, and he looked very much as if he would like to dismiss her immediately. But even a strict Spanish functionary would not insult the queen by turning away her gift.

"What is this, Senor de Alvara?" The Count de Feria himself emerged from the hall, clad in black satin trimmed in fine purple velvet. His dark hair was brushed back from the handsome, harsh planes of his face, and his eyes were narrowed. Around his neck was a large amethyst cross.

"This person is a musician sent by Her Majesty," the majordomo said.

The count carefully studied Kate. She held tight to her lute and met his gaze in return, refusing to fidget no matter how much she itched to. She had to remember her lessons from Rob in the art of playacting.

"Ah, yes. Mistress Haywood," the count said in English. "I remember you from the queen's court. Your music is most delightful."

Kate was surprised he remembered her at all. She hoped it was not from his visit to Brocket Hall last year. "Her Majesty has sent me to entertain your illustrious guests, Count, if it pleases you. I do know some of the newest Spanish songs."

"It pleases me very much. The musicians I have brought from Madrid have much to learn about English style, I think. If you would care to be shown to the gallery . . ."

Kate curtsied once more to the count, and followed the footman up a narrow, winding staircase to one of the musicians' galleries looking down on the great hall. On the way she glimpsed several narrow hallways branching off from the stairs, hidden ways for the servants to get around the enormous house.

She left her cloak with the boy, glad she had worn one of her new gowns of dark blue silk with silver sleeves and embroidered silver ribbon trim. Fine enough for Durham House, but subdued enough not to draw attention.

Kate was happy to find herself alone in the small gallery, the Spanish musicians nowhere to be seen. From there she had a good view of the hall and its inhabitants.

It was a lavish room indeed, marble pillars soaring up to an arched, painted ceiling and three vast fireplaces chasing the January chill away. As she tuned up her lute and launched into one of the Spanish tunes she knew, she studied the people dining at the white-damask-draped tables below.

She didn't know all of them. Few of the "new courtiers" who frequented Elizabeth's court were there. It seemed to be mostly Catholics cast out of their monasteries and convents by Elizabeth and sheltering with the Spanish, and old families disgruntled by their new places. Though the food and wine looked to be almost as lavish as that at court, the talk was quieter. More tense, more secretive, as if a rope held taut around them all and would break at any moment, sending them into chaos.

Then she glimpsed two faces that startled her. Master Hardy, the lawyer, and her friend Anthony Elias. Her fingers fumbled on the strings, but she quickly recovered and went on playing as she watched them.

They sat at the far end of the great hall, with a few other courtiers Kate recognized, cousins of Robert Dudley and the Seymours. They observed the gathering carefully, talking quietly among themselves. Kate couldn't imagine why they were at Durham House at all. Master Hardy was most loyal to Queen Elizabeth, and to a Protestant England. He had been arrested during the last weeks of Queen Mary's reign, taken off to London while his Hertfordshire offices were ransacked. Yet here he was at the Spanish embassy. Kate couldn't fathom it.

She had to admit, though, that her heart gave a glad leap to see Anthony again. He was as handsome as ever, with his lean, elegant face beneath a black velvet cap and alert green eyes watching all around him.

Her attention was suddenly caught by the Count de Feria. He had risen from his place at the head table and was hurrying toward a door half-concealed in the dark wood paneling of the walls. He spoke quietly, intently, with a small group gathered there. One ascetically thin man in cardinal's robes whispered to him most fiercely. They looked as if they were intent on important business.

Impulsively, Kate tucked her lute beneath her stool and hurried out of the lonely gallery. She remembered the maze of hidden corridors they had passed, and she was sure one would lead her to where Feria was in conference. She couldn't learn anything playing her lute alone so far from the guests. She had to try to discover whatever she could in the short time she had at Durham House.

Holding her skirts close to still their rustle, she rushed through the small warren of hallways. They were obviously meant for servants to move quietly through the massive house, and they were mostly empty now. Once she had to duck behind a doorway to avoid a rushing page boy. A few of the closed doors hid faint noises, conversations, tears, a murmured rhythm of prayer. The whistle of a scourge whip.

Kate remembered hearing that Feria sheltered many monks and nuns turned out of their monasteries by Queen Elizabeth and she shivered.

Half-fearing she would become so hopelessly lost in this world behind the walls that she would never get out, Kate at last found another staircase. She followed it down, and discovered exactly what she was looking for—the small chamber where Feria and his friends were talking in confidence.

The servants' door in the paneling was slightly ajar, the tapestry hung before it swung into place to muffle the Spanish voices. Kate pressed her back to the wall as close as she dared to the opening and listened.

Her Spanish was halting, but she could decipher enough words to know they were talking of the queen's court. Their solemn words were punctuated by the clink of silver goblets, the sharp whistle of the winter wind past the window.

For a time they talked of inconsequential things, the health of Feria's new wife, Jane Dormer, who had once served Queen Mary, the abysmal weather, the news from Spain. Then someone asked about "the lady, our friend," and Feria laughed.

"The lady is most offended, I fear," he said. "It is not difficult to keep her very friendly. She served in Queen Mary of blessed memory's household with my wife, and remembers our friendship from those days. She is sweet and biddable, as a lady should be. Unlike her vain and clever cousin."

Catherine Grey—he had to be speaking of her. Kate thought of Lady Catherine whispering with Feria, of Elizabeth's dislike of her cousin, her certainty that the Greys were not to be trusted. That Catherine was angling to be named the queen's heir.

"But what of her religion?" someone asked in a querulous voice. There was the rustle of stiff silk and Kate wondered if it was the ascetic cardinal who spoke. "If she is a heretic, she would be no suitable wife."

"She assures me she has long been a faithful Catholic, and is hated by her family for it," Feria said, most confidently. Kate almost laughed at his certainty. Catherine Grey struck her as no great devout worshipper on either side, unlike her firmly Protestant sister Lady Jane.

"She bears some watching, then," one of the other men said. "Has she been helpful?"

"She knows much of what happens at court, and is not shy to talk about it," Feria said. "She declares she puts her trust entirely in me, and thus in King Philip. It is too bad about our other—friend. She was also most useful, if a bit greedy. It's a shame to have lost her assistance."

Their other *lost* friend? Kate pressed her hand to her mouth in a sudden spasm of worry. Could they mean Lady Mary? Surely not. Just because she had been friends with Catherine Grey . . .

"What does Lady Catherine say about Robert Dudley?" the cardinal asked.

Feria laughed, a most unpleasantly humorless sound.

"Ah, yes. Sir Robert, the former traitor to our dear Queen Mary. He is so much in favor now that he does whatever he likes. Lady Catherine says it is well known his wife has some malady of the breast, and Elizabeth waits only for poor Lady Dudley to die to make him her consort."

"A lowborn cur like Dudley, King of England!" cried one of the men. "The scandal . . ."

"Indeed," Feria agreed. There was a clatter as more wine was poured. "But for now he is in the ascendant. I have advised Lady Catherine to come to an accommodation with Sir Robert, as we all must. He is surely not completely unamenable to us. He fought with King Philip's armies in France."

"To save his own neck after his father was executed," someone grumbled.

"Be that as it may, he owes a debt to our king. Dudley is hated by many with great power here in this benighted country, such as Norfolk."

"Norfolk," someone scoffed. "A mere puppy."

"Young he may be," Feria admonished. "But he is a duke, the queen's cousin, and protective of his place. He hates Dudley, and it is said he favors the French ambassador. If Norfolk decided to throw his weight behind Mary of Scots . . ."

"Better a heretic like Elizabeth than a Frenchwoman like Mary," the cardinal grumbled.

"So we must keep Lady Catherine and her friends close," said Feria. "We must make sure the doors of Durham House are always open to those who share our views."

"What did that Henry Everley want of you, then, Count?" the cardinal demanded. "He looked most wild when he rode in yesterday."

Henry Everley had been at Durham House as well?

Kate shook her head, baffled. It seemed there was no one in all of England not involved in Spanish plots.

Feria was silent for a long moment, and Kate thought he might not answer. She curled her fingers into tight fists to keep from screaming in frustration. She *had* to know what Lord Henry was doing there!

"Lord Henry proposes to be of help to us, but I vow we must be most cautious of him. Such passion can be unpredictable," Feria said at last. "He probably cannot be of help like our lost friend."

A loud clatter from below Kate's hiding place, as if someone had dropped a tray, sharply reminded her where she was. She couldn't be caught eavesdropping on the Spanish ambassador. Elizabeth would be forced to disavow any knowledge of what her musician was doing; then Kate could be of no use to her. She had learned a very good start here tonight, proof that Catherine Grey had befriended the Spanish and that Henry Everley had also been there before he disappeared.

She had also learned that Mary, too, might have been a spy. But that was information she needn't share just yet.

She longed to hear more, but she knew she had to go before she was discovered. Kate carefully backed out of her hiding place and tried to make her way back the direction she had come, to be in her gallery playing her music as if nothing had ever been amiss. But she had forgotten how winding the narrow back corridors of Durham House were.

Kate was certain she was almost back to the great hall, sure she recognized a certain turning, but they ended in walls or blank doors. The more she searched, the farther she got from where she wanted to be, and she could feel her hands becoming cold with impending panic.

As she turned down another corridor, Kate suddenly heard a patter of swift, heavy footsteps coming toward her from beyond a sharp corner. Not wanting to be caught, Kate ran as carefully as she could in the other direction, searching for a place to hide until whoever it was had gone past or turned direction.

But the booted steps kept behind her, moving faster when she did, slowing when she did, but always out of sight behind her. Her heart pounded in her chest, so loud it almost drowned out the steps.

She ran faster, but her unseen pursuer was still behind her. Trying to breathe past the stiff boning of her fashionable court bodice, Kate glanced behind her, but she couldn't see anything. Yet she was sure she heard the sound of breathing, the press of malevolent intentions, slowly and deliberately bearing down upon her.

Do not be fanciful! Kate told herself sternly. Surely it was only a servant going about his tasks. Not one of the dispossessed ghosts of Durham House, not a—a murderer . . .

A flashing image of Mary Everley sprawled dead on a stone floor, blood and torn fingernails, passed through Kate's mind and she bit her lip to keep from crying out.

She ran even faster, and so did the steps. Louder and louder, closer. She was sure they were after her now, but why didn't they just shout after her if she was caught spying? Why didn't they show themselves?

At the head of a narrow staircase, Kate twisted around and frantically scanned the shadows. The steps were still racing closer, echoing in the tall stairwell. There was a sudden swirl of dark cloak, like bird's wings taking flight, and a swift glimpse of a tall figure.

It was all gone in a blink of an eye, and Kate couldn't even think let alone study the figure. She caught a glimpse of a line of fine silver buttons on a black sleeve, glinting, bright, just before a hand landed on her shoulder and gave her a hard shove.

For one sickening, cold instant, she teetered on the edge of the step. Her hand flailed out, blindly seeking a wall, a handrail, anything to break her fall, but she grasped only air. She pitched forward, crying out as she managed to twist around and catch herself before her head could bounce off the hard step.

She rolled, stair to stair, her heavy skirts tangling around her. She was sure she was dead, never to see her father again, never to see anything at all, and a strange calm descended on her. Everything seemed to slow down before speeding up horribly.

At last she lurched to a stop on the landing. Her hair had tumbled from its pins, a dark tangle blinding her. For an instant she was sure she *was* dead, but then a bruising pain flashed down her side, reminding her she was still earthbound.

And someone equally earthbound had shoved her. That hand belonged to no ghost. Who knew she was here, and would want to chase her down and do her harm?

Kate pushed her hair out of her eyes and twisted around to peer up the dim stairway. It was empty now, of course, her attacker vanished.

She tried to stand up, to run back up the stairs and find whoever did this, but her bruised body gave a great spasm of pain and she fell back again.

"God's teeth," she cried, using one of the queen's favorite curses. Gritting her teeth, she carefully moved her arms and legs, and realized nothing was actually broken. Her gown had protected her from the worst. Her neck was intact. For the moment.

"Senora!" a woman screamed. Kate turned to see a maidservant at the foot of the stairs. The girl dropped the tray she held and ran up the stairs, panic written on her plain, olive-complected face. Kate could barely make out her features in the flickering light of one torch high in its wall sconce. She knelt beside Kate amid a flurry of Spanish words, so swift Kate could only make out a few.

"No, I am well enough," Kate said in her own halting Spanish. "I was going to the jakes and took a wrong turn. I fell. . . ."

The girl tried to help her to her feet, but she was as small as Kate herself and they tumbled back down to the hard floor. Before she could suppress it, Kate cried out at the burst of pain.

"I will fetch my lord de Feria," the girl sobbed. "Or Senor Alvara."

"Nay!" Kate cried through her gritted teeth. She knew she was in no condition to face Feria or that stern-faced majordomo Alvara and conceal her real purpose from them. She thought quickly, and remembered a familiar face she had glimpsed in the great hall.

"Could you find Senor Hardy, an Englishman at the banquet?" she asked the girl carefully, desperate to be understood. "An older gentleman, with white hair, with a handsome young friend who has green eyes?"

The girl obviously remembered Anthony Elias. Her olive cheeks flushed. "*Sí, sí,*" she said. "I will bring them. . . ."

"*Gracias,*" Kate muttered. As the maid dashed away, Kate fell back against the cold support of the wall to wait. And to hope desperately that her assailant wouldn't return.

She was quickly finding out just how much she hated the act of waiting.

CHAPTER 16

"Mistress Haywood! What has happened? Do you need a physician?" Master Hardy cried as he glimpsed Kate from the foot of the stairs. She watched, deeply relieved, as he hurried toward her. His fur-trimmed robes swirled around him, and his lined face was creased even more with worry.

Anthony was right behind him, his eyes wide and dark, his movements quick and graceful as he ran up the stairs two at a time. Kate couldn't help but remember the last time she saw him, in the middle of Master Hardy's ransacked office in Hertfordshire, when he'd touched her hand so sweetly. She still recalled how it felt.

"The queen sent me to play for the count's gathering," she answered. Master Hardy took her arm to help her to her feet, and she bit back a moan as all her new bruises screamed. "I took a wrong turn somewhere and slipped on the stairs."

"You should not be wandering alone in such a place as Durham House," Master Hardy fussed. "What can Her Majesty be thinking of to send you here all by yourself, my dear?"

Kate steadied herself against the wall and shook her tangled hair back from her face. She couldn't quite bring herself to look at Anthony, though she could feel his steady gaze on her, studying her closely. It seemed ridiculous to worry about a man she had known for so long seeing her all a-mess, especially with the fact that someone had just pushed her down the stairs at the Spanish embassy. But oh, she did wish that Anthony of all people couldn't see her with her sleeve torn and her hair a snarled tangle.

Kate almost laughed at herself. Surely she was becoming just as silly as Catherine Grey and her friends, giggling over handsome courtiers!

But then again, maybe Catherine Grey was not quite as featherheaded as she seemed. Not if she was whispering openly with people like Feria.

"I daresay Queen Elizabeth sent me because she thought it would be a diplomatic gesture," Kate said carefully as she brushed at her crumpled skirts. "She said the Count de Feria much enjoys music. But you are quite right, Master Hardy, I should not have wandered off by myself. This is an old and confusing house."

"Are you sure we should not call for a physick, Mistress Haywood?" Anthony asked. "You may have injuries you are unaware of."

Kate looked at him and shook her head, touched that he would be worried. But he had not been so worried that he could send her a message in the weeks since they had last seen each other. "I am well enough, just feeling foolish. I need to get back to the palace, but I'm not sure I can ride. . . ."

"We shall see you back by boat," Master Hardy said. "Anthony can see that your horse is returned."

Kate studied the old lawyer in the dim light. The torch in its sconce on the wall flickered; it would soon go out. They had to go soon, but Kate remembered her earlier doubts. Why would an English lawyer like Master Hardy, a man who had suffered much under Queen Mary, be at Durham House?

"Thank you, Master Hardy," she said. "It was very fortunate for me that you happened to be here. But you must be conducting important business of your own, and I should not take you away from it."

Master Hardy and Anthony exchanged a long glance over her head. "Nay, nothing of import, Mistress Haywood," Master Hardy said with an overly hearty laugh. "Merely an errand for a patron of mine, Anne, Dowager Duchess of Somerset. Perhaps you know her at court."

Anne Somerset—mother of Edward Seymour, who was said to be wooing Catherine Grey, who was involved in some dangerous flirtation with the Spanish. The tangled doings of England's nobility were making Kate's head ache. She *did* want to go back to the palace, to find her own bed, but she feared her whirling thoughts would keep her awake when she did finally lie down.

"I have only heard of her," Kate answered. "She seldom comes to court."

Master Hardy patted her arm with an indulgent smile. "Her health is not the most robust, but she still has her small business matters, of which I can sometimes assist her. Nothing for a lovely young lady such as you to worry about. Can you walk, Mistress Haywood? Shall we go now?"

Kate carefully tested her ankles and knees. They creaked alarmingly, but she was sure she could walk. "Thank you, Master Hardy. You are very kind."

"Here, lean on me," Anthony said. He held his arm out to her and she let him support her as they slowly made their way down the rest of the stairs. His body was warm and strong against hers, holding her up so she would not fall again.

"What are you really doing at Durham House?" she whispered to him.

A crooked smile touched the corner of his mouth. "Master Hardy told you, Kate—merely a small errand for the dowager duchess. What are *you* doing here?"

"Playing music at the queen's bidding, of course."

"Playing music in the servants' corridors?"

Kate lifted her chin. "I was trying to find the jakes, if you must know, and took a wrong turn somewhere. Most ungallant of you to ask, Anthony."

He made a strangled sound, as if he held back a laugh. "I have missed you, Kate. But I fear for what you are *not* saying. After Hatfield . . ."

Aye, Hatfield. Where she had nearly died, and would have without the help of friends like him. "I am merely helping the queen, if I can. I seem to be doing a poor job of it tonight. But I have missed you, too, Anthony. You must have a great deal of work to do, and for grand people like the Seymours as well. Your fortunes are rising."

Anthony glanced ahead of them to where Master Hardy walked. "Very busy. If I want my own law office one day, I have a long way to go. But I am still your friend, Kate. If you need my help . . ."

Her friend? Was that all? She knew that was all they could be, of course. She had her work at court, and Elizabeth disliked any of her household marrying. And Anthony needed a wife to keep his house and bring him a fortune and contacts for his career. But the word still stung a bit. "I know I can call on you if I need to, Anthony."

"Can you meet me one day next week? I think we have much to talk about."

Kate nodded. "Send me word of where you will be. I

do have something you could help me with, since you have access to many legal records."

"Of course. Anything."

They went through a doorway and turned from the muffled, narrow warren of corridors into a wider hall hung with tapestries. She could hear voices ahead, and she knew they hadn't much more time.

"I need to find out all I can about a family named Everley," she whispered quickly. "The Earl of Everley, and his son—Lord Henry—and nephew, a man called Richard St. Long."

Anthony nodded. "What sort of matters concerning them?"

"I am not sure yet. Anything out of the ordinary. Quarrels, suits, marriages, land grants."

It was a great deal, she knew that, and rather like trying to find a gold ring in a ripe hay wain. But Anthony just nodded again.

"I will see what I can find," he said, "if you will tell me what trouble you are in now."

Kate felt again the hard shove against her shoulder, the freezing flash of panic when her feet slid from under her and she fell into nothingness.

"I am not in trouble," she said. "But I fear I have friends who are."

Anthony gave a doubtful frown, but he could say nothing more, for they had reached a hall full of people. The doors that led through the gardens to the river were just ahead.

"My lute!" Kate cried, remembering the precious instrument she had left under her stool in the gallery.

"I will fetch it," Anthony said, and hurried away.

Master Hardy took Kate's arm and walked with her from the house, as calmly as if they took such strolls all the time. "It is very good to see you again, Mistress Haywood, even if it must be in such strange circumstances. My wife often asks of you and your father. You must come see us at our new home sometime."

"I would like that," Kate answered, still dazed by her fall.

"Mistress Hardy is much enjoying her new home, though I fear I keep Anthony and my new apprentices too busy to savor it much myself," he said with a laugh. "Anthony is almost done with his studies, you know, and shows much promise. He will go far in his career, if he makes no missteps now. You see what I mean, Mistress Haywood, I am sure. You are making your own court career, I think."

Kate gave him a puzzled glance, but he just smiled back at her. "I think Anthony is too intelligent a young man to make any missteps at all, Master Hardy. He will make a fine lawyer."

"So he will, with a fine list of noble clients to his name. Just as I did when I was his age. My dear wife helped me much then, you know. She was the daughter of my own master lawyer, and knew much about running such a household with such an office. I am sure Anthony will do the same."

Kate suddenly realized what he was telling her. Anthony would soon need to seek a fine wife to help him in his career—and a court musician with no dowry and no knowledge of running a prosperous house could not do that. She suddenly felt as if someone had pushed her down the stairs all over again.

"I—yes, I am sure he will do the same, Master Hardy," she stammered.

"Then I am glad we understand each other, Mistress Haywood. Ah, here are the boats at last."

By the time Master Hardy led Kate to the river steps below the elaborate formal gardens of Durham House and found a boat, Anthony was back with her lute and her cloak. He carefully wrapped it around her against the cold evening and helped her onto the hard wooden seat.

Holding tight to her lute as they slipped out onto the river, Kate half listened to Master Hardy talk of his family and watched the city slide past.

So late on a cold winter's night, most Londoners were tucked away by their fires, but there was still a great deal of life swirling around in the city. The waves of the river rocked the boats that beat against them, and made the queen's sleeping swans bob past in white blurs. Kate could hear the lap of the water against their boatman's oars, the creak of timbers, the calls and shrieks of birds wheeling overhead. From an open window of a dockside inn there was an out-of-tune song. Beyond the bridge she could see the tall masts of the oceangoing vessels where they bobbed at anchor in the tidal Thames, waiting to voyage to faraway lands.

Kate knew that when the tide was high, the water raced through those arches of the bridge like a waterfall, and the waves could bank up several feet higher on one side than the other. The openings were treacherous then, sometimes with a clearance of no more than eight feet, and even experienced wherrymen were reluctant to shoot the bridge then. But at that hour all was quiet and placid—on the river at least.

As they glided under the bridge, Kate heard the bleating of a flock of sheep waiting to cross over from Bankside. Torches flickered from the walls of the Tower, their curls of gray smoke winding into the night sky. She was grateful for the peaceful moment, for not battling the deadly swirling high tides that wrecked boats and people on the stone pilings of the bridge.

"'Tis a different life here than it was in Hertfordshire," Anthony said quietly.

Kate turned her head to smile up at him. "So it is. Do you like living in London, Anthony?"

He smiled ruefully. "I have been too busy since I arrived here to know if I like it or not. My lodgings are comfortable and my work interesting. It seems you are in far more danger than I ever could be."

Kate laughed, then winced as her ribs reminded her painfully of their battered condition. "It has followed me from Hatfield, it seems. But I'm happy to be at court. Queen Elizabeth's court."

"You took part in the coronation festivities."

"Aye, some," Kate said, looking at him in surprise. How did he know what she did?

"I saw you in the procession. Master Hardy has a house in Cheapside now, and I watched from the windows."

What did he think when he saw her in the procession, a brown wren among the peacocks of the courtly ladies? "My father composed much of the music, but he felt too ill to attend the coronation himself. I had to make certain the queen's new musicians performed it correctly."

"But I would wager that isn't all you do for the queen."

"Nay. Not all," Kate said, thinking of her errand that night to Durham House. She wanted to curse herself for being so careless.

The boat bumped at the foot of the stone steps leading up from the river to the queen's gardens, cutting short anything else Anthony had to say to her. Kate let him help her out of her seat, his touch most gentle as he made sure she had her footing on the jetty.

"I will send you word as soon as I can about the Everley matter," he whispered quickly in her ear. "In the meantime, Kate, I beseech you to be most careful! Go nowhere alone."

Kate feared that would be a promise she would soon have to break. But she didn't want to make the worry in his green eyes any deeper. "I will be careful, Anthony."

"Come dine with us soon, Mistress Haywood," Master Hardy called as the boat pushed out onto the water again. "My wife would love to see you."

"I will, Master Hardy, thank you," she called back. She watched them slip back over the blue-black waves until they vanished amid the other vessels, and then she turned to make her careful way through the gardens.

She wrapped her cloak tighter against the cold wind and went over all she had heard on that strange night. She was tired and aching, longing only for her bed, but as soon as she slipped from the kitchens into the corridor that led to the ladies' chambers, she knew something was amiss. Too many candles were lit for so late at night; too many people dashed around aimlessly.

Kate had the sudden terrible, flashing memory of red hair and blood spilled on a stone floor.

She caught the arm of the first person who ran past her, which turned out to be Kat Ashley. Shockingly, the older woman wore her fur-trimmed night-robe out of her own chamber, and her graying hair trailed from beneath her nightcap.

"Is the queen hurt?" Kate demanded.

"Oh, Mistress Haywood, 'tis you!" Mistress Ashley cried. "And just in time, too. Nay, Her Majesty isn't hurt, but this ague has made her sleepless. She wants music and card games, and after everyone was already abed. . . ."

Kate remembered at Hatfield House all the long,

tense nights Elizabeth could not sleep for fear of the bad dreams. For fear of waking up to be dragged to a Tower cell. What did she fear now?

"What can I do?" Kate asked.

"Kat Ashley! Where have you gone?" The queen herself suddenly appeared at the top of the stairs. Her red-gold hair fell loose over the shoulders of her crimson brocade robe, and her cold-ridden nose was almost as red as the fine fabric. She waved the lace-edge handkerchief in her hand impatiently.

"Kate!" Elizabeth said, hurrying down the stairs. Her cheeks were a fevered pink in her pale face. "So you return at last. What news? What hear you of—"

Elizabeth reached Kate's side and touched her shoulder. Kate automatically drew back at the flash of pain, her breath escaping in a hiss, and Elizabeth's frown deepened. She gently turned Kate's arm over and eased back her torn sleeve to reveal a livid blue bruise.

"Oh, Kate," Elizabeth said. She had suddenly gone very still, her eyes flat and dark, and somehow that was more fearsome than her fevered temper. "But it is late, and you cannot amuse me now. Let me see you back to your bed."

"But, lovey, you said you needed music to sleep—," Mistress Ashley began, only to be cut off by a quick wave of Elizabeth's hand. The pearl and ruby ring on her finger sparkled.

"Not now, Kat," the queen said. "Help me see Mistress Haywood to her chamber. Here, take her lute. Hold on to my arm, Mistress Haywood."

Kate let the queen lead her up the stairs, watched by the bemused servants who had been so suddenly roused from their beds to amuse the queen only to be quickly cut off. Mistress Ashley scurried after them with Kate's lute. The queen paid them all no mind. Still perfectly, coldly calm, she led Kate to her chamber and helped her sit on the edge of her high, narrow bed.

After Mary's death, Kate was moved from the ladies' chamber to a little room of her own at the back of the corridor. It was a rare favor in a crowded court where every inch of space was fought over, and she was even more grateful for the quiet now.

"Kat, fetch some hot water, and a posset of spiced wine," Elizabeth ordered. Mistress Ashley looked very much as if she wanted to argue, but the queen shoved her out of the room and firmly closed the door behind her.

"Your Majesty . . . ," Kate began. She shrugged off her cloak and winced.

"Here, Kate, let me help you." Elizabeth quickly helped Kate out of her fine, now-rumpled blue and silver gown until she wore only her linen smock. The queen examined her bruises, frowning fiercely. "Oh, Kate. Whatever happened? Tell me quickly, before Kat comes back."

As Elizabeth helped her lie back on the bolsters, Kate hastily told her most of what had happened that night at Durham House. The dour Spanish mood, what she overheard Feria and his friends talk of, being pushed down the stairs, and being rescued by Master Hardy, who was there on an errand for Edward Seymour's mother.

"The Seymours," Elizabeth muttered. "Of course they would be mixed up in all this somehow. They are as pestilential as the Greys. Always turning their colors."

"Your Majesty?" Kate said. Could it really be the Seymours and the Greys who had done this? Who conspired with the Spanish? But then of course they could. Courtly families were capable of anything to secure their own advancement—she had seen that time and again. But something told her there was more to what happened at Durham House, something swimming just below the surface, like the swirling eddies of the river that hid all kinds of nasty muck.

Elizabeth paced the length of the chamber, her expression most thoughtful. "They once used their pale-faced sister Jane to take what was my mother's, you know. Who knows what they scheme now? And with the *Spanish*."

"I have heard Edward Seymour's mother has some kind of secret business," Kate said. "If he had a gathering of some sort, I could go there as I did to Durham House. . . ."

"Ah, Kate, you cannot think of this now!" Elizabeth suddenly whirled around to kneel beside Kate's bed and tucked the soft bedclothes around her. "You have been cruelly injured again doing me this great service, and now you must rest. You have found out most valuable information tonight already."

"Nay, Your Majesty!" Kate cried. Found valuable information? No, she had failed, caught off her guard in that stairwell. She would not be so foolish again. "I have much more I can do. I am quite sure I can . . ." She struggled to sit up on the bed.

"Not tonight." Elizabeth pressed her back down just as Mistress Ashley returned with a goblet in her wrinkled hands. A maidservant followed with a ewer of steaming water and clean toweling.

"Oh, Kat," Elizabeth said as she stood up straight. "I fear Mistress Haywood does not feel well. I count on you to take care of her tonight."

Mistress Ashley's eyes widened. "But, lovey," she cried. "You are ill yourself, you need me."

"I feel much better," Elizabeth declared. "I will retire now. Mary Sidney can see to me. You take care of Mistress Haywood, as I have commanded. Do not let her leave this chamber until she has rested."

"Your Majesty . . . ," Kate cried.

Elizabeth shook her head. "We will talk tomorrow, my good Kate. Just sleep now."

Elizabeth swept out of the room, and Kate saw she couldn't follow even if she managed to rise from her bed. It was obvious Mistress Ashley was going to strictly follow Elizabeth's orders and "take care" of Kate. She stood over her until Kate finished every drop of her spiced wine, then helped her wash with the warm water. She said nothing about the bruises on Kate's arms. Mistress Ashley had been at court for many years, and was unlikely to be surprised by much at all.

The wine and the heat of the fire in her little grate, along with Mistress Ashley's efficient presence, soon made her feel much better. She sat back in her bed and watched as Mistress Ashley smoothed and folded her gown, clucking over its wrinkled state. Just as she must have done over Princess Elizabeth's garments when the now queen was a child.

"You have been with the queen a very long time, Mistress Ashley," she said.

Mistress Ashley gave a rusty laugh. "Aye, that I have. Since she was a babe barely walking. Poor motherless mite, we couldn't even get enough new clothes and good food for her then. But she was such a proud, determined little girl!"

"You have seen so very much all these years," Kate murmured, the wine flooding through her veins and making her thoughts hazy. But something still hovered at the edge of her mind, something she couldn't quite grasp yet.

"No more than your own father, Mistress Haywood. He has been at court a long time as well." Mistress Ashley told her a few stories of life at court when she and Matthew Haywood were young, which made Kate laugh. Her father seldom spoke of his life before Kate was old enough to remember for herself, and the stories made her forget her aches for a moment.

"Do you know Lady Gertrude Howard as well?" Kate asked. "She seems to remember my parents, though she is most confused. I think she believes I am my mother."

Mistress Ashley gave her head a sad shake. "Lady Gertrude is of a goodly age indeed. She is even older than me, though I would wager a mite like you could scarce believe that possible! She lived with the queen's grandmother Elizabeth Boleyn, who was the Duke of Norfolk's sister, when she was a girl. Sometimes Lady Gertrude thinks she's back there again, at Hever. You shouldn't pay mind to her ramblings, Mistress Haywood."

Kate frowned as she remembered Lady Gertrude's joyful cry—*Eleanor*. "I won't. I just enjoy hearing tales of the old times."

"So do we all. But the best of times is now, Mistress Haywood, with our Queen Elizabeth."

Kate agreed with that most wholeheartedly. After all the years of fear and uncertainty under the reign of Queen Mary, always looking over their shoulders for terror of the stake, it felt like the summer sun had come out again and they could all walk free under its light. That was why the queen had to be protected at all costs. "I think you are right, Mistress Ashley. This is the best of times."

"You just sleep now. The queen will be wanting her music again tomorrow." Kate let Mistress Ashley tuck the bedclothes around her, and, left alone with just the smoldering light in the grate, she drifted down to a dark, drowsy world where images of her strange night slipped in and out of her mind.

Suddenly an image struck her memory, and she sat straight up. The sleeve of the arm that pushed her had been dark but decorated with a line of buttons. *Silver* buttons. Something like the one hidden in her clothes chest, but without that fine braided edge.

It seemed she definitely needed to pay a visit to Master Lucas the goldsmith.

CHAPTER 17

Mad Henry was at his post again as Kate approached the Cardinal's Hat. Even though it was the middle of the day, the quiet time for Southwark, he vigilantly watched the passersby with impassive eyes, his arms crossed over his leather jerkin.

"Good morrow, Master Henry," Kate greeted him. "I trust all has been well here of late?"

"'Tis you again, is it, mistress?" he said, with not a flicker of surprise to see her. She had worn her boy's garb again, to move more easily around Southwark. If she had shown up in a court gown, mayhap he wouldn't even have known her! "Aye, things have been quiet enough. Just the usual trouble. We hear tell that hasn't been so at the queen's fine court."

"Aye, a lady was killed the night of the coronation banquet, I fear. I had a few more questions for Bess, if she is not, er, occupied."

There was finally a spark of something in Mad Henry's flat eyes. He shifted on his massive booted feet. "You think poor Nellie and this court lady are connected?"

"I am not sure," Kate answered. "Probably not. But she and Nell did share a certain look about them. I just want to be sure before anyone else gets hurt."

Mad Henry nodded. "Bess is in her room with that

actor fellow. He's always hanging about now, the bastard. Go around up the outside stairs, no one will bother you."

"Thank you, Master Henry." Kate hurried around to the back of the house. The stairs were rickety wood, hastily built against the plastered wall and facing the yard with its midden heap. But it was indeed private, with no one to watch her hurry past but the chickens scratching about in the dirt.

She ran up the creaking stairs, quick in her boy's garb, and knocked on the door. Bess pulled it open. Her bright red hair spilled in tangled waves over her shoulders, and she wore a yellow satin dressing gown, which she quickly drew up over her shoulders.

"Mistress Haywood," she said in surprise. "What has happened?"

"I'm sorry to come without sending a message, Bess, but so much has happened in the last few days and time is getting away from us," Kate said. "I only have a few questions. I won't take up much of your time."

"You'd best come in, then." Bess opened the door wider and let Kate slip into the chamber.

Rob sat by the fireplace, tugging on his linen shirt. Kate had a quick glimpse of his bare chest, gleaming smooth and gold in the firelight, and she could feel her cheeks turning warm despite the cold day outside. She wasn't quite sure where to look, and she turned away to study the room.

The narrow bed was rumpled, the blankets tossed back, and the remains of a meal sat on the one table. Before she looked elsewhere, Kate noticed that Rob wore only a pair of loose breeches, no boots, and she saw the muddy footwear was kicked under the edge of the bed. The dirt was dried, so he hadn't been anywhere for a while. A doublet hung on a hook next to Bess's red satin gown. It was plain purple-black cloth, no decorative buttons.

"Kate," Rob said. "Is aught amiss? Have you discovered anything yet?"

"Not very much," Kate admitted. "You have heard of Lady Mary Everley at court? She was killed in Westminster Abbey during the coronation banquet."

"We did hear tell of it," Rob said. "But surely it can have nothing to do with me? I have been nowhere near court, and never met the lady!"

"Perhaps not," Kate said. "But Lady Mary was a small, slender redhead, much like Nell."

"A redhead?" Bess cried, startled in the act of pouring out some wine. The dark red liquid spilled over her hand. "Was Nell killed because she was mistaken for this woman?"

"I don't know. Probably it is just a coincidence. But I fear I am quite confused by everything," Kate admitted. And her near-disastrous visit to Durham House had only confused her more. Music she could understand; if done in a logical, proper manner, the notes would come together and yield a harmonious whole. The violence of politics, though, refused to make any sense. And it changed with every instant.

"Perhaps Nell and Lady Mary knew some of the same people," Kate continued. "I just wanted to ask you more about Nell's, er, friends."

Bess frowned as if concentrating, or worried. She perched on the arm of Rob's chair, her hand placed casually on his shoulder as if they were easily intimate. Kate pushed down on an emotion that felt suspiciously like—jealousy at the sight. Which was absurd. She didn't care in the least what an actor like Rob did with his own time.

"Perhaps," Bess said slowly. "But I told you, Mistress Haywood, we don't usually know their names, even those that come around regular. And I didn't know all Nellie's favorites. We shared some of them, but not all."

"Did you see a man named Henry, mayhap?" Kate dug around in the pouch at her belt and came up with the miniature portrait she had "borrowed" from Lord Everley. She handed it to Bess, who held it up to the grayish light from the window to squint at it. "He was Lady Mary's brother, and he vanished from court soon after her death. His father says he sent Lord Henry to woo a rich heiress in the country, but 'tis all most suspicious. He was arguing with his sister at the coronation."

"Aye, I do think I recognize him," Bess cried. "Likes his wine, he does, and he likes to hear the sound of his own voice. A braggart if there ever was one."

Kate thought of Henry Everley, and had to agree he was a braggart. But she hadn't seen him with Edward Seymour and Master St. Long the night she first came to the Cardinal's Hat. "That does sound like Lord Henry. Has he been here recently?"

Bess shook her head. "I haven't seen him since Christmastide. He only visited me once or twice anyway, which was fine with me. A bit too rough for my taste. Preferred Meggie, she likes that sort of thing. Killed his own sister, did he? Nasty."

"But he hasn't been seen around the Cardinal's Hat in the last few days?"

"Nay. You could ask Mad Henry, but I ain't seen him. Have you, Robbie?"

Rob studied the painting. "Not me, but I know the face. He and some of his ruffian friends used to come watch us play sometimes, when we were near Everley Court. Bess is right, he's fond of his wine. Never even shut up long enough to hear my speech as Prince Hector, which is one of my best."

"You haven't seen him since Everley Court, then?" Kate asked. She took back the portrait and carefully tucked it away to slip it back to Lord Everley.

Rob gave a rueful laugh. "Not grand enough for nobility yet, am I? I need a rich new patron now that Lord Ambrose is banished from court."

"But your troupe played for the queen," Kate reminded him.

Rob's handsome face twisted into a scowl. "Without me. I had to hide like a fox."

Bess kissed the top of his head. "Only till we find out who did this for Nellie," she said gently. "Then I vow your troupe will be called the *Queen's* Men, and too grand for us here at the Cardinal's Hat."

"But you can't perform your plays swinging from a gallows," Kate said. Though it seemed most unlikely Rob was involved in either Nell's or Mary's death, one could never be too careful. The authorities would seize on the easiest, quickest solution, just as the royal coroner had with Mary. Better safe than sorry. And Bess was right— Rob had too great a talent to waste, even if he was a wastrel.

And he was too handsome as well.

"Did Lord Henry's cousin ever come here, too?" Kate asked. "His name is Richard St. Long, though I don't have his portrait."

Bess thought again, her brow creased a bit under the tangled swoop of her dyed hair. Kate was surprised to see that, in the light of day, dressed more simply and with her face paint gone, Bess was quite young and pretty. She couldn't be much older than Kate's own nineteen, and she'd said Nell was even younger. The harsh unfairness of it all made Kate angry, and even more determined to find who had done this.

Even if it meant she had to find *two* murderers now, Nell's and Mary's.

"He has his friends he likes to go roistering about with—most of them do," Bess said. "What is he like?"

"Middling height, strong but not stout," Kate said. "Dark hair, a bit longer than fashion. Very blue-gray eyes. He doesn't dress as elaborately as many of the court gentlemen."

"Poor relation, is he?" Bess said. "Mayhap. This man Lord Henry has sometimes paid for a friend or two as well as himself, and he ain't stingy with the wine for anyone. I couldn't say for certain, though. They liked Nell, but they liked the rest of us, too."

Kate nodded. So Richard St. Long may or may not have come to the Cardinal's Hat with Henry Everley. Master St. Long seemed most comfortable "roistering about" in Southwark with Edward Seymour, so she would think he *had* been there. But if she couldn't yet prove he knew Nell . . .

"What of a tall, lean man with very distinctive gold-colored eyes?" Kate asked. "I think his name might be Walter. He may have favored red-haired ladies."

"I don't think so. I would remember eyes like that," Bess said. "I like blue eyes, anyway, don't I, Robbie, love?"

Rob laughed as Bess ruffled his golden hair, but he looked thoughtful. "Golden eyes, you say?"

"Aye," Kate said, suddenly feeling a spark of hope. "Do you know a man like that?"

"Possibly. We played at a country manor once, a place that belonged to a family called Dennis. They had once been allied with the Boleyns, and had fallen on difficult times with Queen Mary. The house was tumbling down, and the lady was quite ill, but she much enjoyed our play. She must have been a beauty once, and she had eyes the color of amber. Cat's eyes."

"Did she have a son? What of her lord?"

"Her lord was fat and gouty, Kate, and that was two years ago," Rob said with a laugh. "He can't be running around London bashing ladies over the head. And we met no one else there but the servants. I think one of the maids said there was a son who had gone to live abroad or some such thing. Many of the followers of the new faith did back then, you know."

"Especially if they were allies of the Boleyns," Kate murmured. "Do you remember anything else? Where was the Dennis manor?"

"Not far from Hanworth, where the Duchess of Somerset lives now. I remember because we also played for her that week. She wasn't as appreciative of our art as Lady Dennis. Other than that, I remember little, I fear. It was long ago, and we've played for many families since then. I wouldn't have remembered if not for Lady Dennis's eyes."

Near Hanworth—and the Dennis family was friends with the Boleyns. "Most interesting. Let me know if you ever remember anything else about them at all, Rob."

Rob sat forward in his chair, his hands curling into fists. "Do you think the Dennises have something to do with this, Kate?"

Kate shook her head. She wasn't even sure yet that Mary's Walter was the same as the Dennis heir, or how they were tied to the Everleys. "It does seem unlikely, doesn't it? But the Seymours do keep coming around in this matter."

Bess snorted. "Like a bad guinea, they are. Especially that Lord Hertford."

Kate looked at her, and almost laughed at the smirk on Bess's face. "Does Seymour come here often?"

"He's known at every bawdy house and bear pit in Bankside," Bess said. "He comes sometimes here to the Cardinal's Hat, but he doesn't play favorites between the houses. He's like your Lord Henry, I think—more in love with himself and his own high place than anything else. I say he should have a care. Look what happened to his uncle Thomas. Got his head on a pike for flirting with royalty."

Kate remembered Edward Seymour's handsome dark head bent close to Catherine Grey's golden one. She would say Bess was right. But the Seymours weren't known for their great caution. "Does Edward Seymour consider himself to be royalty, too?"

"When he is cup-shot, mayhap. Likes to talk about his aunt the late queen." Bess laughed harshly. "Queen Jane Seymour was long dead before he came whining into the world, I'd think. Not that it matters to his self-regard. He never swived my Nellie, though. He likes the blondes."

Blondes like the royal Lady Catherine? "I see. Most interesting."

"Anyone else you need to know about?"

Kate thought of her other errands, of the evening at Durham House, the ride on the river with Anthony. "Do you have many Spanish customers?"

"We used to have crowds of them," Bess said. "When King Philip was in England. Couldn't understand a word any of 'em said, but they paid well enough. Good-looking, too, some of them. Not so many of them around now."

"Did any of them visit Nell often?"

Bess thought again before she shook her head. "Not especially. There was one man who came sometimes— fair hair he had, and a beard. He always wore a mask. One of the girls said he was King Philip himself in disguise, silly cow. Nell liked that idea, though."

Kate remembered wild rumors of the Spanish king's lusty nature, while poor, sad Queen Mary pined for love of him, and let Spanish wickedness spread via the smoke of the Smithfield fires. "Perhaps it was him. But I doubt King Philip has crept back to England to murder ladies."

"This bearded man, though, he did bring friends with him. One was very handsome indeed, dark—he seldom came near the ladies. Mostly he drank wine and kept a watch on the fair man."

Could it be Feria? It was said he was the king's closest confidant. But all that would have been long ago. Kate sighed, deeply discouraged. It seemed the more she examined the tangled skein of this terrible matter, the more opaque it all became. She had to most carefully pick it apart, strand by strand.

"It could be almost anyone, I fear," she said. "I will come back when I can. In the meantime, Bess, you will talk to the other women and see if they remember any unusual customers of late?"

"Of course I will," Bess said. "But I think it would be stranger to hear of a man who was *not* unusual. I'll do anything to find who did this to my Nellie."

She suddenly stood up and hurried across the room to rattle at the washbowl, as if to cover a spasm of emotion. Rob looked after with a concerned frown.

"Where do you go now, Kate?" he asked. "Back to court?"

"Soon. First I must visit a goldsmith in Cheapside

called Master Lucas," Kate said. She had the silver button tucked into her pouch with Lord Henry's portrait.

"I will walk with you," Rob said. He pushed himself to his feet and reached for his dusty boots.

"Nay, Robbie, 'tis not safe!" Bess cried. She spun around from the washstand, and her face was indeed splotched with tears.

"I need some fresh air, my Bess," he said. He shrugged into his doublet and raked his tumbled golden hair back from his face. "No one will attack me in daylight in a respectable street like Cheapside. I have to help Kate, if I can. Not cower indoors like the veriest knave."

Kate looked between Rob and Bess, feeling strangely as if she were in the playhouse, watching a scene. She didn't want to know what was between Rob and Bess, how many women had fallen violently in love with him. She only knew she could never let herself be one of them.

"Fine, go, then!" Bess said. "Get a dagger between the ribs and see if I care one farthing for it."

Rob went to her and kissed her cheek. "You won't lose me as you lost Nell, Bess, I vow it. I must do something now, though. I'll be back for supper, bring some pies or something."

Bess sniffed. "I might be here and I might not. Some of us have to earn our coin, you know."

Rob kissed her again, and left the room with Kate. They went down the main corridor rather than the outside staircase, past groups of women standing around whispering and laughing, their bright satin gowns falling from their shoulders, their hair tangled down their backs. Any one of them could be Nell. All of them deserved to make their own lives.

A plump woman laced tightly into a faded green silk

gown stood in the small front hall talking with Mad Henry. She had hair of an even brighter red than Bess's, piled high atop her head and fastened with fine Spanish ebony combs. But her lined face, heavily rouged, showed her to be at least two decades Bess's senior. Her blue-gray, slightly slanted eyes, rimmed with kohl, must have once been her great beauty. Now they were bloodshot, dull, hard with all she must have seen in so many years in Southwark.

Those eyes flickered over Kate, not giving any indication besides the tiniest of smiles that she saw past her boy's disguise.

"Brought a friend to visit us, eh, Rob?" she said. Her voice, unlike most of the other bawds', sounded sharp and refined at the edges.

Rob shrugged, a half smile tugging at his lips. "Apprentices must be shown the way of the world, Mistress Celine."

"So they must. Just remember, the ways of the world don't come free. Bess and poor Nell might have a weakness for your pretty face, but I still have debts to pay. This house doesn't run itself, you know."

Rob caught up the woman's plump, reddened hand and kissed it. A finely wrought silver ring set with an amethyst winked on her finger. "You shall have my rent on time, never fear, Celine. Never you fear."

"I'd better." Mistress Celine turned back to her conversation with Mad Henry, but Kate could feel those pale blue eyes watching her back as Rob led her away.

"Who was that?" Kate asked as they turned the corner into the crowded street and walked toward the more respectable environs across the river.

"Mistress Celine. She owns the Cardinal's Hat, and a harder landlady you could never find," Rob muttered.

"But she keeps the place clean enough, and never over-works the girls."

"Has she been there a long time?" It seemed to Kate that most of the bawds were young, and soon worn-out. Celine must be a strong woman indeed.

"Very long," Rob said without much interest. "They say before she ran a house in some country village. Then a rich lover set her up here. Why are you looking for this goldsmith, Kate?"

Kate fished the button from her pouch and showed it to him. "Master St. Long said his cousin Henry Everley often borrowed money from Master Lucas. I want to see if this shopkeeper has met with Lord Henry lately, and if he knew who made this. The jewelers of London must know each other's work, I think."

Rob nodded. "I know a shorter way. Turn here."

They dashed across the muddy road, leaping over the midden trench that ran down the middle and dodging around a cart laden with turnips. Rob led her down a narrow side alley, with dingy plastered walls looming to either side, his steps so swift she almost had to run to keep up. But she knew she had to. Without Rob, she would surely be lost.

CHAPTER 18

Master Lucas's shop appeared to be a most respectable, most ordinary one, Kate thought as she studied it from across the lane. The large front window was thrown open to reveal an enticing array of wares, pretty rings and brooches, shining in the dull gray day. A painted sign swung over the door, a picture of the Moor's head, the symbol of the goldsmith's trade. A plump, fair-haired older lady in a fine dark green wool gown leaned out of the window, laughing with a customer.

Kate glanced at the tall, timbered buildings to either side. One was a draper's, with bolts of cloth spread over the front counter, and one a bookbinder. She doubted any of the Everleys were great readers, but their clothes were fine enough. Perhaps if they patronized Master Lucas, they called on the draper as well.

"Are you sure this is the place, Kate?" Rob asked, frowning up at the shop's top-floor windows. "They don't look the sorts to be involved in the murder of a bawd."

"I don't think Master Lucas had anything to do with Nell or Lady Mary," Kate said. Not yet, anyway. "I merely want to ask him something. You needn't go in with me if you have another errand."

Rob flashed a smile down at her. Despite the strain of

the last few days, his unshaven jaw and rumpled hair, he was still one of the most handsome men she had ever seen. He was also a merry spirit, a man of hidden depths she had glimpsed at Hatfield. She hated to think he could have done anything so cruel as kill one of his lovers, not after the way he once saved her own life.

"I will do whatever I can to find who did this to Nell," he said fiercely. "Shall we go in?"

Kate nodded and led the way across the lane, weaving through crowds of housewives with market baskets on their arms, children clinging to their skirts as they did their day's shopping. There were soldiers hurrying to their posts, merchants in their warm furred robes, beggars lingering in the meager shelter of the walls, quickly driven away. A new queen might be on the throne now, but households must still be fed and commerce go on.

Kate pushed open the door to Master Lucas's shop, setting the bells jangling. Aside from the customers the lady was gossiping with over the open front counter, the shop wasn't busy. It had a well-kept, well-polished air about it, the wooden floor swept, the wares carefully displayed. A metallic smell hung in the air, combined with the sweetness of lemon and beeswax polish.

A back door swung open and a man emerged, looking most harried. His sparse gray hair stood on end, and he wore a leather apron over his shirt and fine wool breeches.

He shot an annoyed glance at the woman, who went on obliviously with her chat. "How may I assist you?" he asked shortly.

Kate tugged her cap lower on her brow, hoping the dimness of the room would help her boy's disguise hold. Behind her, Rob waited, silently, with his arms crossed.

"Are you Master Lucas? I come from—Sir Robert

Dudley at the queen's court," she said in a low voice, struck by a sudden inspiration. "He has heard you do some very fine work."

The man's impatient expression vanished in an ingratiating smile. "Aye, Sir Robert indeed! A most discriminating man of fashion. I am sure I have some wares he would admire. Perhaps he looks for a gift for someone? For Lady Dudley? Or mayhap—Her Majesty?"

"If he was pleased, my master's patronage would know no bounds," Kate said. "He much admires these, and was told they were your own work."

She pulled out the silver button and handed it to Master Lucas. He took it to the light from one of the windows and carefully examined it.

"Aye, 'tis mine," he said proudly. "That braid work on the edge is one of my own trademarks. 'Tis most complicated to work."

"Sir Robert said he saw it on the garments of Lord Carew, or mayhap of Lord Henry Everley, he could not recall. He much admired the fine effect."

"I have not had the fortune to work with Lord Carew yet, but the Everleys are patrons of mine. Most particular about their adornments, they are."

And particular about how they paid for them? Kate remembered Richard St. Long saying Lord Henry came to Master Lucas for loans as well as adornments. "Who would wear these particular buttons? A young man like Lord Henry, or someone more old-fashioned in their tastes like Lord Everley?"

Master Lucas gave an overly affable laugh. "I only make the buttons, young sir, I do not tailor the garments. It could have been any of them, or perhaps one from another family. I have many patrons at court. Sir Robert would never be shamed by my work."

Kate nodded. She knew she had to be careful in her questions and not rouse any suspicions. She casually examined a tray of poesy rings, delicate bands of flowers engraved with forget-me-not messages.

"Mayhap Lord Henry has not been here in a while, anyway," she said.

Master Lucas glanced to the side, his jaw tightening. The merest flash, but she knew he hid something. "Not that I recall. We have been most busy of late, and I am kept busy working with the wares in the back."

"That kinsman of his was here not so long ago," the woman at the window suddenly said. "Brought a woman with him."

Kate glanced over at her. The woman watched them with avid eyes, bright under her respectable headdress. Definitely the sort to enjoy a fine gossip. "Did they buy anything then, mistress?"

The woman snorted. "Nay, not him. And she didn't look like the kind who would find our work to her tastes."

"A redhead, was she?" Kate said, taking a wild guess. When the woman frowned suspiciously, Kate looked down and scuffed her boot along the floor as if suddenly shy. "'Tis just that I saw Lord Henry's cousin with a red-haired lady once. Beautiful, she was."

The woman's frown turned to an indulgent smile. "Ah, young infatuation. So sweet. Nay, brown hair she had. But who knows? Everyone wants red hair like the queen. The apothecary does a great business in dyes now, he says. Anyway, they seemed most ale-shot, giggling all over the place. I thought he might have come on an errand for his cousin."

"Hush, Ann," Master Lucas cried. "We wouldn't want Sir Robert Dudley to think we cater to Bankside geese."

Kate had the feeling she had heard all she could in

that shop for the day. She couldn't overplay things. "Sir Robert knows you have good-quality wares, Master Lucas," she said. "I will tell him of the fineness of your goods and what you have on display."

Master Lucas beamed. "Tell his lordship I would be most happy to bring my goods to court at any time, my boy."

Kate nodded and made her way out of the shop just as the door opened to admit more customers. It seemed clear she would get no more information out of Master Lucas; the man was too intent on keeping his good business name. Mistress Lucas, on the other hand, looked as if she was fairly bursting to talk more. Kate thought it might be worth her time to come back when the lady was working alone.

Or maybe she should send Rob, she thought as she watched him bow to Mistress Lucas and the lady giggled back.

"Did you get what you came for?" Rob asked as they headed back down the street.

Kate shook her head. "It is most maddening. When I think I come close to an answer, it only slides further away. At least I know the button *could* come from the Everleys, but it could come from other courtiers as well." She kicked out at a loose cobblestone in frustration. "Perhaps if I could find Richard St. Long's dark-haired doxy . . ."

Rob laughed. "I fear there are more dark-haired whores than red, Kate. And they don't always stay one hair color or the other." He grew more somber as they reached the narrow walkway that ran along the water's edge. The smell of the river was stronger there, sickly-sweet and fishy. "You don't think I really had anything to do with these women's deaths, do you, Kate? I should hate to think such vile suspicions were between us now."

Kate tipped her head back to study him from under the brim of her cap. He looked older in the daylight, his golden beard roughening his fine-hewn features, his eyes red-rimmed.

She remembered how suspicious she had been of him when they first met at Hatfield. How strange it was that he had shown up just as Queen Mary's agent was wreaking such havoc in Princess Elizabeth's household. How he was *too* charming, too easy-mannered, too capable of hiding his thoughts behind a player's mask.

But then she had glimpsed some of the kindness he tried to conceal, the care he so strenuously denied. After his uncle was killed, that mask had dropped for an instant. And then he had saved her life on that rain-swept lane.

She thought of how Bess held on to him, smiled at him so fondly. Bess was no innocent simpleton. She knew the darker ways of men better than Kate could. She surely wouldn't behave so if she believed Rob capable of killing her sister.

"Nay," Kate said. "I know you did not, Rob. You haven't got it in you."

He gave a crooked, humorless smile. "You think I could not kill?"

"I didn't say that," Kate said. They walked along the river path, past fishermen mending their nets, women washing bits of laundry in the icy water, grubby beggar children chasing one another. "You could kill. If you were angry enough, to take revenge or protect yourself. But to harm a woman, especially one you were—fond of. Nay, I think not."

She suddenly thought of the unknown Walter with the golden eyes. Had he loved Mary—or loathed her? Was he one of the family of Boleyn supporters, out to take revenge so long after the feud between Seymour and Boleyn had faded?

· Rob's smile withdrew and he looked solemn again. Older, harder. He nodded, and stopped to buy them some warm ginger cakes from a barker's cart. Kate realized she had eaten nothing that day, and the spicy warmth of the cake chased some of the chill of the water away.

"I was fond of Nell. She was a merry girl," he said. "And a sweet one. She would never hurt anyone."

"And she favored you? As her sister does?"

Rob laughed ruefully. "I am an actor, Kate. 'Tis hard to settle for one sort of woman when there is such a delectable banquet in life."

Kate shook her head. Rob did like women, aye. It was part of his charm—and part of why she knew she could never get *too* close to him. "You are a great rogue, Rob Cartman. But not a cruel one. You might break a woman's heart, yet you could never be violent to one."

"Thank you for that, Kate," he said quietly. "I am honored you would have such faith in me. Many would not. That you can see people so clearly sometimes. You are truly a most extraordinary lady."

"I wish you were right, Rob. I wish I *could* see people as easily as looking through an open window." Kate wiped her gingery fingers on her boy's breeches and watched two of the queen's swans glide past. "Then I could easily pick out the villains amongst us. Yet I think almost all of them look like villains right now. The queen has many enemies."

They walked onward, looking for an empty boat to carry Kate back to the palace.

"I will ask around the stews," he said. "Bawds and pimps see everything around them. You stay at court, Kate. It is safer there."

Kate laughed, thinking of the fine stairs at Durham House. Safe indeed. "Courtiers see everything, too. We all must sing for our suppers in our own ways."

They found an empty boat at last, and Rob took her hand to help her climb aboard the creaking planks. His touch was warm and steady on hers, his fingers roughened and callused from an actor's stage sword-craft. Before he let her go, he suddenly pulled her close for a quick, hard kiss.

He tasted—surprising. Sweet and dark all at once, his lips soft and firm as they moved expertly over hers. His arms close around her kept her from falling as the world spun around her.

But his kiss was over as suddenly as it began, and the freezing day closed in around her again.

"I mean it, Kate," he whispered. "There is no other woman like you, I vow."

Then he let her go, and Kate sat down hard on the narrow wooden bench. The grizzled old wherryman said nothing; he surely saw even stranger displays every day.

But Kate was not kissed every day. Her lips still tingled from the touch of Rob's, and she could taste him, ginger and ale mingled with some darkness that was only him. He was a very good kisser. Her head still swam with the feeling of it, and she couldn't quite fathom it yet.

Of course there was no time for worrying about kisses now. A killer was still out there, or mayhap two killers, and somehow Kate had the terrible feeling that he needed to be found most quickly. Before something else tragic could happen.

She glanced up as they neared the bridge, and saw that

even though no heads now adorned the waiting pikes, crows wheeled around them still, waiting for their future feast. This was no time to think about romance at all.

"Rob . . . ," she began, unsure of what she should say to him. What had just happened.

Rob laughed carelessly, as if he kissed girls every day. And probably he did. "I am sorry, Kate. I meant you no insult. We are friends, are we not? I should not want anything to mar that. You just looked so very . . ."

"Aye," Kate murmured. Friends. It was only a strange moment. "I know, Rob. No insult meant at all."

CHAPTER 19

Queen Elizabeth was walking in the gardens when Kate made her way toward the palace. Though the ladies who trailed behind her were shivery and miserable-looking in their thick cloaks, Elizabeth was striding briskly down the graveled pathway. Her fur-lined mantle swirled around her, stirring up the dead leaves on the ground. The only sign of the head cold that had confined her to her bedchamber was a reddened nose.

"So you have returned at last, Kate," Elizabeth said. She waved to her impatiently, leading her farther down the path where the others could not hear. "How do you fare today?"

"Much better, I thank you, Your Majesty," Kate said. She had to concentrate on hurrying to keep up with the queen. "The salve your physician sent via Mistress Ashley worked marvelously well."

Elizabeth shook her head. "'Tis a den of lions, that Spanish house, and if I could, I would clear it out altogether. But I fear I must always have dealings with my former brother-in-law. He is ever a thorn in my side, just as Mary of Scotland and the Greys are. Families are one infernal nuisance, Kate."

Kate nodded, suddenly grateful her own family was so very small. That they had no secrets from each other.

Her father was never a thorn of any sort, and she realized how much she missed his quiet company these last few days. The two of them working on their music together by the fireside, away from tangled webs of families that hated and schemed against one another.

"Hopefully I will not have to send any more innocent souls into Durham House soon," Elizabeth said. "Tell me what you discovered today."

Kate quickly recounted what had happened at the Cardinal's Hat and Master Lucas's shop, including her suspicion that Bess's and Mary's deaths might be linked in some strange way, and that Edward Seymour and his friends often visited the stews of Bankside—despite his obvious liking for Catherine Grey.

"That damnably foolish girl," Elizabeth muttered. Bright red spots rose up in her pale cheeks and her dark eyes blazed. "She never knew her place, never knew what was good for her, just like her whole grasping family. I should have known she was scheming something. At least she is not in my confidence, and can have nothing of great value to tell them. It will be easy enough to detect any scheme she conceives—she is not bright enough to long conceal herself."

Elizabeth glanced back at the ladies who followed in her wake: Kat Ashley, and Mary Sidney, who was Robert Dudley's sister; Lady Clinton; and Mistress Radcliffe. They huddled together for warmth near a silent stone fountain, laughing at the barking antics of a little lapdog. Catherine Grey was not among them now, nor was her mother, but the youngest Grey daughter, Mary, was. Mary Grey was tiny and malformed, her back crooked, but her eyes were always alert, watching everything around her.

"Perhaps I was mistaken in keeping my cousins at a

distance," Elizabeth said thoughtfully. "I could keep a much closer watch on them as Ladies of the Bedchamber, mayhap. Did you hear anything else at Durham House, Kate?"

Kate hesitated, thinking of what Feria said about their "lost friend," the spy who was better than any other.

Mary Everley was dead now; it seemed cruel to darken her memory in any way. Yet her dealings at Durham House, if indeed it had been Mary who was the spy, could have led her to that death.

"I think perhaps Mary Everley was also in the pay of the Spanish in some small way," Kate said carefully. She told Elizabeth of Feria's words.

Elizabeth gave a sad sigh, and sneezed. "Poor Lady Mary. Why can these girls not keep their wits about them?"

"Perhaps she had some great need of money."

"Aye, 'tis said Lord Everley is a purse-pincher. And most of what he has goes to that useless son of his. Sons always fare better than daughters, I fear. But there can be no excuse for spying among my household. I will always find out, and everyone should know that. I have eyes and ears everywhere."

"Your Majesty?" Kate whispered. Elizabeth had gone so quietly fierce it was almost frightening. The queen's long, graceful hands curled into tight fists, her eyes positively snapping sparks. She looked as if she was on the verge of one of her famous Tudor tempers, where items were thrown at heads and people were banished forthwith from the royal sight.

Kate wondered how anyone dared angering such a queen. She could almost feel sorry for Catherine Grey.

"Knowledge is essential to survive in this world," Elizabeth said. "I learned that long ago. Know all; reveal nothing. Cecil and my new man Walsingham have most of the country in their pay between them. Treachery will always be found out. If Lady Mary was indeed in the pay of the Spanish, her reasons will soon be discovered."

"And Lady Catherine, Your Majesty?"

Elizabeth gave her ladies another glance. "I think she bears further watching. After all, given enough rope . . ."

A foolish person was likely to hang themselves. Kate shivered.

"What else have you learned, Kate?" Elizabeth asked, walking onward.

Kate quickly told her about her visits to the Cardinal's Hat and the goldsmith, of what Master Lucas said about the Everleys' "patronage" of his shop.

"I think Lord Henry must be found quickly. He is gone from my court without leave, after all," said Elizabeth. "His father's tale of sending him off to woo a rich lady when his sister is new in her grave is most odd. Cecil will dispatch a man to Everley Court within the hour. But what of their cousin, this mysterious Master St. Long?"

"I can find little enough about him," Kate said ruefully. "He has also been to the Cardinal's Hat, and Bess, the dead woman's sister, says Lord Henry may have helped pay for his cousin's pleasures there. He also seems friendly with Edward Seymour. That cannot be a cheap thing to be, I think."

Elizabeth gave a harsh laugh, ending on a loud sneeze. "Nay. The pretty Lord Hertford does not practice thrift. I have been thinking a diplomatic post abroad might do him some good, the vain peacock. Yet I do feel for Master St. Long. He is a handsome young man, and it's never easy to go a-begging for one's supper. He is a cousin to the Everleys, yes?"

"He told me his mother was Lord Everley's sister and died long ago."

A frown flickered over Elizabeth's face. "I do not recall hearing Lord Everley had a sister, but then they have never been a family that was much at court until now. All families have their scandals—perhaps he is one of them."

Kate's thoughts raced as they flew over the possibilities. "A bastard of Lord Everley's own?"

Elizabeth laughed. "Quite possibly. Most of our noble names have such things littered around. The Howards, the Cavendishes, the Herberts. Some are not hidden away at all. My father doted on his son the Duke of Richmond, born of Katherine of Aragon's lady-in-waiting Bessie Blount. He gifted him with estates and titles, a noble wife. But not all bastard children fare so well."

Elizabeth grew quiet for a moment and stared out over the winter gardens of her fine palace as if she was seeing something else entirely. Kate remembered how Elizabeth herself had been called "bastard" after her mother died, and of the rumors that the red-bearded Lord Hunsdon was not the son of Mary Boleyn's Carey husband but of King Henry himself. No one *really* knew how many children the old king had scattered around. Most noblemen were the same way.

The queen suddenly shook her head and smiled, back from wherever her mind had wandered. "You have been most resourceful, Kate. Let me know what else you discover. For now, you should find your chamber and warm yourself by the fire. You must play for my banquet tonight. I expect the French ambassador as my special guest, and I wonder what you will think of him compared to Feria."

"Of course, Your Majesty," Kate said. She curtsied and hurried toward the palace, leaving Elizabeth to her solitary contemplation of the garden. Or not so very solitary, for her ladies waited nearby, ready to leap into action at the queen's smallest sigh. One of them was the young Duchess of Norfolk, cradling the little dog in her arms. Lady Gertrude Howard lurked behind her, leaning on her cane.

Kate dashed past, too tired to try to puzzle out Lady Gertrude's cryptic certainty that Kate was Eleanor Haywood come back to life. She had enough to puzzle out about parents and children, about the sticky web of families, already.

As she stepped into the dark coolness of the narrow back corridor off the kitchen garden, she saw a page boy leap up from his stool and run toward her, as if he had been waiting for her.

"This message came for you, Mistress Haywood," he said, handing her a neatly folded and sealed bit of parchment.

"Thank you." Kate turned the note over in her hand, half-afraid it was from the Spanish embassy or perhaps Lord Everley, denouncing her as a spy. But the writing was in a neat, strong lawyer's script, and the signature at the bottom was one that was most welcome.

Anthony Elias.

Kate began to read.

I have discovered some information that might be helpful to what you seek. Meet me when you can, send word to me here at Master Hardy's house.

—Anthony

Kate carefully tucked the note away in the sleeve of her doublet. She couldn't help but smile, though she told herself sternly that it was only at the prospect of discovering more pieces of the puzzle. Not at the chance of seeing Anthony again.

CHAPTER 20

A nthony Elias rubbed his hand over the back of his aching neck as he finally looked up from the ledgers scattered across the table. It felt like many hours indeed since he had locked himself away in the small closet at the back of Master Hardy's house to examine every legal record he could unearth concerning the Everley family.

It was a great deal of information indeed. The Everleys were a very old title, made more solid by the fact that a great-great-uncle had died fighting for Henry VII at Bosworth Field, but they had not much coin to help maintain their estate at Everley Court. But lack of funds didn't stop them from being litigious.

Anthony studied the open ledgers scattered around him like hovering black-winged birds. There, in faded, cramped law clerk's handwriting, was column after column of the saga of the Everleys. It was a fascinating tale, but one he feared would take much longer to untangle than he had.

The Everleys, starting with the current earl's father, as many earlier records had vanished into the maw of destroyed churches, loved to feud with their neighbors and relations. They had retained lawyers and clerks to bring suit with the earl's uncle (for keeping a set of valuable tapestries meant to go to Everley Court), his late wife's family (for failure to turn over a dower property), and with any neighbors within two counties.

As Anthony traced the branching lines of the earl's suits, he could see a pattern of complicated alliances and feuds emerging. Very often the earl's co-litigants or witnesses were members of the Seymour family. And after the catastrophic fall of the Boleyns after Queen Jane supplanted Queen Anne, the Everley/Seymour suits became even more aggressive, going after the property of vulnerable Boleyn allies.

Surely Queen Elizabeth knew nothing about Everley's actions against her own relations or she would not allow him and his children at court now. Or perhaps she did—Elizabeth Tudor knew how to play a long game indeed.

There was also a case from the second year of Queen Mary's reign, when Lord Henry Everley spent a few nights in Newgate gaol after stabbing a man to death in a brawl in a Bankside tavern. Young Edward Seymour had come forward and testified that Lord Henry had acted only in self-defense, and Queen Mary herself ordered his release. The victim was a young man named Oliver Dennis.

And that was not the Everleys' final dealings with the Dennis family.

Anthony sat back in his cross-backed chair with a satisfied smile. His eyes would never be the same after the long hours of reading the cramped script, but he would have interesting news for Kate. And that was the most important thing.

Anthony pushed himself back from the table and stacked up the ledgers before he went to open the window. The cold winter wind, smelling faintly of fish from the river, swept into the stuffy chamber and cleared his head.

In the courtyard below, two of Master Hardy's new young apprentices were playing a spirited game of battlecock, shouting exuberantly as they ran along the narrow gravel pathways, swinging their rackets.

Mistress Hardy, trailed by a maidservant as she trimmed back the dry winter roses, scolded them when they knocked over an Italian statue of a small cupid. But then she laughed as they scurried to apologize and set cupid aright. The wind swept around her fashionable plum woolen skirts and tugged at her graying hair. Master Hardy appeared, a book in his hand, and kissed her cheek.

It was a pretty scene, peaceful and domestic, and prosperous after all their long struggles. The Hardys were safe in their own house, their own livelihood, again, and Anthony's career was about to begin. One day he would have just such a place for himself, as he had worked so hard to obtain. A law practice with fine patrons, a house.

A wife? He smiled as he watched the Hardys stroll the pathways together, arm in arm, laughing as the apprentices tumbled back to their game. The Hardys had never had children, but their affection for each other was clear to everyone who saw them. Their long separation under the reign of Queen Mary had only strengthened that bond.

Anthony's father had died so long ago, and his mother had relied on her only son ever since. Their small house in Hertfordshire was often bare and cold, until his studies led him to this place. He had never seen such a marriage as the Hardys, a real partnership. And suddenly he had the dagger-sharp realization that he wanted that for himself. A friend, a confidante—a home.

And the only woman, the only person, he could ever

really confide in was Kate Haywood. From the first moment they met at a small banquet at Hatfield House, where they talked for many hours, he had thought about her. Wondered about her.

But would Kate ever want to trade court life for an existence as a respectable lawyer's wife? A housewife like Mistress Hardy? Would she wait, perhaps for years, until his career was established and he could afford a wife and family?

Helping her find this information could surely only help his suit with her. He couldn't woo her with pearls and perfumed gloves, not yet, but he could do this for her. And stay close to her, make sure she was safe, at the same time.

He quickly scribbled a note to Kate, telling her he had much to share with her about his discoveries, before he hurried down the stairs into the courtyard garden.

"Anthony!" one of the apprentices called. "Come play battlecock with us."

Anthony laughed and tried to refuse. It had been many months since he had time for such games, and he was sure he was rusty. But he also felt as if a strange, burning energy was flooding through him, forcing him to move.

"Go, Anthony, go," Master Hardy said. "You cannot spend all your days at work."

Mistress Hardy sighed. "Young men must have their pleasures. I think we should look about for a wife for Master Elias, my dear. Someone with a great deal of spirit, yes?"

Master Hardy patted his wife's hand as he studied Anthony with narrowed eyes. "There is plenty of time for that. Anthony has much work to do first, and we must be most careful to find him the right lady."

The right lady. Anthony feared that no matter how much he craved to hear Kate's laugh, their lives could not fit. Not yet, anyway. Not until he could earn her. Yet he couldn't wait to see her smile when he told her what he had discovered.

He caught up a racket and launched himself into the game, snatching up the ball and laughing as he dashed down the length of the garden. For just that one moment, knowing he would soon see Kate, he felt free.

CHAPTER 21

Kate stared up at the house before her, tall, narrow, most respectable, with freshly plastered, half-timbered walls and solid chimneys wreathed in gray smoke. It was near to the shops, including Master Lucas's establishment, but not too near. They were at the quieter end of the street.

Master Hardy's house spoke of professional, proper prosperity, a place such as she had never lived in before. The tiny, diamond-shaped panes of glass in the windows stared down at her blankly, reflecting back the slate-colored sky.

She held Anthony's note in her hand, asking her to meet him there, but somehow she couldn't quite bring herself to go knock on the door. She stood across the street on the narrow walkway, jostled by hurrying passersby, loath to disturb the solid silence of that house.

Suddenly the front door flew open, and two young men, probably apprentices, tumbled out and chased each other down the lane, shouting. Anthony came to shut the door behind them. He wore no cap, and his dark hair was neatly trimmed to reveal the carved, sharp angles of his handsome face, his slightly crooked nose and bright green eyes. He was grinning, as if at some joke, and the sight made Kate's heart beat faster. He so seldom smiled.

"Kate!" he called. He ran across the muddy lane, dodging carts and a herd of pigs being driven to market. The cold wind tousled that dark hair, and he impatiently shook it back out of his eyes. "Why are you standing out here? Come inside where it's warm."

"I—I don't want to be in the way of your work," she said, suddenly strangely shy. This was *Anthony*, her friend. Surely she should not be uncertain around him?

"Master Hardy has gone out on business," Anthony said. "And Mistress Hardy would be most angry to lose the chance to show off her new home to you."

Kate nodded and let him take her arm to lead her through the front door left ajar by the apprentices. The front hall smelled of lemon polish and fine wax candles, the floor buffed to a high sheen and the paneled walls hung with pretty painted cloths. Herbed rushes in the corner scented the air. Mistress Hardy was indeed a fine housekeeper.

She followed Anthony into a small sitting room where a fire crackled in the grate and a long table was piled with thick ledger books.

Anthony looked almost boyishly eager to show her what he had discovered, and she found herself excited, too, her nervousness forgotten. Hopefully something in those ledgers would help her untangle some of the puzzle of what happened to poor Lady Mary. They sat down beside each other on the bench drawn close to the table and Anthony opened one of the books. Kate's eyes almost crossed as she stared down at tiny columns of cramped, faded humanity.

"Your Everleys have been most busy for a few years," Anthony said, pointing out one of the columns.

"Mary always gave the impression they lived quietly

in the country," Kate said. She felt a pang of sadness to remember how Mary loved to dance at court.

"They may have lived in the country in recent years, but not so quietly," Anthony said. "Once they were great friends of the Seymours and enjoyed some favor, but of late they have spent their time bringing several lawsuits into the courts."

"Lawsuits?" Kate asked, surprised. Surely retaining the services of many lawyers would make the coin in short supply—and court life was expensive.

"Indeed," Anthony answered. He told her a litany of quarrels with neighbors and relations. Dowers and tapestries, jewels, money, disputes over herds of sheep wandering onto land where they did not belong. "The latest suit should be of much interest to you, Kate. Lord Everley has been feuding with a neighbor of his, the Dennis family."

"The Dennis family?" Kate cried. A name she was becoming most familiar with of late, thanks to Rob and his visit to the golden-eyed Lady Dennis's manor.

"You know them?"

"Nay, but I have heard of them lately. What have they to do with the Everleys?"

"It seems the matter began long ago, over a disputed piece of land between their estates. Lord Henry even spent a few days in gaol after killing a Dennis cousin in a brawl, though Queen Mary saw to his release. But last year Everley's daughter, Lady Mary, tried to elope with the son of the Dennis family, a certain Sir Walter, and was dragged back home by her brother. Her brother then tried to kill Sir Walter, and the Dennises in turn brought suit. Lord Henry seems to be most strong-tempered."

"Walter!" Kate cried.

Anthony glanced up from the ledger page, his brow raised. "You do know of this matter."

"Not of this matter specifically, no, but I have heard these names much of late. I saw a man at Lady Mary's bier when I went to see her body. He ran away before I could talk to him, but someone called him Walter."

"Do you think this Walter killed her in a lovers' quarrel, since their elopement was thwarted?"

Kate closed her eyes and remembered her few half glimpses of Walter Dennis. Embracing Mary on the Tower ramparts, lingering near her body in that cold chapel. "I don't want to think so, not if he loved her enough to try and run away with her."

Something unreadable flickered in Anthony's green eyes. "Perhaps she had found a new lover and he was angry with her. Not everyone is as kindhearted as you, Kate."

"Oh, I do know about acts taken in anger and regretted after," Kate said quietly. "But Walter and Mary didn't look angry with each other. Lord Henry has vanished from court. His father says Lord Henry has been sent to woo an heiress, but it seems more likely now he killed his sister and ran away. Don't you think?"

A wave of cold anger suddenly broke over Kate that a man could do such a thing, could destroy Mary's happiness and life in a fit of temper. And then just run away from it.

"God's teeth!" she cursed, bringing her fist down hard on the table. The ledgers tumbled from their piles.

Anthony laid his hand over hers, bringing a calm over her anger. "Kate, you cannot go after Lord Henry Everley yourself. He has already shown himself to be of a bad temper."

Kate thought of Lord Henry, the way he grabbed his sister's wrist, the fire in his eyes. Anthony was right; she would gain nothing from confronting Lord Henry herself. He would never confess to her, if indeed he was the one to kill Mary, and she might end up dead herself. She nodded and drew in a deep breath. "What of Richard St. Long? What did you discover about one of that name?"

"Very little. It appears that he may not be a natural relation of the Everleys, as the earl's only sister died many years ago, and Master St. Long did not come to Everley Court until many months after she was gone. I could find no record of her married name."

"Then who could his mother be?" Kate said, puzzled.

They searched through more of the ledgers, but could find no answers to the origins of Richard St. Long, or any more useful connections to the Everleys. There was a record of a wealthy wool merchant who had purchased the estate next to Everley Court, which could have been the family of the heiress Lord Henry was supposedly sent to woo.

When they at last looked up from their work, the light at the window was turning a soft amber. Kate rubbed at her aching eyes, and gave Anthony a rueful smile.

"I fear I have kept you from your real work too long," she said. "I should return to the palace."

"Surely this *is* real work," Anthony said with a laugh. He pushed away the ledger in front of him and rubbed his hand over the back of his neck. "Finding a villain who means the queen harm—surely nothing could be more important."

As Kate studied him in the pale gold light, she was struck anew by how handsome he truly was. He didn't have the flashing, bright beauty that made Rob Cartman such a focus on the stage; Anthony's face was thinner, more sharply sculpted, starker. His dark, almost black hair was cropped short, making his green eyes seem even lighter. Intelligence shone in those eyes, a close attention that Kate knew missed little of the world around him.

Kate was sure he would make a fine lawyer, with a practice that would attract noble families who needed his quiet perception. He would have a successful and prosperous career.

She remembered Master Hardy's words, seemingly uttered so distractedly, but she knew he had meant a message for her. Anthony was at a critical stage in his budding career, where he was just beginning. He needed good connections, plentiful funds—eventually a good housekeeper and hostess. Things Kate could not have or be.

Anthony was her friend, a friend she valued highly for so many reasons. And, as his friend, she knew she had to wish what was best for him—even in a wife. No matter how much it would hurt to lose him in her life.

But he was not gone yet. He was still here, with her.

"Aye," she said. "The queen is all that is important. I must go and tell her what we've learned today."

"You should stay for supper first," Anthony said. "Mistress Hardy would be disappointed if you don't. She is most proud of the fine table she keeps, and there are no ladies in the household for her to converse with."

Kate took a deep breath, and her stomach did rumble with the sweet scent of roasted meats in cinnamon sauce that floated up from the kitchens. The Hardys were always kind and polite to her, but she was too tired now to face them across their own table and know what they were really thinking. That her friendship was not as beneficial to Anthony as his was to her.

"That is very kind of her, but I have duties at court this evening," Kate said. "I must return there before dark."

"Then I will walk with you."

"Nay, you have your own work...."

Anthony gave her a stern look. "I can't let you walk by yourself. After all that has happened, it is too dangerous."

Kate nodded, and let him help her with her cloak. His hands were warm and strong on her shoulders as he settled the heavy wool around her, and for an instant she was tempted to lean into him.

Only friends, she reminded herself as he led her out into the cold evening. But she had to admit she was glad to have his company for a little longer.

The lanes were crowded with people trying to make their way home before the dark winter's night closed in around them. They hurried and jostled on the narrow walkways, the frosty ground crackling under their boots and pattens, and Anthony kept her close to his side so she wouldn't be knocked into the gutter.

They talked of his work as they made their way toward the palace, of the new music Kate had been writing for the queen's revels, and of her father's health. Only when they reached the looming royal gatehouse with its sentries in the queen's livery did Anthony face her with a most solemn look on his face. He rested his hands gently on her shoulders.

"Kate," he said quietly. "You must take care. If you think to go and ask questions again in places where enemies could lurk, I hope that you will come to me first and let me help you."

She had just been thinking that very thing, that she should return to the draper's shop near Master Lucas's establishment and ask them if they had seen anything strange of late. But she could not say that to Anthony. She had already asked too much of him.

"I will confine most of my questions to court, and I am quite safe there," she said lightly. "I am always surrounded by people. And Master Hardy is right—you must mind your own work."

"I can see to my own work *and* help a friend," he insisted. "I hope you always know that, Kate."

Kate swallowed hard and nodded. Friends. Just as she and Rob were friends? "I know. I do hope we shall always be friends, Anthony."

For an instant, his hands tightened on her shoulders. He pressed a kiss to her forehead. Even though it was light and soft as the brush of a feather, it made her shiver.

"Send me word whenever you need me," he said. Then he turned and vanished into the crowded street.

Kate watched him until she could no longer see his dark head above the river of people. Only then did she straighten her back, square her shoulders, and steel herself to go back into the whirling maelstrom of the court once more.

CHAPTER 22

"La volta!" The cry echoed in the crowded great hall as all the gentlemen dancers lifted their ladies high in the air and twirled them around. Bright silken skirts swirled and flared.

Robert Dudley lifted the queen higher and held her longer than any of the other dancers. Elizabeth held on to his shoulders and threw her head back in laughter. Her loose red-gold hair spilled down her back, over the darker red silk of her gown.

William Cecil scowled at the couple, almost as much as the Count de Feria did. It seemed Sir Robert was not admired by everyone at court.

Kate's fingers ached on her lute strings as she played the Italian song faster and faster. She almost laughed aloud out of the sheer joy of the music. The rush of the notes, tumbling over one another, whirling and shimmering.

The dance wound and wound, more and more wild, until it all ended on a great crescendo.

"Most excellent, Mistress Haywood!" one of the other lutenists said.

"I do like the new Italian songs," Kate agreed, trying to catch her breath. For those long, sweet moments she had been able to forget death and cruelty in the bright alchemy of music. Nothing ever overcame her like music could, and the volta was so quick and fiery it carried her away like a warm wave.

She watched as Sir Robert lowered Queen Elizabeth slowly to her feet, the two of them laughing with their heads bent together. He led her toward the dais at the far end of the hall, where her chair and canopy of estate waited. Elizabeth leaned on his arm as the other couples swarmed around them.

For just an instant, Kate wondered what it might be like to be one of those dancers herself. To feel a man's strong hands on her waist, twirling her high in the air, looking up at her with a flirtatious smile.

But whose hands would she want?

She took a deep drink from a goblet of wine offered by a page boy, then launched into a quieter madrigal. Servants carried in the next course of the banquet, winter vegetable salads dressed in vinegar and cinnamon-laced chicken. Everyone found their seats again at the long tables laid with fine white damask cloths and lined with tall silver saltcellars. Merriment still hung in the air, a cloud of laughter.

Suddenly the exuberant scene was shattered by a piercing scream that rose even above the laughter.

Kate's heart leaped with a hot rush of fear. She hopped up from her stool and ran through the shifting confusion of the hall, toward those screams that went on and on, moving only on instinct, feeling. Robert Dudley was behind her, drawing his dagger, his cronies closing in directly behind him.

Kate glanced quickly over her shoulder to see the queen standing on her dais, her guards surrounding her even as she impatiently tried to push them aside.

Outside the great hall was a long corridor lined with

tapestries that made the sound of screams echo, carrying them into the hall. At the end a door stood open, diffuse rays of silvery moonlight sparkling on the wooden floors in a strange beauty that contrasted with the terror of the screams.

Kate tumbled out into the night to find Lady Catherine Grey standing at the foot of the outdoors stairs, her pale blue gown and golden hair shimmering in the darkness. Her hands were thrown out in front of her as if to hold something away, her mouth open on a scream that had faded to a hoarse hiccup.

Kate took in the whole scene in one horrified glance. She felt a scream crawling up her own throat, clawing to get out, but she managed to shove it back down and look at the tableau as if it were a mere tapestry.

A woman was sprawled out at the foot of the stairs. Her fine, dark red satin skirts were spread around her, and her head was arched back as if to stare at the clouded night sky. Her hair, even more red than the dress, was piled on her head and held in place with a gold wire headdress. The fine metallic embroidery of her bodice gleamed. It was the same color as the gown the queen wore in the volta.

The woman looked almost as if she had just wandered away from the royal party and fallen asleep there. Except for the garish red-purple gash slashing her throat, and the glazed, silvery, looking-glass gleam of her wide-open eyes.

For one instant, Kate thought it was Queen Elizabeth. Then she heard a shout from behind her.

"God's blood! What is the meaning of this?"

Relief rushed through Kate until she realized that if this was not the queen, it was still *someone*, someone murdered and left on the queen's doorstep. She glanced back to see Elizabeth standing behind her. The queen tottered on the threshold on her heeled velvet shoes, held back by Robert Dudley. He and the queen's guards had drawn their swords, and Elizabeth's dark eyes were burning as she glared out into the garden. Bright pink spots flared in her pale cheeks.

Kate spun around again and ran down the steps to where Catherine Grey still shrieked in little hiccup noises. Kate wasn't at all sure what to do with shocked, shrieking people, but she did remember a nursemaid she once had as a child who was very strict—until her father found a sweeter girl to look after her.

Sweet would not work now.

"Be quiet now, Lady Catherine," Kate said, stern and loud. She gave Lady Catherine's arm a hard shake, which seem to surprise the woman into silence. Once Lady Catherine covered her face with her hands, sobbing, Kate went to study the terrible sight laid out on the dry, frosty grass.

She pressed her fingers to her mouth to hold back a sudden sick rush. It was Bess who lay there so still, Bess— the sister of the murdered Nell. Bess who wore the fine, rich gown and gold headdress on her curled red hair.

And pinned to her bodice was a piece of expensive parchment. Written across it, in bold, black, scrolling letters, was a simple message:

Bastard queen, Elizabeth Tudor. You are next.

CHAPTER 23

"Tell me where he is!" Kate grabbed a handful of Harry's rumpled shirt and shook the apprentice actor hard. He was so surprised by her sudden move that she yanked him to his feet before he could stumble and pull away from her.

"I don't know what you mean," the young man muttered as he backed away from her. He ran his hands through his tangled hair, eyeing her warily all the time. "You should be declared mad, woman, breaking in here like that and hurling accusations!"

"I haven't hurled anything yet," Kate said fiercely. She had spent the morning dashing up and down the crowded, stinking lanes of Bankside, looking for Rob Cartman. He wasn't at the Cardinal's Hat or any of the taverns nearby. None of the actors she had found there had seen him in days, though most of them were ale-shot and probably couldn't even remember their own names.

The queen's wardrobe ladies had no knowledge of the gown Bess wore being stolen, but when they looked for it amid the cases and cases of gowns, underskirts, and sleeves, it was gone. No one at the Cardinal's Hat had even realized Bess was missing, and Kate could find no clues in her chamber. She had looked around while Mistress Celine stood in the doorway and screeched about missing her rent. The bed was made, and Bess's few clothes hung on their pegs. The grate was cold. There had been no struggle there, so surely Bess was snatched someplace else, possibly for her red hair, or possibly because she knew Nell.

Or maybe she went with someone she knew. Someone who offered to take her somewhere away from the Cardinal's Hat.

Kate had to find Rob. She had risen at dawn after a terrified, sleepless night amid a chaotic court, put on her boy's clothes, and slipped out of a tightly guarded palace to go in search of him. She'd finally found Harry, the young actor who had appeared in the play that night at the Tower, in bed with a drowsy-eyed bawd at the Sign of the Hart.

"If I do not find him soon, Dudley or Cecil will," Kate said. "With all their spies throughout London, it won't take long for them to find out he was connected to both Nell and Bess, and they will come after him to question him about their murders. Wouldn't you rather I found him first?"

Harry's eyes went wide. He fell back another step. "Bess is dead, too?"

Kate nodded tightly. "And her body left at the queen's palace, dressed in a fine embroidered gown."

Harry breathed out a foul word. His face went as white as his shirt had once been, and the bawd who had been listening behind the door the whole time let out a shriek. Southwark would soon know the doings at the queen's court.

"If Rob did this . . . ," Kate began.

"He never would!" Harry shook his head fiercely. "He likes a brawl sometimes, but you know he wouldn't hurt a woman, especially not Nell or Bess."

Kate nodded. Harry reflected her own earlier feelings about Rob, her surety that he couldn't kill a defenseless woman. But what if a woman made him very, very angry? Or what if Rob was hurt as well, by whoever was killing red-haired women?

Kate could almost see Harry's thoughts scrolling across his smooth brow. Surely an actor ought to be able to conceal his inner feelings. Finally he nodded. "I think I know where we can find him."

"Rob is *there*?" Kate cried, appalled as she stared up at the black, stark walls of the Clink Prison. "For how long?"

Harry shrugged. He tried to act careless, as if such things happened all the time. And to actors, who always seemed embroiled in drunken, high-emotion quarrels, perhaps they did. Yet Kate could see the shadow of concern in his eyes. The Clink was notoriously filthy and gaol-fever ridden, a cesspit stop on the way to the gibbet that stood just outside its walls.

"Yesterday, so I heard," Harry said. "He went looking for the villain that did for Nell, furious he was. Nearly killed a man in a brawl at the Rose and Crown tavern that he heard had been seen hitting Nell before. So he got tossed in here."

Kate clenched her fists, so angry and frustrated with Rob she could hardly see clearly. Losing her temper would never help him now. "Well, he will not be here for long." She gathered the heavy folds of her cloak around her and marched up to the ironbound doors. Harry scrambled behind her, but by the time he reached her side, she had already tugged hard on the bellpull.

After several long, heart-pounding moments, the rusty locks and bars on the doors at last squealed and the portal swung open to reveal a cadaverously thin, waxy-skinned guard. He peered out at them with ratlike eyes from behind a curtain of long, greasy hair.

"Aye?" he said.

Kate swallowed hard, and tried to imagine she was the queen. She needed some imperious manners now. "We are sent by one of the queen's own courtiers to see a man who had been unjustly imprisoned here. A Master Robert Cartman. At once, if you please."

The guard eyed her fine cloak and implacable expression, and the tall, handsome man who lurked silently just beyond her shoulder. "The queen's court, is it? How can I be sure of that? I can't let visitors in without telling the governor, now, can I?"

Kate dug a coin from her purse and held it out to him. "You may be sure of our complete honesty. And of Her Majesty's most acute displeasure if we are turned away."

The coin swiftly vanished between his skeletal fingers. "Follow me, then."

Harry took Kate's arm as they stepped through the door and it slammed behind them, like the gates of hell. A thick, damp darkness closed in around them, and Kate shivered. The guard had already almost vanished in the gloom, and she hurried to keep up.

They turned down a narrow corridor lit by a few flickering torches set in iron holders on the dripping stone walls and lined with barred cell doors. Pale faces pressed to the tiny grilled openings, shrill cries following them as they passed. The smell was overpowering, appalling, a mixture of damp rot, human waste, and rancid food.

"Just keep walking, Mistress Haywood," Harry whispered, and she nodded as she pressed the edge of her cloak hood to her nose. She couldn't help but be most alarmed at the thought of Rob locked away in here, all his vibrant laughter and life buried in noxious odors and disease.

To her relief, they were not taken to one of those cells but to a large, open courtyard. Surrounded by arched walkways, the patch of dirt was surmounted by what was surely the only glimpse of sky in the whole cursed place. It stretched, gray and flat and pitiless, over the scene of prisoners milling aimlessly about. Their grubby faces turned eagerly toward Kate and Harry, but the presence of the guard seemed to hold them back.

"Over there," the ghoulish man said, gesturing toward the high wall at the end of the courtyard. "You have ten minutes."

He held out his hand again, and Kate tossed him a coin before she hurried toward the man who stood with his back disdainfully to the rabble.

Even in the gray-brown crowd, Rob could be seen. He was taller than most, his hair bright even though it was already tangled and tinged with dust.

"Rob!" Kate called, and he turned to her with a smile breaking over his dirt-streaked face. As he took her in his arms, she could smell the tang of prison on his unfastened doublet, his rumpled shirt. He had only been there a few hours, if Harry was to be believed. She had to get him out of there soon.

"How did you know I was here?" he said, pressing a quick kiss to her forehead.

"Harry told me, when I came looking for you," she answered, scanning his fine figure quickly to make sure he was not hurt. There was dried blood on his shirt, but it did not appear to be his, and a bruise above one eye.

Rob scowled over her head at Harry, who just shrugged again. "You should not have brought her here."

"Could *you* have stopped her?" Harry said. "If I had

let her go alone, she would have scoured every inch of Southwark until she found you."

"Never mind that now," Kate cried impatiently. "How did you end up here?"

Rob gave a bitter laugh and ran his hand through his hair. "I had a bit of a misunderstanding with a man in a tavern. I was looking for Bess, no one knew where she had gone, and he said something most insulting about her. I had imbibed a bit of ale by then, and well . . ." He shrugged. "Next thing I knew, I was being tossed in here. Not to worry, Kate, 'twas not the first time, nor will it be the last."

Kate stared up at him, sadness washing over her. She knew he lied, for Harry had told her the truth. Did he try to protect her? She held on to his sleeve, keeping him with her. "Oh, Rob. You do not know? I fear Bess is dead."

Rob stared down at her, his eyes bright with shock. He tried to laugh, to brush her away, but slowly she saw the truth of her words work its way into his mind. Then anger replaced the shock.

She quickly told him of the terrible events in the queen's garden, about how she had been desperately seeking any clue to Bess's death. Rob tried to pull away from her, but she held him tightly, aware of all the avid listeners who were close to them. The queen would not want word of this to spread so quickly.

"Bloody hell!" Rob groaned. "May God damn whoever did this. Bess—and Nell . . ."

"The killer *will* be found," Kate said firmly. "At least we know you could not have done this, since you were in here all night. But we must find who it was, and quickly. Did you see nothing at all last night? Hear nothing?"

"Nay, of course I did not!" Rob shouted. "If I had, I

would have—" He suddenly broke off, his eyes widening as he went very still.

"What is it? What do you remember?" Kate asked urgently.

"There is a man in here, a thief. He tried to talk to me in the cell last night. He was raving about the haunted shop he tried to rob before he ran off and was caught," Rob said slowly. "I thought he was merely ale-shot and listened to him but little, since I had my own problems to think on. He said a ghost was in the attics and shouted at him, giving him a deathly fright."

Kate was most confused. "A ghost? How could this link us to Bess?"

Rob gave a rough laugh. "The shop he tried to rob belonged to the goldsmith named Lucas. Lucas was said amongst the thieves to have rich pickings in his shop, as you and I know to be true from our own visit. But no one was meant to be in the attics."

A ghost in the attics of Master Lucas's shop. Kate's thoughts raced. "Can I speak with this mad thief?"

Rob gestured toward a man who paced back and forth beneath the moldy stone arches. He didn't look as if he could coherently describe what he saw in Master Lucas's attics, but if something was lurking there, she needed to know about it. "If you can, Kate."

"I think we must," she said decisively. "So far he is the only hint of where Henry Everley might be lurking. I will *make* this thief talk sense. . . ."

CHAPTER 24

"**I** will not be a prisoner in my own house!" Queen Elizabeth's shout thundered along the crowded corridor, silencing the flock of whispering, fluttering, pale-faced courtiers. "Not now. Not again."

Kate elbowed her way through the crowd, her lute cradled against her. She'd returned to the palace just in time to receive the queen's summons. She had quickly washed off the grime of her search through Southwark and changed into her new blue silk gown before dashing through the presence and privy chambers, down this corridor toward the chamber where Queen Elizabeth waited.

The fear, that iron-tinged tang of incipient panic, hung thick in the air, greater than the flowery perfumes and the smoke from the massive marble fireplaces.

The queen was in a sitting room, the door to her bedchamber open in the corner of the paneled wall and a flock of worried-looking ladies gathered around her. Their pretty faces looked wild and uncertain as they dashed one way and then the other, not knowing what they should be doing. The whole ordered world of the court, where everyone knew their place, be it in privy chamber or presence chamber, was upended and destroyed.

Kate glanced around the room. The queen's desk was

set up by the fire, piled high with documents of state requiring her attention. But her cushioned chair was shoved back from it, as if she had leaped up, unable to sit still any longer. A quill lay abandoned in a little pool of ink. The hassocks and pillows where the ladies usually sat to do their embroidery and gossip were abandoned.

In the corner was a stack of coronation gifts, gleaming bolts of silks and velvets, chests glinting with hints of gold and silver, garnets and pearls. A black-robed clerk held a scroll, as if he was trying to inventory it all, but it was clear the man could not concentrate. Guards in the queen's livery, their swords obviously displayed at their sides, stood behind him.

The heavy brocade draperies were drawn over the window, closing out what little daylight there was. The only illumination came from dozens of candles set around the room, which only added to the stuffy oppressiveness.

One of the ladies' lapdogs dashed across the floor after a tiny scurrying object that fluttered across the fine carpet. A woman screamed and clutched at her skirts.

"Vile creatures!" she cried. "How shall we bear it?"

"Oh, do be quiet, Lady Helen," the queen shouted. "It is only a mouse. The palace is infested with them today."

"If only that was the worst of our troubles," William Cecil muttered.

"Aye. If only," Elizabeth said with a sigh.

Kate turned to find the queen standing near the fire, her white, bejeweled hand braced on the marble mantel. She wore a fine green and silver gown, but her hair was undressed and fell over her shoulders in tangled waves. Her green velvet shoe tapped out a staccato rhythm on the floor.

William Cecil stood across from her. He wore his usual somber garments, dark gray velvet trimmed with brown fur, his silver-streaked beard hiding his expression and a black velvet cap on his balding head. He leaned on his walking stick, the only hint of weariness about him.

Kate thought again of her long-ago strict nursemaid, the one who had inspired her to get Lady Catherine Grey to stop screaming. Lady Catherine wasn't among the women dashing around the chamber now, but even if she had the megrims today, she *had* quieted down last night.

Kate grabbed Kat Ashley's arm as the woman hurried past, her skirt hems held up against the mice. "Mistress Ashley, what is happening?"

Mistress Ashley gave a deep, harried sigh. "Ah, Mistress Haywood! There you are. Perhaps a song could soothe Her Majesty. Though I doubt it." Mistress Ashley eyed the chaos of the room uncertainly. "Sir Robert Dudley has sent his men out into the city to make inquiries, and Master Cecil has ordered the queen to stay in her chambers until the villain who left *that* in the garden has been found."

"Ordered?" Kate said in surprise. That did not seem like the best course to take with a Tudor.

Mistress Ashley sighed again. "I know. Most unwise. You would think he would know by now, he has worked with her for so long. But men can be ever foolish."

Kate nodded, remembering the tales of royal courts past that Mistress Ashley had distracted her with after Durham House. "It would not be a good thing for the whole city to hear of what has happened. Everyone is celebrating the new queen. There might be a panic in the streets."

Mistress Ashley studied Kate's face for a moment, then nodded. "Very true, Mistress Haywood. Nothing can blight these days, not after all the strife it took to get here."

So they understood each other. The queen's coronation was a time of hope, of looking forward, of moving on from the dark days of fear. "What is meant to happen tonight?" Kate asked, even though she knew very well, for she had arranged much of the music for it.

"A masque. *The Triumph of Diana*."

Kate nodded. "Then it must go on. Who is to play Diana?"

"Lady Helen." Mistress Ashley gestured toward the lady who was still shrieking about mice.

"Take them to rehearse their songs, then, Mistress Ashley, and I will play a soothing tune for the queen."

Mistress Ashley nodded, and hastily set about herding the ladies out of the room like a flock of ducklings. Soon only Mary Sidney stayed, sitting on a stool with her pretty dark head bent over her embroidery in the dim light. The little dog leaped up onto her lap, as if quite satisfied he had chased the evil mouse away. The clerk went back to his inventory of the gifts, unpacking a crate of finely chased silver saltcellars and goblets, and another of fine Malmsey wine, the queen's favorite.

Elizabeth looked as if she didn't even notice the sudden silence in the room, but her shoulders slumped a bit and she sighed. Her fingertips tapped on the marble mantel, the quick, unsteady rhythm of raindrops.

Unsure of what to do now, Kate sat down on a stool in the corner closest to the queen and set her lute across her lap. She had much to tell Elizabeth about what she had learned in the gaol, but Cecil still stood with her. He scowled and stiffened, as if bracing himself for a new storm.

For a moment the room was so silent Kate could hear the skittering sound of the terrified mice, the low whine of the dog, and Mary Sidney's soft murmur. Then Elizabeth's voice rang out like a whiplash.

"Kate," she said. "What think you of marriage?"

"I—er . . ." Kate thought quickly. She wasn't at all sure what the queen wanted of her, or what marriage had to do with the murderous matter at hand. "It is a necessity for many, of course, Your Majesty. But I look for it not myself."

"Exactly so," Elizabeth said with a small smile for William Cecil. "Some are called for higher purposes. But my good Cecil thinks that, despite the fact that it is God Himself who has put me in this place, my seat on the throne is a mere aberration. That I must find a husband to rule for me while I get on with the task of bearing heirs to supplant me."

A red flush flared in Cecil's craggy cheeks above his beard. "I only urge you to do what is right and natural, Your Majesty. You *must* marry, for England must have an heir if the country is not to fall into civil war."

"An heir." Elizabeth gave a weary sigh and dropped down onto her abandoned chair. "The country has no shortage of possible heirs, it seems. The Grey girls, Mary of Scotland, Margaret Douglas. And I am only twenty-five. I plan to keep my crown on my living head for a long while."

Cecil's fist curled around the carved head of his walking stick. "Life is most uncertain. . . ."

"Believe me, no one knows that better than I do," Elizabeth snapped. "I shall do as God bids me when the time comes. In the meantime, we have more urgent matters to see to than my marriage. We must first find who is trying to kill me."

Cecil's eyes narrowed, but he seemed to know he was pushed back for the moment. And besides, if there was no firm Protestant Tudor on the throne, even if it *was* a woman Tudor, all he had worked for so hard and so long would be lost. Elizabeth had to stay alive.

"It is clear I am not the first victim of this villain," Elizabeth said. "There was the red-haired bawd Nell, that poor wretch in my garden wearing my stolen gown. Lady Mary also, mayhap? She had red hair."

Before Kate could open her mouth to tell Elizabeth what she had learned in the gaol, Cecil said, "My man returned from Everley Court this morning, Your Majesty. It seems your suspicions were correct. Lord Everley did not send Lord Henry home; in fact no one from the family has been seen there in weeks. Master Walsingham is talking to Lord Everley now, but he steadfastly claims he didn't know where his son has gone. He says he sent him home, and if Lord Henry has instead run off, it is no fault of his."

"A fond father, I see. Well, Walsingham will have the truth from him soon enough," Elizabeth said. "God's teeth! But I will never show kindness or mercy to such families again, not if they repay me in such a vile fashion. They are worse than these mice scurrying across my carpets."

"I think I might know where Lord Henry has gone, Your Majesty," Kate said quietly.

Elizabeth and Cecil both turned to her with wide, startled eyes, as if they had forgotten she was there. Before they could say anything, a messenger stepped into the chamber and gave a low bow.

"The Count de Feria waits without for your audience, Your Majesty," the boy said.

Elizabeth nodded, and a catlike smile spread over her

face. "You will tell us all later, Kate. Right now I must speak to the Spanish ambassador. He has been so eager for an audience, and I have put him off too long. Who knows, my dear Cecil? Perhaps your matrimonial hopes will come true sooner rather than later."

Cecil's flush flared even brighter red over his face. "Nay, Your Majesty! Not Spain, I beg you . . ."

Elizabeth just laughed and gestured for the ambassador to be admitted. She smoothed her skirts and shook her hair back from her shoulders.

Feria came into the room and bowed low over Elizabeth's offered hand as Cecil retired with a muttered curse. The clerk and guards followed him. Kate half rose to follow, nervous that Feria would remember her from Durham House, but Elizabeth gestured to her to remain. Kate lowered herself to a stool, bending her head over her lute.

"Nay, Kate, play us a pretty Spanish song," Elizabeth said. She smiled amiably up at Feria, yet she didn't offer him a seat. "Perhaps you would also enjoy some wine, Count? I have some fine Malmsey here as a gift, as you can see."

Feria smiled smoothly, but his eyes were cold. "Nay, Your Majesty, I thank you," he said amiably. "I require nothing but assurances that your health has quite recovered. King Philip was most distressed to hear that you had taken to your chamber so soon after your coronation."

"His Majesty is most kind," Elizabeth said. "A good and true brother. As you can see, I am well. It was a trifling winter cold."

"I am relieved to hear it, as my master shall be." Feria didn't mention the other "indisposition" Elizabeth had found of late—the body in the garden. The Spanish had not been at the banquet that night, but surely he had heard all about it. "He is most concerned about you, Your Majesty."

"He has no need to be. I am perfectly healthy." Elizabeth's smile never faltered. Kate watched her carefully as she played a soft Spanish love song.

"It is no easy matter to wear a crown, Your Majesty," Feria said. In his stark black clothes, he looked like a large, dark crow circling over Elizabeth's bright, small kestrel. But kestrels had dagger-sharp talons. "King Philip knows this very well, and he is eager to be of assistance to you in any way he can. He has long been very fond of you."

"As I said, Count—the king is a good brother, and I am happy to think we can be allies now," Elizabeth said.

"The king would hope to be much more to you than that, Your Majesty. If you would but listen to his proposal, he could relieve you of those labors which are only fit for men."

Elizabeth blinked, and that blazing light in her dark eyes that always signaled trouble flared out. "As he *relieved* my sister? I think not!"

"Your Majesty . . ." Feria held out his hands as if in supplication. But his careful smile seemed to say how unreliable a female monarch truly was. How prey to emotion.

Elizabeth rose from her chair and paced to the window in a rustling flurry of green and silver skirts. She pulled back the heavy draperies covering the glass, letting in a burst of gray-yellow light.

"You may tell your master that I already feel myself married." Elizabeth spun around and held up her hand to show the coronation ring on her finger. "To my country. It is indeed a heavy task, but 'tis mine alone, and I must take care of my people as a mother would her children. England has shown she does not care for a foreign husband with no time for her. Surely King Philip remembers that."

Feria's jaw tightened, but he had been too long at court to show any other hint of emotion. "Spain surely has much more to offer England than vice versa, Your Majesty. An empire that stretches across the globe, in fact. Alliances with the oldest kingdoms in Christendom. If you would but consider . . ."

Elizabeth sat back down and nodded. "Parliament meets next month. I can do nothing without their consent. I will consider King Philip's words most carefully."

"Thank you, Your Majesty. I am sure God will turn your heart as He sees fit." Feria bowed again. "My master is a strong man, and could protect you from many dangers. Even ones on your own doorstep, mayhap? Family matters, even. The king is your family too, as you know."

Family matters? Kate studied the queen's face, and was sure Elizabeth was wondering the same thing. Did Feria refer to the body on the doorstep, or to someone like Lady Catherine? Family matters indeed.

Elizabeth's fingers clenched in the fabric of her skirts. "I will keep such in mind, Count. Now I must beg my leave of you."

"If we could speak further soon . . ."

"I shall send for you."

Feria clearly saw he would get no further that day. He bowed and backed gracefully from the chamber.

Once the door closed behind him, Elizabeth leaped to her feet and sent her chair toppling over with a fierce sweep of her hand. Cushions went flying, and Mistress Sidney's dog yelped. Kate's fingers faltered on the lute strings and the song went silent.

"God's blood, but I hate the Spanish!" Elizabeth shouted. "Like spiders hiding in the grass, hissing with my own relations." She kicked out at a cushion and gave a strange laugh. "If only Feria knew I am meeting with the French ambassador later. Monsieur Castelnau is most eager to negotiate after Calais, which my sister so foolishly lost. Wouldn't *that* set Philip awry?"

"Your Majesty, you are overset," Mary Sidney said in her low, soothing voice. She gave a gentle smile, and for a moment her large, dark eyes looked like those of her brother Robert Dudley. "You should rest. Let me send for some sweetmeats. Maybe those fruit suckets you like?"

Elizabeth shook her head fiercely, but some of the hectic red color leached from her cheeks. She sat back down on her chair. "Nay, I am well enough, sweet Mary. Now that the Spanish infestation is cleared of my rooms. I want to hear where you went today, Kate. You have found Henry Everley?"

"Nay, not yet, but I think I am close," Kate said. She quickly told the queen of her adventures through Bankside, and finding Rob Cartman in the festering gaol cell with the thief. She had no certainty that the frightened man's "ghost" was Lord Henry, but the fact that the Lucases were hiding something in their attic seemed most suspicious. She needed to see for herself what was there before she could tell the queen more.

Elizabeth frowned thoughtfully, tapping her fingers again on her skirt. "So that handsome young actor is in gaol, is he? We must have him out again as soon as possible. He has done us more than one good turn of late. And I suppose you were planning on going to search the Lucas shop yourself?"

Kate had in fact been planning to do just that. If Lord

Henry was there, he would have some of the answers she had been seeking for so long. "I did think—"

"You cannot go by yourself," Elizabeth interrupted sharply. "It would be too dangerous."

"But there shouldn't be panic spread in a respectable street, as it would if an army marched in," Kate said. "Henry Everley must be made to go quietly."

Elizabeth pursed her lips. "You are right, of course. My people need peace now, security. The celebrations must not be marred. Very well. I trust you to go, Kate, but you will wait until Robert Dudley returns. He can go with you and see to this troublesome matter." The queen smiled, and it was nothing like the cat-with-the-cream smirk she had given Feria. It was soft, gentle. "There is none I would trust more to keep the peace of my realm than Sir Robert."

Kate nodded. "Aye, Your Majesty. I will wait for Sir Robert."

The queen slumped back as if suddenly weary. She rubbed her fingertips over her brow. "Now I think I might be in need of some wine before I must face the French ambassador on top of all else. Kate, Mary, will you join me?"

Elizabeth rose in a graceful sway of her glittering skirts and hurried to the corner where the clerk had been inventorying gifts. She reached for one of the silver-gilded bottles of Malmsey wine and twisted off the wax seal.

It all happened in an instant. Kate suddenly realized the wine was still closed, not yet tasted, and she opened her mouth to call out to the queen when something warm and furry and terrible brushed her ankle and she shrieked like Lady Helen had.

Startled, Elizabeth whirled around and the bottle fell

from her hands to crash on the floor in a cacophony of splintered glass.

Elizabeth lunged back as some of the wine splashed on her skirts. Mistress Sidney screamed and jumped to her feet. Her dog barked merrily and ran around in a circle at all the sudden excitement. The noise seemed to flush out more of the mice that had set the ladies aflutter earlier, and that made the dog even more giddy. It chased one of the mangy bits of gray fur onto the sticky puddle, where the mouse fell and rolled as if drunk on the fine wine.

"Oh, bad dog!" Mary Sidney cried. She snatched up the dog and cradled it against her violet satin bodice. "Now you'll need a bath."

"What a waste of good wine," Elizabeth muttered. She held up her hem to examine her green shoes, scowling at the stain on one toe.

But Kate stared in growing horror at the mouse that drank the wine. It staggered a step, let out an unearthly yelp—and fell over dead. All in a moment.

"Your Majesty!" she shouted. "Come away from there right now. Take your shoes off."

Elizabeth looked up with a scowl. "Kate! Who are you to say . . ."

Kate didn't know where her boldness was coming from—she just knew she had to move. With one hand she grabbed the queen's thin, silk-covered arm and pulled her away, and with the other she pointed at the dead mouse.

Elizabeth gasped in understanding. She tore off her shoes and examined her stockings and skin for any stain of wine. Poisoned wine.

It seemed that "Elizabeth Tudor, bastard queen" was indeed next.

CHAPTER 25

Twilight was gathering over the spires and chimneys of London as Kate made her way with Robert Dudley through the streets.

The crowd of retainers who usually followed him were nowhere to be seen. There were only two guards following them at a discreet distance, somberly dressed in plain russet doublets, the iron hilts of swords and daggers glowing with quiet but lethal strength at their belts.

Sir Robert was different here than he was at court. At the queen's palace, he was all laughing charm, all sparkling dark eyes, richly dressed gallantry. Now he scanned the street with a close, hardened gaze, a small frown creased between his black brows. The people on the walkway, hurrying on their own errands and quarrels, instinctively dodged out of his path.

Kate remembered that he had been a soldier, that he had fought in France with King Philip in order to save himself and his family after his father and brother were executed. The Dudleys had been hardened courtiers since the days of King Henry VII; they had played the dangerous games of crowns to the highest of heights and the lowest of lows. His father had been declared a traitor for raising Queen Jane Grey to the throne in Queen Mary's place.

Yet Robert Dudley had survived. He had to be a man with a soul of steel to do that. A soul that matched the queen's own. As Kate looked at him now, in his somber black wool and leather doublet, his black hair disarrayed by the wind, she could see why Queen Elizabeth would risk gossip to be near such a man.

But he somewhat frightened Kate. He was most unpredictable—like the man they hunted now.

She shivered as she studied the street past Sir Robert's shoulder. It was a very cold night, the wind icy as it swept around the buildings and caught at cloaks and hoods, but the sky was clear. Tiny diamond-like stars flickered on against the dark blue velvet sky, just as torches flared to life outside the houses. Shop windows were being closed for the night, and everyone seemed in a hurry to reach their own firesides.

It was a most respectable street, only a few lanes over from Master Lucas's shop, but still Kate had the prickling feeling of being watched. She shivered again.

Sir Robert's frown transformed into a smile as he looked down at her. "Cold, Mistress Haywood? We will soon be there. Then this foul business can be done."

"If the man in the gaol was telling the truth and Lord Henry is indeed at the goldsmith's shop."

"Did he seem to be lying? What would be in it for him?"

Kate thought about how the man had looked. Worse for drink, certainly, and most willing to trade secrets to get more. But there had been no shifting of his gaze, no fidgeting. None of the usual signs of lying.

And he had not been a smooth-voiced courtier who had learned to hide all his true feelings like Robert Dudley.

"I don't think he was lying," she said. "The Lucases are hiding something."

"Then we will find Lord Henry, make him tell us how he did these murders, and be done with it." Sir Robert led her across the street toward Master Lucas's shop. Their window was already closed, the building dark except for a shimmer of candlelight in one window.

Sir Robert swept a grim glance over it. "The queen must be kept safe at all costs."

"Of course." Kate completely agreed with that. No one wanted the dark days of Queen Mary to return, or the civil war that would surely erupt amid the many claimants to the queen's throne.

Yet something nagged at her from the back of her mind, something that told her Lord Henry was not the whole story to these foul deeds. Perhaps he *had* killed his sister in a fit of rage. And Lady Mary did have red hair, like Nell and Bess. Like the queen.

But Nell and Bess seemed planned, calculated. Lady Mary seemed different. Chaotic.

If anyone could get answers from Lord Henry, it was surely Robert Dudley. Kate only feared that Sir Robert might lack the subtlety needed to discover if Lord Henry was capable of planning all of the murders, planning this cat-and-mouse game with the queen.

Then again, she thought as she watched Sir Robert bang on the Lucases' door with a grimly determined look on his dark face, he was surely a man of infinite subtlety. He had to be, to have survived so long.

He had to pound on the door several times before there was finally the thunk of a bar being pulled back. The door opened a crack.

It was Master Lucas himself. He wore no leather work apron now, but other than that, he looked much as he had when Kate visited the shop before. His sparse gray hair stood on end, and his shirt was rumpled despite its fine linen fabric. His eyes were startled and red-rimmed as he took in the people on his doorstep, the stone-faced Robert Dudley and his two burly guards, with Kate lurking behind.

"You are Master Lucas the goldsmith?" Sir Robert demanded.

"I—yes, I am Master Lucas," he stammered, his fingers white where they curled around the edge of the door. Kate could tell he longed to slam and bolt it again, but he didn't dare with such an obviously powerful person.

"I am Sir Robert Dudley," he said, his tone perfectly flat and expressionless.

Master Lucas's face flushed and his mouth fell open. He snapped it closed and quickly bowed very low. "Your lordship, I am honored by your visit to my humble shop. But I fear we are closed for business at the moment. If you would care to—"

"I am here on an errand for Queen Elizabeth." Sir Robert reached out and shoved the door open. Master Lucas fell back a step, his creased face turning stark white as Sir Robert and his men marched into the empty shop. "We have heard you are harboring a man who is gone from the queen's court without license."

Master Lucas made a visible effort to draw himself up, to remain calm, but Kate could see his hands trembling.

"There is no one here, my lord, only my wife and servants," Lucas cried. "If some foul villain has broken in and hidden himself . . ."

"If that is indeed what happened, then you should be grateful if we flush him out," Sir Robert said brusquely. He gestured to his men to search the shop while Master Lucas twisted his hands in his sleeves and bleated desperate protests.

Kate stood back and carefully studied the room. A torch placed hastily in a wall sconce was the only light, and the corners behind the counters were in shadow. From behind a closed door could be heard the sound of hurrying footsteps, as if the servants Master Lucas mentioned were in a rush to find their beds. The faint, metallic, smoky smell of metalwork still hung in the air.

As Sir Robert's men searched behind the counters and poked their swords through bundles and packing crates, Master Lucas scurried after them. Kate noticed a tray set on a nearby table. It was a display of rings, finely wrought silver set with amethysts and amber. They looked familiar in their delicate style, and she frowned as she tried to remember where she saw something like that.

An image flashed through her mind. Mistress Celine, the plump, red-haired landlady at the Cardinal's Hat. She had worn just such a ring, a silver band of flowers with an amethyst stone. Yet another link to Master Lucas's wares.

But who had given the ring to Celine? Lord Henry? The bawd didn't seem his style.

Kate felt the strange prickling sensation at the nape of her neck that always seemed to mean someone was watching her. She spun around to see a narrow staircase against the back wall. The steep steps led up into darkness, but there was a glimpse of a pale face, a twitch of skirts. A patter of footsteps on the floor above sounded like the mice at the queen's palace.

And Kate remembered all too well what had happened to *them*.

She caught Sir Robert's attention and gestured toward the stairs. He nodded, which she took to mean she should explore them further, and she quietly slipped out of the shop. Master Lucas didn't even seem to notice, he was so busy entreating the guards not to break any of his wares.

Kate ran up the stairs, following the retreating footsteps. At the landing she glimpsed a sitting room one way, a comfortable, firelit space with an embroidery frame and open workbox that looked hastily abandoned. It was empty. The other way lay more stairs, which was where the steps were vanishing.

Kate followed, moving quickly in her boy's clothes. At the top of the stairs, under the sloping eaves of the house, the lady who had so cheerfully gossiped with customers on Kate's last visit was carefully opening a door.

"Mistress Lucas, I assume?" Kate called.

Mistress Lucas gasped as if in shock, even though Kate had not tried to be particularly stealthy in running up the stairs. Mistress Lucas whirled around, letting the door slam behind her.

"I am sure your husband could use some assistance in the shop," Kate said quietly. "It's not every day Sir Robert Dudley comes calling, I would think."

Mistress Lucas had surely been a pretty woman in her youth, blond and pink, probably often laughing if the faint lines around her eyes were any indication. She had been very merry with the customers on the day Kate and Rob came to the shop. She was not laughing now. She opened and closed her mouth as if she couldn't decipher what to say. Her hands twisted in her skirts.

"Or perhaps you already have company that urgently requires your attention now? In that very room?" Kate said.

Mistress Lucas snapped her mouth closed. "I don't know who you are, young man, but our shop is closed. It was rude enough for Sir Robert to come here so late, but for him to send his servants into our private quarters is—is . . ."

The lady's moment of attempted bravado collapsed, and her chin quivered.

"I am not a servant," Kate said. "And Sir Robert is here on the queen's own business. If you are hiding something, you had best reveal it now."

"I'm not!" Mistress Lucas cried. "I am the queen's loyal subject, I would never—oh, what have I done?"

The door suddenly opened behind her, and the soft click of the latch made her shriek. Her hands flew up to cover her face as she sobbed.

Much as Kate had suspected, Henry Everley stood there, backed by lamplight from his hiding-hole.

He looked far from the fashionably dressed court gallant, the brash young man who tossed coin around so carelessly and just as carelessly bullied his sister. His reddish gold hair was grimy, tousled, his beard untrimmed, and his eyes were sunk in purple shadows. He wore no doublet, and his shirt was dusty and wrinkled. He looked as if he had been run to ground by the devil himself.

But his voice was gentler than she had ever heard from him as he said, "All is well, Mistress Lucas. You needn't hide me any longer. I can't stay in your garret forever."

"But, Lord Henry . . . ," Mistress Lucas sobbed.

Henry shook his head. He frowned as he peered closer at Kate, and she remembered the way he roughly shook Mary's arm. She glanced behind her down the darkened stairs. Sir Robert wasn't there, but she could hear his voice floating up from the shop as he argued with Master Lucas.

"I know you," Lord Henry said. His voice hardened, his face turning cold and blank. He took a step toward Kate, and she moved back. "You are no boy."

Kate stiffened, steeling her bravery in order to face him. "Nay. I was Lady Mary's friend."

Lord Henry scowled, the coldness cracking the merest bit. He still stood close to her, tense, as if he would snatch at her at any moment. "Mistress Haywood. The musician. What are you doing here?"

"Looking for you, of course, Lord Henry. The queen is most interested in your whereabouts, after everything that has happened."

"Everything?" He frowned as if puzzled, and Kate had the sudden thought that, for all his bluster, Lord Henry was perhaps not the brightest man in the world. But he was still tall and powerfully built. If he became angry with her, felt threatened . . .

"All the red-haired women," Kate said quietly.

He looked even more confused, almost like an overgrown boy. Without his minions behind him, he was not so swaggering. "Nay, I—I know only about Mary. Is she not why you're here? Why you have come for me? I would rather be at the queen's mercy than that of Walter Dennis."

Kate studied him carefully, searching for any sign his confusion was mere playacting. She could find none, but she knew she couldn't let down her guard. "You are hiding here from Walter Dennis?" Mistress Lucas went on sobbing, and Kate had to force herself not to shout at the woman to be quiet at once.

Lord Henry shook his head and ran a trembling hand over his bearded jaw. "Being drawn and quartered by the queen's men would be better than what *he* would do. He fought in France with the Spanish, and surely learned many methods of torture from them. After all I have done . . ."

Kate's thoughts raced. Walter Dennis must be a formidable man indeed, for Lord Henry to be so frightened of him. Or mayhap Lord Henry was merely a rank coward. "You mean killing the woman Walter Dennis loved, after murdering his cousin in a duel? Aye, I would say you should be wary of him."

Mistress Lucas shrieked again, and Lord Henry turned to her with a gentle smile that Kate would never have thought he even possessed.

"Go now, Mistress Lucas," he said. "You have been a good friend to me, but I can impose on you no longer."

Mistress Lucas, still sobbing, ran back down the stairs. Kate was left alone with Henry Everley—a murderer.

She curled her fingers tightly around the hilt of the dagger at her waist. She could feel the cold touch of fear, but she forced it down again. She could hear the voices from below and knew Sir Robert and his men were a shout away. Perhaps Lord Henry would tell her more with no one else nearby. She was a mere woman, after all, as delicate as his sister had been.

"So you knew about Oliver Dennis?" he said. His tone was musing, careless, but she didn't trust the overly bright sheen of his eyes. She had seen mad panic like that before. She knew she had to press him for all the answers soon.

"I know you killed him in a duel, that you are a murderer. That will not look good for a queen's jury," Kate said carefully, keeping her distance from him on the landing. "And that you were freed on the orders of Queen Mary herself. A great kindness, considering your family's friendship with the Seymours."

A strange, humorless smile touched Lord Henry's lips. "She was glad enough to be rid of one of the friends of the foul Boleyns. But Oliver Dennis was the one who found *me* in that tavern. His family had hated ours for years, had attempted to take land that was rightfully ours, but we tried to live with them in peace."

Somehow Kate much doubted that. She had seen the many columns of legal records for the Everleys' habit of bringing suit against all who crossed them. *Bastard queen Elizabeth Tudor*—bastard Boleyn spawn, hated by the Everleys?

"It is a hard thing to be so persecuted by near neighbors," she said, carefully sympathetic.

"So it is. I was merely drinking an ale with some friends when Oliver Dennis swaggered in and confronted me. He was ale-shot, he wouldn't be calmed. When I tried to leave, he attacked me from behind like the coward all Dennises are. I had no choice but to defend myself."

His words had the ring of truth, but of course they would. Henry Everley was exactly the sort of man who thought himself always the injured party. "It must have been a great blow when your own sister eloped with a foul Dennis."

His eyes narrowed. They glittered like those of a wild animal trapped in a menagerie cage. "So you knew about that, too? Of a certes you do. You were Mary's friend. Perhaps you knew she was still meeting with that hedgepig and you kept her secret?"

"I was Mary's friend, aye, but she didn't confide in me. She kept her secrets close."

Henry laughed. Suddenly he spun around on his bootheel and went back into his hiding chamber. Kate heard the sound of objects being carelessly tipped to the floor, as if he searched for something. A weapon, mayhap? She stiffened, bracing herself to flee.

But he was back before she could run, and he held a letter in his hand rather than a sword. He had pulled on a doublet over his shirt and pushed his hair back from his face.

"I found this in Mary's possession, the day of the procession from the Tower," he said. His tone had a pleading sound to it, almost as if he were a schoolboy beseeching for mercy after some prank. Most strange for a hardened duelist. Kate didn't trust it.

He held out the letter, and she took a small step back. That mad glitter was back in his eyes, and she did not like it.

"It's from the Spanish embassy," he said. He stared down at the paper he clutched as if he couldn't quite believe that his sister, a mere woman, had outsmarted him. "She was in the pay of the Spanish. My own sister!"

"But if you were allies of Queen Mary, close enough for her to pardon you, surely that is not so very unheard of," Kate said calmly, even as she could feel the cold stab of disappointment. True, she had suspected her friend of consorting with the Spanish. But to have it confirmed shattered all hope that she could be wrong. Especially if Mary's beloved Walter had once fought for the Spanish.

"Queen Mary is dead!" Lord Henry shouted. "We must make our way in the world of Queen Elizabeth now, and my father and I put all that's left of our fortune at her service in hopes of rising again. Mary was even given a place as one of the queen's ladies, which took a great deal of coin. And this was how she repaid us! Meeting in secret with a Dennis. Taking Spanish money to spy."

Kate couldn't tell which of these offenses he found worse—eloping or treason. "So she had to be shown the error of her ways. That was why you followed her back to the Abbey from the banquet."

Lord Henry's face twisted in rage. Kate hadn't been

completely sure he killed his sister before, but now she was beyond doubt. He crumpled the letter into his fist and took another sudden step toward her, as if he was eager to have someone hear his tale now.

"Why should I kill my own sister?" he said. "She was only a woman. She could have been silenced. . . ."

Kate felt her own anger flare up, anger that he thought his sister so disposable when she did not do as he wished. "And you did silence her, did you not? Perhaps you hoped to blame her lover. Perhaps you thought the queen would not mind losing one more lady-in-waiting. But I am sure Robert Dudley and his men can get the answers from you speedily enough. The rack, mayhap? The spike?"

Henry crumpled at the mention of instruments of torture, of how easily Sir Robert could break a patent coward like him.

"She had to be stopped, before she ruined us all," he growled. "I only meant to find her, to see that she was locked up until she could be sent back to Everley Court. When I found out she was writing to Feria . . ."

He shook his head and went silent, as if the remembered fury choked him.

"You lost your temper," Kate said quietly.

"She was my sister! An Everley," he roared. "Yet she cared nothing for our honor. She laughed, and said how else could she get a dowry to bring to her lover, since Father would give her naught. She turned away from me, and I . . ."

Kate shivered. "You killed her."

"I never meant to!" Lord Henry's face went bright red, and he clutched at a handful of his hair, making it stand on end like Master Lucas's. "I reached out to bring her back, and she fought me. She fell and hit her head on the stone pillar, and she—she was so still. I could do naught to help her then."

Kate was overcome with another surge of anger, like a red mist before her eyes. "She was your *sister*! And you just left her there. Is that what you did to the others as well? Did they fight you, too, and you couldn't bear that?"

His face, crimson and creased with fury, crumpled even more. "Others? What are you talking about? I am no killer of women!"

"Only your own sister!" Kate cried. It would be so easy to blame all the murders on him, but even in her anger she feared she could see why he was right. Why would he kill Nell and Bess? What connection did they have with the whole matter? Her head was spinning with it all.

"She was a traitor! She deserved it." Lord Henry suddenly lunged for her, like a bear maddened by the pit dogs. He grabbed her sleeve and she tottered off-balance, the same cold rush of panic she felt at Durham House flooding through her. She knew she was perilously on the edge of tumbling down the stairs and meeting her own demise on those hard wooden boards. Lord Henry's hand snatched at her arm, pushing her backward even harder.

She screamed, and instinctively pulled the dagger from her belt. She drove the blade into his arm and felt it sink sickeningly through fabric and skin, hitting bone. Lord Henry roared, and Kate was sure she was about to tumble down the stairs—again.

Through a strange, misty haze, time seemed to slow down and she saw that Lord Henry's sleeve was decorated with silver buttons, but these had no fine braided edge. They were plain.

"Mistress Haywood!" Robert Dudley shouted, and at last she heard him running up the stairs behind her. He caught her by the waist just as she swayed backward, and set her on her feet again. "What happened?"

"He tried to attack me, so I stabbed him," Kate said. Her breath seemed caught somewhere deep in her chest, but other than that, she felt strangely calm. Almost as if she watched a scene on a stage, distant and apart from her.

Lord Henry reared up, as if he would come at her again, but Sir Robert kicked him down and one of his men held him there with the point of his sword. Master Lucas looked on in horror from the lower landing, his wife sobbing out of sight.

Aye, Kate thought. Very dramatic. She would have to tell Rob Cartman about it; he might want to write a scene just like this.

"He killed Lady Mary, though he claims it was an accident," she said quietly. "I suspect he killed the others as well."

"Nay!" Lord Henry roared, even as he bled onto Mistress Lucas's scrubbed floor and the guard's sword pressed to his chest. "There were no others, I vow. I don't even know what you speak of, you vile she-wolf."

"We'll soon have you in the Tower, Lord Henry, and then we'll see what you have to say," Sir Robert said grimly.

Lord Henry was still shouting as Sir Robert's men dragged him down the stairs. Through that strange haze, Kate could hear the commotion, even Mistress Lucas's sobs and Master Lucas berating her about where her "infatuation" had gotten them, but she felt removed from it all. There was something about what Lord Henry said, the way he disavowed any knowledge of any other woman. . . .

Something about his appearance?

"Are you well, Mistress Haywood?" Sir Robert asked.

"Aye. I am not hurt." Kate stared at the dagger on the floor. Bright red blood gleamed at its tip. "I've never stabbed anyone before."

"'Twas neatly done," Sir Robert said admiringly. "It went right through. And you made him confess as well. The queen can sleep better tonight knowing the vile killer of red-haired women is gone."

Kate slowly shook her head. "I am not sure he *is* gone."

"What do you mean?"

Kate spun around and ran down the stairs. If it wasn't Lord Henry who killed Bess and Nell, who was hunting down red-haired women, then the person who threatened the queen was surely still out there. She reached the shop just as the guards were shoving the villain out the door. Mistress Lucas wailed behind the counter as her husband went on berating her for daring to hide a fugitive from the queen's law under his very roof.

"Lord Henry," Kate cried frantically. "Where is your best doublet, the one with the silver buttons with the braided edge?"

He went suddenly still, looking at her as if she were the mad one. Even the burly guards seemed bewildered.

"I gave it to Richard—it had a wine stain, and was no use to me," Lord Henry snarled, so startled he actually answered her.

He gave it to Richard St. Long? But when was the last time he wore it? "Your cousin?"

Lord Henry gave a hard, humorless bark of laughter. "He is no cousin of mine. The son of an old whore of my father. But he was useful for a time."

Useful? Kate opened her mouth to demand he tell

her what he meant, but the guards were pushing him out the door again. She started after him, stopped by a firm hand on her arm. She whirled around to see Sir Robert holding her back.

"God's teeth, but he is getting away without telling me . . . ," she cried. She wanted to kick something, throw something! Suddenly she knew how the queen must feel when the frustrated rage came over her. She wondered that Queen Elizabeth had been able to restrain herself sufficiently to stay alive long enough to gain her throne.

"Never fear, Mistress Haywood, he will tell us all he knows," Sir Robert said. He grinned, and Kate realized how very good-looking he truly was, with his white teeth and dark eyes. No wonder the queen liked his company so much. "You looked so very much like another warrior-lady I know, just then."

"Who?" Kate said, puzzled.

"The queen, of course. You were truly splendid to-night, Mistress Haywood. Indeed, you could have been her very sister. . . ."

CHAPTER 26

"Back again, are you?" Mad Henry said. He sounded fierce, but his eyes sparkled as if Kate amused him as she ran toward the Cardinal's Hat. At least she knew not to be afraid of him anymore.

"They're busy tonight," he went on. "No time for you to be lurking around here."

Kate shook her head. She stopped for a moment to brace her hands on her knees, trying to catch her breath. She hadn't stopped running ever since she crept away from Sir Robert at the palace gates and set out for Southwark on her own. Something urged her that there was no time to lose, not now.

Obviously, she was going to have to start joining the queen on more of her brisk walks if there was going to be much dashing around London. Sitting over music scores for hours was no help in getting into running condition.

"I need to see Mistress Celine, right away," she gasped. Celine seemed to be the only one who might hold the key to the murders. Richard St. Long had lurked in the background for too long. Kate had no time to go to Everley Court itself, so Celine it had to be.

Mad Henry crossed his beefy arms over his chest and shook his head. "I told you, 'tis busy tonight. More than my skin is worth to bother Celine when she's trying to manage things."

"But don't you care what happened to Nell and Bess?" Kate cried in frustration.

A frown flickered over Mad Henry's scarred face, but he looked away. "Aye, 'tis sad. But such happens every day here. We couldn't make a living if we took to wailing over it all."

"I'm not talking about wailing! I'm talking about justice!" Kate shouted. She was jostled by a drunken group making their loud, laughing, shoving way into the house.

Kate stepped back and studied the Cardinal's Hat. Mad Henry was right—it was a busy night. Despite the icy chill in the air, the windows were thrown open to let out light and noise. Shrill laughter, shrieks, growls, and the loud click of tossed dice flowed out into the darkness.

Where other parts of London were tucking themselves up safe by the firesides for the long night, Southwark was just coming to life. The lanes were crowded, full of people hurrying past looking for their own brand of pleasure. Ale-shot men tumbled into the gutters while brightly clad women howled with laughter. It was the perfect place to go unnoticed. To slip through the teeming, heaving crowds and commit foul murder.

Kate just didn't yet know to what purpose those murders had happened, but she was determined to find out.

One of the newcomers was arguing with Mad Henry, weaving wildly on his feet as the burly guard stood firm against him. Kate took advantage of the distracted moment to slip into the house.

The corridors and winding chambers of the Cardinal's Hat were packed so full that there was not a hint of the night's chill in the stuffy air. It smelled of cheap tallow candles, ale, flowery perfumes, and sweat, and the laughter was deafening. Through the haze of smoke, Kate could barely see faces, only a blur of reddened cheeks and kohled eyes, bright gowns, hands reaching, and wine pouring.

She tugged at a yellow satin sleeve. "Where is Celine?" she gasped.

The bawd shrugged and pointed up the stairs with a cackling laugh. "She don't do the actual work on her back no more, lad. You'd best be staying here with us."

One of the other women giggled and reached out to grab Kate, but Kate evaded her and ran up the stairs. She found herself in the long, narrow hall that once led to the chamber of Nell and Bess. Shouts and cries echoed from behind closed doors, along with the slap of a leather flog on flesh and broken, excited pleading.

Kate decided not to risk peeking behind any of those doors, not yet. Luckily she found one door open. Celine sat behind a writing table, muttering to herself as she scribbled notes in an open ledger. Her hair, the brilliant orange-red of a sunset, gleamed in the light of a sputtering torch. Her silver and amethyst ring flashed as she wrote.

Kate slipped into the chamber and closed the door behind her. Celine looked up with a gasp.

"What are you—," Celine began indignantly.

But Kate had no time for niceties. "Is Richard St. Long your lover, Celine?"

Celine, who had started to push herself up from her stool, sank back down again. Her eyes narrowed, and behind the thick rim of kohl Kate saw they were a pale blue-gray.

Golden eyes. Blue eyes. Dark Boleyn eyes. They seemed to be only the outward signs of deeper, darker familial inheritances.

Celine gave a harsh laugh. "My lover? A young man like that?"

"He is something to you, I know."

"So he is." Celine studied Kate's face carefully, and whatever she found there seemed to convince her that Kate was not going away. "I am fond of him, despite myself. But how did you know we were connected?"

"Your ring." Kate gestured toward the silver band of flowers on the bawd's finger. "Everything kept coming back to Master Lucas's shop, his fine silverwork. Of course, you might have been blackmailing Lord Henry Everley over something and got the ring from him, but that doesn't seem likely. A bad word about your house from one courtier could ruin your prosperous trade here, and Lord Henry hasn't enough coin to make up for that."

"Most clever, my lady," Celine said, a note of grudging admiration in her smoke-roughened voice. "But mayhap Lord Henry *is* my lover, and thus disposed to giving gifts?"

Kate laughed. "I hear that he likes blond hair. Much like his friend Edward Seymour."

Celine laughed, too, and leaned her elbows on the edge of the table. "So he does, when he can afford them. I quit giving him credit, despite Richard's pleading for his kinsman."

"Are you Richard's mother?"

Celine's laughter faded. "Now, how could I be the mother to the cousin of a lordling like that?"

"Everyone did think Master St. Long was the son of Lord Everley's long-dead sister. But Lord Henry tonight claimed Richard St. Long was no true cousin of his, but a son of his father's old doxy."

"Lord Henry talked to *you*?"

"Not willingly. And not nearly enough," Kate said. "He was arrested tonight at Master Lucas's shop, accused of killing his own sister. But he claims no knowledge of Bess and Nell. If he killed them, a stay at the

Tower will soon have the truth out of him. If not—the killer might still be here in the lanes of Southwark, looking for women with red hair."

Celine smoothed her hand over the elaborate arrangement of her vivid hair. Kate let the silence stretch out for a long moment, let Celine think over her words.

"You have built a profitable business here," Kate said quietly. "'Twould be a shame to let it crumble away. . . ."

Celine sighed. "True. I am above all else a woman of business. I have to be, in my position, or I'll starve and all my girls and servants with me. Nay, I am not Richard's mother. He is my nephew."

Kate frowned, quickly working out the possibilities in her mind. "I take it you are not somehow related to Lord Everley's sister. Your sister was the earl's leman? And Lord Everley is Richard's father?"

"I fear it is not so simple as that. If it was, my Richard might have had a happier life, as would my sister—and her other child."

"Other child?"

"Richard had a twin sister, an angelic little girl. But she died young. Mayhap it was a blessing."

Celine suddenly pushed back her stool and leaped to her feet, as if she couldn't stand to sit still a moment longer. She paced to the fireplace and stared down into the flames. By the golden light, Celine looked younger, softer. Sadder, as she lost herself in the past.

"I lived with my sister, Nan, and her babes when they were young, in a cottage given by Lord Everley on his estate, and I came to love them like they were my own," Celine said.

"You didn't live here in Southwark?"

"Nay, not then. We were country girls born, fresh as new milk, and Nan was so very pretty. Pretty, but innocent. Our parents had no money, but they did what they could for us before we had to go seek our own bread." .

"They must have done better than most parents," Kate said, gesturing to the ledgers. "You can read and write, do sums."

"I was always good at numbers, though Nan wasn't. She could barely write her name, but she was sweet. She took up for a time with Lord Everley, and he was good to her. Infatuated with her, everyone said."

"But he is not Richard's father?"

Celine sighed. "Nay. Sweet and pretty Nan was, but not clever. She wanted more than a little room in the country. I had come to London by then, so she left Everley and came to stay with me. After a time she found another lover, and I seldom saw her. She became most secretive, and every time I met with her, she wore finer and finer clothes. Until she was with child, and this new lover cast her off."

It was a sad tale indeed, Kate thought, and one far too common. But who was the secret lover, the one with the fine gifts? "She did not tell you who this lover was?"

Celine shook her head. "She kept that secret forever. Poor, stupid Nan. Whoever he was, he was a right hedge-pig for casting off his own children like that. I wrote to Lord Everley when Nan lay here sick and pregnant."

"And Lord Everley took her back?"

Celine glanced back at Kate over her shoulder, a small smile on her painted lips. "You think him only an ill-tempered old coin-pincher now?"

"He seems to care little for his own children, or his neighbors and relations. He has spent most of his time bringing lawsuits in recent years."

"Aye, he was dour enough even back then. But he had a soft heart for my Nan. He was good enough to her,

gave us a cottage to live in at Everley Court, saw that
Richard was educated. All he asked was that Nan stay
with him, and she did until she died of the sweating sick-
ness. No one is all bad, my dear. A woman like me, you
see where people are vulnerable."

"And your nephew is your own vulnerability?"

Celine's face hardened. She kicked out at a fallen log.
"I've been a fool where he's concerned, but I see my
poor Nan in him. When she died, my little niece was already gone and Lord Everley said he would look after
Richard. I thought Richard would be better with a man's
influence in his life—he was such an angry, bitter little
person. So I came back here, built up this house. I sent
money and letters to Richard when I could, but I hadn't
seen him for a long time until he showed up late last
year. I was happy to see him, so tall and handsome,
but—well, he wasn't the boy I remembered. Not entirely."

Celine twisted the silver ring on her finger for a long
moment. Suddenly she turned to face Kate. "Do you
truly think he might have done these murders?"

Kate thought of everything she had learned at Master
Lucas's shop. "Aye, I think perhaps so. Though I don't
know why yet. I only know he must be found and ques-
tioned before anything else happens."

Celine nodded, looking suddenly old and sad. Tired.
"How can I help you?"

"When was the last time you saw him?"

"Before Bess disappeared. He came here one night
with that young ruffian Edward Seymour and his friends.
They spend their coin freely enough, but 'tis always a
mess when they leave. I have warned Richard that Seymour is not as clever as he thinks, that he is a vain peacock overly proud of his family. But Richard just laughs

and says he must get ahead at court as best he can for a man with no coin and no family."

"Did he talk with you that night?"

Celine frowned as if she tried to remember. "For a moment. He seemed in a merry mood. He gave me this ring, and said soon his fortunes would be made."

"Made how?"

"That he did not say. 'Twas a busy night, and I didn't see him again."

"Was he fond of Bess or Nell? Show a preference for red hair?"

Celine shook her head. "He wasn't so very selective. Besides, I should think he *wouldn't* care for red-haired bawds. His mother and sister both had red hair, as I did. Do. He seemed to like dark hair."

Parents—it always seemed to come back to that. But why had Richard suddenly been in a good mood that night? "Are you quite sure you know nothing about your nephew's life now? Nothing about his real father?"

"I have heard court gossip sometimes, that is all. Who is in favor, who is not, who loves who. Nothing substantial. As for the twins' father . . ." Celine shook her head again. "He must have been a wealthy man. When Nan was with him, she had fine gowns and hoods, jewels even. Once she wore a bracelet I thought had a crest of some sort on it, but she drew her sleeve down over it and refused to show it to me. She said she should not be wearing it in public anyway."

"What happened to the jewels?"

"Most of them were sold, after she came to me, sobbing and pregnant. Cast off by her fine lover with a bruise on her pretty cheek. She did have a small, locked casket she gave to Richard right before she died. But he was just a boy then. Who knows what he did with it?"

If it was indeed a crest that Nan once wore, surely it could be used to help identify Richard's father? "You never saw the bracelet again? You can remember nothing about it?"

Celine closed her eyes tightly. "Nay, nothing. It was bright-colored enamel, set in gold. Framed with pearls, mayhap. I do know my jewels."

From the corridor outside the room, heavy footsteps thudded on the floor and Mad Henry came running in.

"Trouble with Master Carew again, Celine," he announced.

"A pox on that man, he is more trouble than his coin is worth," she said. She pushed back from the fire and shook out her red striped skirts. "I'll be there in a moment. Fetch my dagger, will you?"

As Celine passed Kate on her way out of the chamber, she glanced up at her. Her painted eyes were stark, sad, shining with tears that she would never let fall.

"Do you really think Richard did these things?" Celine said quietly, not quite meeting Kate's gaze. Such uncertainty, such hopeless hope, from the bold bawd was disconcerting.

"You know what he is capable of more than I do," Kate answered. "But I think it rather likely now. You should take care."

Celine laughed, putting on her careless mask again. "Me? I am never alone here. He couldn't get close. You, though . . ."

"I will be careful." Kate had a sudden thought. "If you can wait for me but one moment?" She quickly went to Celine's writing table and scribbled a note on a scrap of parchment, addressed to Anthony. She handed it back to the bawd. "Can you see that this gets to the house of Master Hardy the lawyer, in Cheapside?"

Celine studied the paper in her hand. "Of course. Godspeed to you."

"And to you."

Kate made her way down the back staircase into the chaos of a Southwark night again. She knew where she had to go next.

CHAPTER 27

"'As Vesta was from Latmos hill descending, she
spied a maiden queen the same ascending, at-
tended on by all the shepherds swain. . . .'"

Kate peered down at the great hall far below the narrow gallery walkway, hidden from the glittering court in
the shadows. The music was not quite as perfect as she
would have made it, but no one seemed to notice the flat
notes and wobbly crescendos amid the shimmering
white and silver of the elaborate costumes and the painted
sets that soared toward the ceiling.

A bejeweled moon rose over the tableau of Diana
and her nymphs, their faces hidden by white masks as
they sang of purity's joys and danced gracefully with
their hands joined and white satin skirts floating. The
queen sat on her dais, also dressed in white brocade with
diamond moons and stars in her loose red hair.

Robert Dudley, hastily changed from the stark black
he had worn to raid the Lucas shop into peacock green
velvet, sat beside her, laughing and whispering into her
ear.

Anyone watching them now, as almost everyone in
the court was, would never know he had just chased
down a murderer and tossed him into the Tower. Robert
Dudley looked like a man who cared for naught but the

cut of his doublet and the wine in his goblet. Kate knew she could learn much about concealment from him.

From her perch high above the masque, Kate could scan the gathering with no one watching her in turn. There were rows of cushioned benches behind the queen for those of the highest rank, and Kate saw the Greys among them.

Lady Frances had even left her sickbed to attend the performance, though she looked pale and out of sorts. Her husband, young Adrian Stokes, kept pressing wine and sweetmeats and handkerchiefs on her, which she waved away with a frown. Little, crookbacked Lady Mary Grey sat beside him, watching the masque closely with her hands neatly folded in her lap.

Lady Catherine, though, was obviously restless, twitching at her skirts, craning her neck to peer behind her, until her mother gave her arm a little shake to make her be still.

Kate saw what she was looking for—Edward Seymour, who sat with his mother, the Dowager Duchess of Somerset, in one of her rare appearances at court. Edward was most attentive to his mother, but when the duchess wasn't looking, he would grin at Lady Catherine.

Neither of them seemed terribly concerned that their friend Lady Mary Everley was dead, or that her murderer could still be running free among them. Nor were their friends Feria and his Spanish cohorts at the performance. But the French ambassador seemed to be enjoying himself immensely.

Kate examined the crowds standing at the back of the room, but she could catch no glimpse of Richard St. Long. Perhaps he had already heard of his cousin's arrest and thought it best to be discreet. Perhaps he hoped Lord Henry would be blamed for everything.

One of the palace guards had told her that Lord Everley had departed already, with most of his servants, though whether it was to return to Everley Court or to meet his son at the Tower no one yet knew. Kate couldn't help but feel a pang of sadness for the old earl, despite the thoughtless way he treated his children. Once he had loved a woman, Celine's flighty sister, and he had kept his promise to her when she died to look after her child. Surely such a man could not be all bad?

But it seemed the same could not be said of his adopted nephew. Kate felt sure he had killed Nell and Bess, even if Lady Mary was not a part of it. Yet—why? She was baffled.

She studied the crowd again, tracing the family alliances, the furtive romances. She needed proof, something solid she could take to the queen. If she could find the bracelet Celine's sister wore, the finely wrought one of enamel and pearls with a mysterious crest, perhaps it could tell her who Richard St. Long's real father was.

Perhaps, since the Everleys had vacated their rooms so quickly and Richard hadn't been seen at the palace that night, some of his possessions were left behind. Kate backed away from the gallery railing, leaving the glitter of the masque behind her, and quickly lit a candle before she ran down the narrow back staircase.

She came out into one of the twisting corridors that made up the vast rabbit warren of the queen's palace. All the secrets and passions and schemes of hundreds of courtiers were hidden behind those doors, just like the doors of the Cardinal's Hat. Tonight they were silent, though, as everyone was in the great hall currying favor. Even the servants were gone on their own errands, and there was an almost eerie silence hanging heavy in the air.

Kate thought she remembered where Lord Everley's rooms were, after her last visit to him, but she took a wrong turn on one staircase and found herself staring at a blank wall hung with a tapestry depicting Diana's hounds tearing Actaeon apart for daring to watch the goddess at her bath. It almost made her laugh, finding the furious virgin at every turn when it looked as if all the trouble began with faithless lovers of all sorts.

At last she found the right apartments, at the far end of another branching corridor. She carefully tested the door handle and found it unlatched. Holding her breath, she pushed it open and peered inside.

Lord Everley had been gone for only a few hours at the most, but the unmistakable staleness of abandoned rooms rushed out on a breath of cold air. It was dark and silent, yet Kate knew she had to hurry. She put her candle down on the nearest table and looked around her.

It seemed Lord Everley had packed in a hurry, for a few stray garments still trailed over the floor and torn documents were piled on the table. Some of the furniture had been removed, but the valuable bed was still there, though the hangings and bedclothes were gone.

Kate quickly sorted through the papers, yet saw nothing of interest. She peered into the connecting chamber, whose door was ajar. Lady Mary had been housed with the other ladies, of course, and it looked as if Lord Henry and Richard St. Long had shared this room. There was one narrow bed with a truckle half-shoved beneath it. A few clothes, in the bright colors and elaborate decorations Lord Henry favored, were hastily abandoned on the bed and spilled out of an open chest.

Another clothes chest, plainer and not carved, sat beneath the one window. It wasn't locked, and Kate hastily threw it open and searched through the meager contents.

It appeared to be Richard's, with a dark doublet she remembered him wearing once, and the short, embroidered cape he wrapped around himself at the coronation procession.

Crumpled in the bottom corner, she found the velvet doublet she had noticed Richard wearing before, the one that seemed to fit him so ill. The fastenings were plain bone buttons. She studied he fabric closer. It was finely woven and well dyed, but she found a stiff spot in the nap where wine had spilled and been sponged away. Just as Lord Henry had said when he claimed he gave the damaged doublet to his cousin.

Kate held it up to the light and saw faded places where other decorations had been removed. The silver buttons? But why take away such a fine decorative element? Unless Lord Henry removed them before discarding it. But then how had they been found in Nell's and Mary's hands?

She laid the doublet aside and peered back into the chest. At the bottom was a much smaller box. This one was elaborately carved, in a pattern of roses and twining ivy leaves, and bound in iron bands. A lock held it closed.

Kate frowned as she examined it. It was a stout lock, not one to easily force open with a bone hairpin.

"I shall have to get one of Cecil's men to show me how to open such things," she muttered. She had seen them so easily and smoothly open locks and replace them again so none would know they had been touched. But it was too late for such training at the moment.

Kate took out her dagger and used the hilt to pound as hard as she could at the lock. She winced at the loud metallic sound in the silence, but kept on until the lock fell away.

The small box was half-empty. Kate hastily examined

the contents. A letter, the red wax seal old and brittle, the ink faded. A miniature painting of a girl with pale red hair and a sweet, heart-shaped face. She looked like a younger, more fragile version of Celine, and was finely dressed in an ivory-colored, fur-trimmed gown and old-fashioned French hood. The style of the painting looked familiar, as if Kate had seen work by the artist before.

Beneath the painting was a folded slip of parchment, and tucked inside was a sight that made her shiver. Four curls of hair, all different shades of red, tied with black ribbons. One was faded and pale, like the lady in the painting, and one was the light strawberry of Lady Mary. One was obviously dyed. Bess's?

Fearing she would be ill, Kate quickly tucked the hair and the portrait back in the box. At the bottom was a handful of silver buttons with a braided edge. She counted them. Fourteen, not enough for all the decoration she had once seen when Lord Henry wore the doublet. There was also a pearl earring, like the one all the court swains wore in imitation of Robert Dudley, and at last she saw the bracelet. It seemed Nan St. Long had luckily not sold it after all.

It was rather heavy. Kate held it up to the light of her candle, and gasped at what she saw. It was a fine piece indeed, colored enamels beautifully worked and set in a frame of gold and pearls. Blue, green, and white depicted the crowned double rose, white in red, the badge of Henry VIII.

Kate stared at it, hardly believing what she was seeing. *Some bastards are not hidden away at all. My father doted on his son the Duke of Richmond, born of Katherine of Aragon's lady-in-waiting Bessie Blount. He gifted him with estates and titles, a noble wife. But not all bastard children fare so well,* she remembered the queen saying.

Could Richard St. Long's father be the king? She tried to remember the old king, but she had been a child when her father served Queen Catherine Parr. The king had seldom left his own room by then—he was too ill, too unwieldy, and the queen's apartment was a world of ladies, lapdogs, embroidery, and books of philosophy and the new religion.

The few times Kate glimpsed King Henry were at banquets, and she had been terrified of him. He seemed like a waxy-pale mountain swathed in satins and furs, his blue eyes hidden behind rolls of fat, a stench of decay and heavy perfume about him. Kate could hardly fathom that Princess Elizabeth could embrace him, that Queen Catherine could spend hours reading to him, so close to his side.

Richard St. Long was a handsome man, with none of the old king about him that she could see.

But then, everyone declared King Henry had been a fine specimen of manhood in his youth, the most glorious prince in Christendom.

Bastard queen Elizabeth Tudor. Was that what all this horror could be about? Vengeance?

The sudden sound of a door swinging closed down the corridor sharply reminded Kate where she was. She quickly replaced the bracelet with the buttons and the locks of hair in that chest, and gathered it up. She had to show it to the queen.

Hardly daring even to breathe, Kate hurried out of the chamber and carefully closed the door behind her, hoping it would look undisturbed long enough for her to give the box to the queen. The corridor was blessedly empty, everyone still at the banquet. Once she reached the turn, she breathed a little easier.

But she found her path suddenly blocked by Richard

St. Long, who was coming up the stairs. For an instant, he looked as startled to see her as she was to see him. Then a slow smile spread over his handsome face, and he crossed his arms over his chest.

Her dagger was lost in the room behind her.

"Mistress Haywood," he said. "How kind of you to call on me here. But I must point out that those are *my* possessions. I'm sure that a fine court lady like yourself would never be so ill-bred as to turn to thieving. Just give it back now, and we shall part friends. Aye?"

Kate stared at him, studying his smile, the cold ice of his eyes. She had seen someone look exactly thus once before, at Hatfield House. Just before a murderer attacked her.

Well, she refused to go quietly, not this time. Never again. Summoning up all her strength, Kate threw the box at his head. He ducked out of the way, but his startlement at her sudden movement gave her a precious instant to run.

Richard recovered quickly. He lunged and grabbed the sleeve of her doublet just as she swung out the door. She knew that part of the palace was deserted, but she opened her mouth and screamed as loud as she could.

"Bloody witch!" Richard's arm, hard as an iron band, wrapped around her waist and jerked her off her feet.

Kate twisted around, cold panic rising up inside of her like a suffocating storm cloud. She could taste the metallic tang of it in her mouth, cutting off her breath.

But she refused to give in to the fear. This man had killed before. She wouldn't be his next victim. Visions flashed in her air-starved brain, of her father, the queen, Anthony, Rob. The half-finished musical score in her chamber.

Nay, she would not die now!

She screamed again past his fingers, and kicked back at Richard as hard as she could with her booted foot. He cursed and clamped his hand tighter over her mouth to silence her.

Kate managed to work her jaw free enough to bite down on his palm, so hard she tore away a piece of his leather glove. She tasted the coppery sharpness of blood, and it made her even angrier.

"Witch! No more of that," Richard shouted. His arm tightened around her and he threw her to the floor. She twisted her leg free from the heavy weight of his body over hers and kicked him square in the chest.

He reared back from her for an instant with a satisfying grunt of pain, but then he grabbed her again. He smiled down at her, his eyes glittering as if he was excited by her fear.

"I said enough of that," he whispered in a horribly cold voice. She tilted back her head just in time to see a gloved fist descending toward her.

There was a thud, and a sharp, terrible pain. Kate screamed, and tumbled down into waiting darkness.

CHAPTER 28

Kate slowly came awake. She felt as if she struggled up from some black underground cave toward a distant, wavering spot of light. Her limbs ached. They didn't want to move, to drag her forward one inch, yet she knew she had to struggle onward. She had to reach that one pinpoint of light, to not sink back into darkness.

She pried her gritty eyes open, and that one movement made her head pound as if it would split open. At first she thought she really was in a cave, with sloping black walls all around her. She couldn't see anything but that pinpoint of light, and didn't feel anything but a painful jolting beneath her.

She made herself breathe slowly, evenly, and she realized that light above her was a star. She looked up at the night sky, a heavy, dusty black, lightened by only one star peering out from behind the clouds. A cold wind swept over her face, catching at her hair, and she remembered.

She'd been knocked unconscious by Richard St. Long, who had very likely killed Bess and Nell, and would go to any length to see the queen dead as well. Richard, who was possibly the bastard son of Henry VIII, had obviously inherited the old king's madness and cruelty.

But where was she now? More important, where was *he*, and what was he going to do with her?

The hard surface under her back jolted again, sending a wave of pain over her body. A metallic-tasting fear crawled up her throat.

She fiercely pushed that fear away before she could cry out with it. She would *not* give in to a murderer! She had to get back to Queen Elizabeth and tell her all she knew.

Slowly, as she took in careful breaths, some of the pain faded. The air was icy cold, and smelled of fish and decay. She realized she was lying in the bottom of a boat, jolting down the river. She shifted carefully, hoping Richard or any ally he had would think her still unconscious while she deciphered the situation. Unless he had just abandoned her there . . .

Her hands were tied behind her, resting in a puddle of cold water, but her feet were unbound. She could hear the slap of oars on the water, yet no voices. The rush of the water was too loud, the waves too choppy as they slapped against the boat, for her to hear anything else.

It must be close to high tide, Kate realized in alarm. No one would be foolish enough to be on the river at such a time, especially not in winter when the tides could surge and foam and flood, dashing boats and bodies against the bridge. No one would ever rush the bridge—unless they were mad.

Frantic, Kate found a splintered chunk of wood behind her and started sawing at the ropes that bound her hands.

"Well, well. Awake now, Mistress Haywood?"

Richard St. Long sounded as affably polite as if he greeted her at a court banquet. Somehow that was more frightening than any growling or shouting. Kate pushed away the fear as it tried to surge forward again, and wriggled her way to a sitting position. She felt the ropes at her wrists slacken, but kept holding them tight behind her back.

Richard was rowing, fighting against the high, choppy waves with a grin on his face. Ice bumped against the sides of the boat, and Kate quickly studied her surroundings. There were no other vessels on the water, and she could see why. The lighted windows of the city were bouncing past at an alarming speed.

"Take me back to the palace at once," she demanded, in her best imitation of the queen at her most imperious.

Richard just laughed. His eyes gleamed in the night, and he seemed not to feel the cold even though he wore only a linen shirt and no doublet or cloak.

"I think not, Mistress Haywood," he said with a smile. "Unlike my poor, love-struck cousin Mary, you have been clever enough to decipher my secret. I can't let you go now."

"I know nothing at all about you, nor do I care to," Kate said, struggling to stay calm. Somehow it felt like time had slowed to a crawl, even as the boat sped up. "You are the one who has given away the fact that you even have secrets tonight."

Richard shook his head. "You have been gossiping with my aunt Celine. I always knew my foolish mother told her more than she would admit. If only she had been more clever, she could have spent her life in comfort and riches, like Bessie Blount."

Bessie Blount—the mother of the king's one acknowledged bastard, the Duke of Richmond. "Told her what?"

"About my father, of course. Isn't that why we are here? What my whole worthless life has been about?"

Thoughts tumbled through Kate's mind, memories of families and parents, enameled badges, flashes of anger quickly hidden. "I don't know what you are talking about, Master St. Long. I was merely bringing a message from the queen to your uncle...."

Richard laughed, and pulled harder at the oars. They were moving even faster now, the boat tossing and swirling like a child's toy on a pond, and Kate fell back hard against the wooden side.

"You have been inquiring into matters that are none of a mere musician girl's business for days now. If you were talking to my whore of an aunt, and saw my mother's bracelet, then you should know who you are really meddling with. I've waited a long time for my rightful due. I won't let *you* stop me now."

Kate thought of Mary, of all her romantic, foolish hopes, and felt so angry that someone like this could take away *her* due. Even if it was Lord Henry who had done the deed in the end, she was sure Richard had something to do with it, and especially with the deaths of Nell and Bess. Richard who sought revenge against the queen. Maybe if she could make *him* angry, too, he would confess. "I care not a whit who your godforsaken father is! You murdered women in cold blood, including your own cousin."

Richard's smug smile faded, and a furious scowl covered his face in the instant before his careless mask dropped back into place again. "I never killed Mary. She was kind to me."

"Then why was your button in her hand, as well as Nell's?"

"Nell was a mistake," he said grudgingly. "She tore it off before I could realize it. Then when I found Mary ..."

"Found her? Did you ..."

"I said I did not kill Mary! 'Twas Henry, that wooden-headed peacock. He was drunk and furious that night, kept raging about Mary and that Dennis man, about how she thought to dishonor the family by eloping. As if she could have brought any more dishonor onto the cursed name of Everley. I went to help her, and found her—there. With Henry standing over her, weeping. He thought I would help him get away."

"Wasn't the earl kind to you, as Mary was?" Kate said. She scanned the passing riverbanks, searching for any escape route. She could swim a bit, but all she had ever tried was a placid lake in summer, not a wintry river at high tide. She had to keep Richard talking, keep him distracted. "Didn't he take you in, educate you?"

Richard laughed and shook his head. "Only because he thought my parentage would help his fortunes. He found it to be the opposite, just as my mother had. But by then he gave her his word, and he loved her as all men did. He made me his son's watchdog, his whipping boy. I knew one day I would have my revenge. And I have."

"By killing two Southwark geese?"

"To send a message to Elizabeth Tudor! Redheaded wenches dead all over her kingdom, she couldn't help but notice," Richard shouted. He sounded perilously close to losing what little patience he possessed. The boat swung wildly toward one side, but he managed to right it. "She is as much King Henry's bastard as my sister and me, but she sits on her stolen throne while I live ignored and in poverty. My mother and sister are dead because the king cast us off like muck on his shoes. Why should she not pay for her father's sins?"

"If he *was* your father, then his sins are yours as well," Kate argued, pressing down her fear and anger. The only way she could get out of this mess was to stay calm. "King Henry killed Queen Elizabeth's mother even more surely than he killed yours. You should have gone to her, told her your tale. . . ."

Richard's face twisted into something unrecognizable, like a carved demon on St. Paul's stone towers. "So she could cast me out of her court? I have seen how she treats her relations. The Greys, excluded from her favor. Lord Hunsdon, her brother by Mary Boleyn, denied his true rank. Mary, Queen of Scots, the true queen by legitimate birth—Elizabeth won't even speak to her."

"Baron Hunsdon claims no other position but the queen's cousin. In fact, he claims loudly he looks very like his father Master Carey," Kate argued. "And he is given estates and titles, pensions. If you spoke to her . . ."

"Enough!" Richard shouted. His eyes glowed in the darkness. "I have planned my revenge since I was a child. My mother told me about my father before she died. She told me her name was blackened with the king by his greedy children, Mary, Elizabeth, and Richmond, and she was sent away with nothing, after she worked so hard to gain his attention. Elizabeth herself is naught but a bastard, yet she thinks herself so high above everyone else."

The oars dipped into the water again, and one was caught by the swirling tide and broken in half. Kate gasped, but he just gave a wild laugh. "She didn't look so haughty when she saw what I left her in her own garden."

They were moving even faster now, dizzyingly so. To her horror, Kate saw tall church spires fly past, which meant they were probably close to the bridge. She heard a roaring in her ears like a great waterfall, louder and louder, and she knew the fatal stone piers of the bridge were not far at all.

The boat tilted beneath her, and she heard a crack. If they were caught in the frothing whirlpool under the bridge, they would surely break up. She had to do something quickly.

"But Elizabeth is still queen!" she cried. "You may

have frightened her in that moment, but you cannot defeat her. Her mother was a queen, and yours was—"

Just as she had hoped in her desperate plan, Richard gave a roar of rage and lunged across the boat at her. She shook away the frayed ropes from her hands and threw herself to one side. Her elbow hit the wooden railing and sent a bolt of pain up her arm, but she ignored it. She had to get away from the madman and jump into the freezing water if she was to have any chance.

"You should have died at Durham House," Richard growled as he grabbed for her again. Luckily she was smaller than him, able to maneuver better in the small boat, and his rage made him clumsy.

"So that *was* you who pushed me there," she said, kicking him away. "Conspiring with the Spanish?"

"If a woman must have the throne, why not Catherine Grey? She's legitimate, not like the red-haired witch Elizabeth. She knows her place."

"And is also conveniently in love with your friend Edward Seymour?"

"I've learned to make my way in this world as best I can, denied my birthright," Richard grunted. He tripped over the oar that was left as he lunged for her again, and swept it up like a club. "If Elizabeth had died like she was supposed to . . ."

Kate screamed when he swung the oar at her head. She rolled away from the shattered railing, and water rushed through the hole. Her skin went numb at its icy touch, but she made herself keep moving.

"Kate!" she heard someone shout. For an instant she thought Richard had succeeded in hitting her over the head and she was imagining things. She twisted around to see the bridge looming before them.

From high up, silhouetted against the torches, she saw

two men leaning from a window overhanging the river. One of them was Anthony, his cropped dark hair uncovered. She caught a glimpse of the horror on his face. So Celine had gotten her note to him after all, and he had managed to track her down, but too late.

"Kate! Jump now!" he shouted, tossing a rope down. He climbed out onto the window ledge, as if he would climb down to her.

"Anthony!" she shouted. Richard grabbed at her ankle, dragging her back into the foaming, freezing water that rushed in around them as the boat cracked apart.

She kicked out with her free leg with all her strength, and out of sheer luck caught him on the side of his head. He staggered back, giving her just enough time to launch herself into the river.

The cold stole her breath, almost paralyzing her, but she knew she had to move if she was to survive. The current was powerful, catching at her, twisting her around, determined to drag her down. But she was even more determined to live.

She pushed herself hard to the surface and kicked out until she felt slick, rigid stone under her flailing hand.

She held on with every ounce of her strength. When she shook back the wet, slimy strands of her hair from her eyes, she saw she had reached one of the stout stone supports of the bridge. High above her was the dark canopy of the bridge itself.

Clinging to the stone, just out of reach of the greedy river, she watched in horror as a wall of water engulfed the wrecked boat and Richard St. Long all in one swallow. Richard shouted, a high-pitched, primitive, animal sound. Then he was sucked down under the bridge, and she couldn't see him any longer. Every bit of him and his boat was gone, as if they had never been there.

But she was alive.

Kate held tight to the stone, her teeth chattering so loudly she could hear nothing else. All she could do was keep holding on, and wait for Anthony to find her.

Kate rested her bruised forehead against the cold stone and whispered the only words she could think of. The queen's own favorite oath: "God's blood!"

"Kate! Are you hurt?"

From behind her closed eyes, she heard the thud of a rope swinging against the stone pile, and suddenly warm arms closed around her and drew her close to an even warmer, strong body. *Anthony*. He *had* come for her. She wasn't alone there any longer.

"Nay, I—I am not hurt . . . ," she gasped, but her words dissolved in tears she had held back too long. Tears for Mary, for Nell and Bess, tears of fright that she would die in the cold waters, never to play music, or dance, or laugh again. Never to see her father or the queen again.

"Sh, I am here," Anthony said softly. "You are safe now, I swear it. Thank God I got your note in time, and was able to follow the villain's trail to the river. He made little effort to cover his tracks. Master Hardy thought we could see more from the bridge. Oh, Kate, if I had lost you . . ."

Kate held on to him as tightly as her numb hands would let her. She could almost think she felt the press of a gentle kiss on her temple. But perhaps she was merely dreaming it.

CHAPTER 29

Kate opened her eyes, gasping for air. For an instant she was sure a cold wave of water was closing over her head, sucking her down and down to the bottom of the Thames. Then she realized she stared up at the dark blue curtains of her own bed at the queen's palace. She was safe. She was alive.

She fell back onto the bolsters and made herself take a deep breath and then another. The bedclothes and her smock were twisted around her, damp with sweat, but she hadn't the strength to tug them aright. Her whole body ached, and the image of Richard St. Long screaming as the river seized him wouldn't leave her mind. The horrible cracking sound, like thunder, as the boat broke apart.

The boat she had been in only an instant before.

Nay, she thought fiercely. She wouldn't think of that now. She was alive. And Richard was a murderer who had killed innocent women simply as some mad revenge against the queen—his half sister?—who had stolen what he saw as his right. That the river had claimed him was only a sort of justice.

She wouldn't think of him now. She would think of the moment when Anthony had so daringly climbed down that rope to gently pry her frozen hands from the stone pier and take her in his arms. He had held her, whispered to her, wrapped her in his own doublet until her sobs quieted. He waited with her until they could be rescued by Master Hardy's boat, and then he had made sure she was brought here. The queen's own physician came, and then ...

Then what? Kate could remember nothing else after that, just flashing images of roaring fires, Mistress Ashley holding out a goblet. The queen's dark eyes as she bent over the bed? There was also discordant music jangling in her head, shrill laughter, images of masked visages and Diana's deer chasing her down. What was real, what a dream?

Kate held her breath and made herself sit up against the bolsters, pushing away the aching protest of her bruised limbs. When summer came, she would have to practice swimming. The view outside her small window was only blackness, punctuated by a few swirling flakes of snow. Night, then. How many nights had passed while she lay there in bed, dreaming? She had to find Queen Elizabeth and tell her what she had learned. That no red-haired ladies need be afraid to walk in the garden now.

She saw two goblets on the small table beside her bed, and she reached out for one, but her hand was still stiff, clumsy. She knocked the heavy silver vessel askew, and cursed as she looked down at her rebellious fingers. Surely they would be better soon? She needed them so much, for the music that was everything to her.

A sudden movement near the fireplace made Kate twist around with a gasp. She felt foolish to let herself be so unobservant as to not realize she wasn't alone. After all that had happened ...

Then she saw who it was, and she sat back again. The woman who slowly rose from a seat by the fire wore a black gown and old-fashioned gable hood, and she leaned heavily on a walking stick. Lady Gertrude Howard.

The elderly lady moved carefully across the small room. She smiled, and her faded eyes seemed clear, with none of the dazed confusion she usually wore as she followed the young Duchess of Norfolk around court.

"Here, Mistress Haywood, let me help you," she said. "I have been dosed with Mistress Ashley's possets before, they can be most disconcerting. It is good that you are awake now. How do you feel?"

"Tired. Confused." Kate watched as Lady Gertrude's thin, twisted hands carefully poured out a measure of wine. Pale Malmsey, the queen's favorite. Just like the kind that poisoned the mouse. "How long have I been here? I must tell the queen what happened!"

"You have been here three days. And the queen knows what that mad Master St. Long did—your friend Master Elias told her. It is good that you wake now. We are to move soon, so the queen can be ready for the opening of Parliament next month." She gently pressed the cool silver into Kate's hands. Her fingers were warm on Kate's chilled skin, strangely comforting. "Her Majesty sent you this wine herself. She has been to look in on you every day. She has sent messages to your friend Master Elias telling him you are recovering, and to the actor Master Cartman to tell him of the poor women's murderer. His troupe has gone to Whitehall to prepare a celebration performance for the queen's return."

The queen had taken the time to look in on her? And she was to see Rob again soon? Kate's head spun so much she could not take it all in. "Thank you, Lady Gertrude." Kate stared down into the golden liquid, still seeing that mouse—and that terrible moment they realized the queen was truly in danger from some unseen foe.

And now it was known that particular danger was from sins committed long ago. The sins of parents, visited on their children, never dying.

Kate took a sip of the wine. It was soft and soothing on her dry throat. Lady Gertrude sat down carefully at the foot of the narrow bed.

"I know you are not Eleanor," Lady Gertrude said quietly. Her fingers twisted over the handle of her stick, and Kate saw it was carved in the pattern of lions and crosses. The badge of the Howards. "I am old, true, and I often feel closer to things that happened decades ago than now. But I know you are not her, though you look so much like her. I was startled at first."

Kate took another sip of the wine, turning Lady Gertrude's words over in her mind. Her father had also told her she looked like her mother, but she sometimes thought it was only his wishful thinking. The wine seemed to fortify her. "You knew my mother when she was young?"

"Aye. We were friends. Well, perhaps not *friends*." Lady Gertrude laughed, and set about straightening the blankets around Kate's legs. "I was older than her, so perhaps it was more like we could be a mother and daughter, since neither of us had such. I was only one of dozens of Howard girls, you see, and had no dowry, so I never married. And your mother's mother died when she was a small child, barely out of leading strings. That was when she came to Hever Castle."

"Hever?" Kate cried in surprise. That was the home of Anne Boleyn's parents, where it was said King Henry courted Anne with letters, jewels, and gifts of fresh venison for her table. "What was my mother doing there?"

Gertrude's eyes narrowed in her lined face. "What exactly do you know of your mother, child?"

Kate's gaze flickered to the lute on its stand near the

fire. The elegant instrument that was her only connection to the mother she had never met. That, and her thick, heavy dark hair, which her father said looked just like her mother's. Her hair and her music, inherited from Eleanor Haywood. That was almost all her father told her about her mother.

"Not very much," she admitted. "She died when I was born. I think it wounds my father to talk of her. Would you tell me what *you* know, Lady Gertrude? Anything at all. I do so want to know her."

Lady Gertrude bit her lip uncertainly. "I am not sure—if your father has not said . . ."

"Please, Lady Gertrude!" Kate begged. Somehow being so close to death in that icy water made her long to know even more about her past. About her mother, who sometimes felt so very close to her and sometimes impossibly far away. "I must know. Wouldn't *she* want me to know her?"

Lady Gertrude studied Kate carefully, her head tilted to the side like a fragile, inquisitive little bird. "Aye, I know she would. And I am old. Soon I will see her again, and I will have to tell her of my dealings with you. Here, let me brush your hair, and I will tell you what I can."

Kate obediently sat on the edge of her bed while Lady Gertrude fetched her comb and set about gently untangling the knots in Kate's long, dark locks. Her old hands were careful, soothing, and Kate fell into the rhythm of it and of Lady Gertrude's tale of the past.

"Do you know anything at all of your mother's family?" Lady Gertrude asked.

"Nothing at all. I know my father's family were always court musicians. His grandfather came from Italy to serve King Henry VII."

"Your mother's family were also musicians, but not to

royalty. They served noble families for any entertainments when royalty visited their estates. They were very well-known for their skill."

"Is that why she was at Hever? Her parents were employed by the Boleyns?" Kate was rather happy to know her family was somehow connected to the Boleyns, however distantly. Ever since that night in the chapel of the Tower, kneeling with the queen next to Queen Anne's grave, she had thought about her.

Lady Gertrude's steady sweep of the comb paused for an instant. "Aye, in a manner of speaking. Her mother played the lute, that very one you have now. When she died, Eleanor was brought to Hever so she could learn music as well. She was the loveliest little girl, Mistress Haywood—Kate. All dark, curling hair and large green eyes, so full of curiosity. She could play the lute and sing like an angel. I had been sent to Hever to serve Lady Elizabeth, the sister of the Duke of Norfolk who married Thomas Boleyn, and I was lonely there. Eleanor followed me everywhere, always asking questions, but I didn't mind. I loved her company. I always wanted a child, you see, and she was like my own in many ways."

"And when she got older?"

"She was even more beautiful. There was some talk of sending her to serve Lady Anne, when she went to the French court, but Eleanor was still too young for that. I was glad of it. I would have missed her too much. As it happened, we both ended up in the train of Anne Boleyn, when she became queen in 1533. She wanted Eleanor as her privy chamber musician."

"And that is where she met my father?" Kate asked.

"Aye, at the court of Queen Anne. Matthew Haywood was so very handsome! All the ladies giggled over him, following him about, trying to catch his eye, but he could see naught except his music. Until he met Eleanor. Queen Anne didn't want Eleanor to marry and leave her, yet we could all see there would be no parting them. If ever two people were meant to be together, Kate, it was your parents. They would spend hours in the corner of the great hall, absorbed in some bit of music they were composing, no one in all the world but the two of them."

The image Lady Gertrude painted made Kate smile. Her father, young and handsome, no gray in his hair or worry in his eyes, no gout crippling him, scribbling down musical notes while her beautiful mother played the lute to his tune. "When did they marry, then, if Queen Anne objected?"

Lady Gertrude's hand went still. "Not until after the queen died. Then they left court for a time, as I did. I heard they worked under the patronage of Lord Evensham in the north of the country, until your father came to serve Queen Catherine Parr. Your mother had died by then, and I fear I never saw her again. The reign of Queen Anne was too brief, but it was glorious, for all of us. She loved your mother as I did. There was never anyone as beautiful and sweet as Eleanor."

Beautiful and sweet. So her father had lied when he said Kate took after her! But she relished the description now; it made her feel she could see her mother in her mind. "Why did Queen Anne favor her so very much? Because of their childhood days at Hever?"

Lady Gertrude carefully set aside the comb and turned Kate to face her. Her face was very solemn in the firelight. "Oh, my dear girl. You truly do not know, do you?"

"Know what?" Kate asked, confused. "I knew almost nothing of my mother until tonight, thanks to your kindness."

"Then I should not be the one to tell you."

Kate was desperate to know more now, to know everything. "Please, Lady Gertrude! I beg you. I need to know my mother, and you are the only one who can help me. If there is some secret, I shall never share it with anyone. I vow that."

Lady Gertrude caught Kate's face between her hands and looked deeply into her eyes. In her faded gaze, Kate was sure she could see all the past. The truth of who her mother was, who *she* was. She had seen just such a truth drive Richard St. Long to madness. Could she bear it any better?

But she knew she could. She had survived murderers not once but twice now. She was learning her own strength. And knowledge, truth, was the foundation of all real strength.

"Please," she whispered.

Finally, Lady Gertrude gave a sad nod. "Queen Anne loved your mother because Eleanor was her own sister. Thomas Boleyn once took your grandmother as his mistress, and Eleanor was their daughter. When her mother died, Thomas vowed he would take Eleanor into his household at Hever and raise her to be a musician, as her mother's family were. His wife, Elizabeth, who was my own cousin, could not object. And she became fond of Eleanor, too, as everyone did who knew her." Lady Gertrude gently touched a long wave of Kate's hair. "You have her Boleyn hair. Queen Anne's hair."

Kate stared at Lady Gertrude in stunned, numb silence. The firelight flickered and danced, turning her from a normal, placid old lady in old-fashioned clothes into something twisted and strange. Frightening. "You are lying," she whispered.

Lady Gertrude smiled, a sad, pitying smile. If she had smirked, or laughed, Kate would have known she did indeed lie. Or that her words were a mere figment of the madness of an elderly mind, as when she had first called Kate by the name of Eleanor. But her eyes—so dark and shining, sunk deep into her lined face—were clear and steady. They were eyes that had spent decades watching everything, knowing everything, saying nothing.

Until now.

Aye. Kate knew, deeply and instinctively, that Lady Gertrude told her the truth. Kate's own mother, the mother she had never known and always dreamed of, was the bastard sister of Queen Anne Boleyn.

Suddenly dizzy, Kate fell back against the bolsters and closed her eyes. Her whole past, the past she had imagined, anyway, seemed to shatter like the stained-glass windows of Queen Mary's old-religion churches. The shards, sparkling green, red, blue, yellow, exploded outward and scattered, landing in a pattern of chaos. She could make no sense of it.

"'Tis well, my dear, I promise," Lady Gertrude said, so horribly gentle. Kate felt Lady Gertrude's trembling hands smooth the blankets over her shoulders and tuck them around her. The soft gesture made her want to cry. "I loved your mother like she was my own daughter, just as she would have loved you. She would never want the truth to hurt you, but to set you free. To help you know her, and yourself."

Kate opened her eyes and stared up again at the dark blue of her bed-curtains. They *were* like the water, but this time instead of drowning in it she could break free of its hold. Free of the past. If she wanted to. If she was strong enough.

And Kate suddenly realized she *was* strong enough. She had survived murderers, twice. She had survived the merciless, careless river. She had helped the queen.

Queen Elizabeth, who was now closer to her than she ever could have imagined.

Lady Gertrude was right. She could come to know herself.

"Does my father know?" she said.

Lady Gertrude shrugged. "I know not, my dear. I know Thomas Boleyn gave her a dowry of sorts, though it was after the Boleyns' disgrace, so it could not have been much. But I saw your parents together when they first met, Kate, and you must know how very much in love they always were. It was never arranged in any way; he never took her for her connections, which at that time could only have done him ill in his career. I never saw two people more adoring of each other."

Kate thought of those few times her father spoke of her mother. His eyes would grow soft, faraway, as if he saw only things that happened long ago, faces that were vanished. He spoke of Eleanor's beauty, her sweet smile, her rare musical talent. Once, he even told her of how Eleanor had sung to Kate before she was born, as she grew larger and larger in her mother's belly. Of how Eleanor had blessed Kate with her music.

But he never spoke of where Eleanor came from, where he met her, even what her surname was. Surely he had known. If all he and Lady Gertrude said was true, the Haywoods were a couple with a rare love. Yet he kept her secret, even now when she had been dead nigh on twenty years.

"What was her name?" Kate asked. "Before she married my father."

"She was called Eleanor Thomasin," Lady Gertrude said. "You are not angry with her, are you, my dear? Or with your father?"

Kate shook her head. She was not yet entirely sure

how she felt, but it was not angry. "Nay, I cannot be angry with them. I only wish they thought they could trust me to keep their secrets. But now, as you said, I can know them better."

Lady Gertrude smiled. "And I can have my friend Eleanor back in you. I will tell you everything I remember of her, when you are strong enough to walk in the garden with me. You really are very like her, you know. You have her kind nature. But you also have some of her sister's vinegary spirit." The old lady suddenly laughed. "Oh, aye, you do have some of that!"

Kate had so many questions tumbling over in her mind she hardly knew where to begin. Before she could open her mouth to demand to know *everything* about her mother, there was a soft knock at the door. The sound of it was startling so deep in the night, and Kate sat up straight.

But it was no enemy. It was the queen herself who pushed open the door.

Elizabeth wore a sable-trimmed green brocade bed robe, her hair in a long, loosely woven braid down her back. The candle she held in her hand turned her marble white skin a pale gold, and the ruby and pearl ring on her finger, the ring that once belonged to Queen Anne, sparkled.

She was alone, but for Kat Ashley, who hovered just beyond her shoulder with a worried look on her face. Elizabeth waved her away.

The queen stepped slowly into the chamber, and seemed to notice that Kate was not alone for the first time.

"Lady Gertrude," Elizabeth said. "It was kind of you to sit with Mistress Haywood as she recovers." Her tone seemed to say, *Lady Gertrude, do you really know where you are?*

Lady Gertrude bobbed a wobbling curtsy, which Elizabeth quickly stopped before the lady could fall. "I wanted to make sure she drank her posset, Your Majesty. The freezing wind can bring on an ague so quickly."

"Quite so. But you need your rest as well, Lady Gertrude. Mistress Ashley will see you to your chamber," Elizabeth said, leading Lady Gertrude to the door. "I will look after Mistress Haywood now."

Lady Gertrude let Kat Ashley lead her away. At the threshold, she glanced back at Kate and gave her one more secret smile. Then she was gone, the door closed behind them, and Kate was alone with the queen. Her cousin.

Elizabeth poured out more wine into the goblet and held it out to Kate. "Lady Gertrude is quite right. You must take care with your health, Kate. I could not do without you."

Kate took the goblet and sipped at the sweet, rich wine even though she could feel drowsiness slipping over her again. She didn't want to sleep, not yet. "I will take care to not have any more midnight swims in the river, Your Majesty, I promise."

Elizabeth laughed. "I should hope not. Robert Dudley and his men have been searching for Master St. Long's body for three days now, but it isn't likely to be found at this point. The river is greedy, Kate. I am grateful it did not claim you."

Kate remembered the freezing black water closing over her head, sucking her down, and she shivered. "As am I, assuredly. Did you know of his supposed parentage?"

Elizabeth shook her head. She poured herself a goblet of the wine and took Lady Gertrude's seat by the fire. She looked impossibly rich and remote as she sat there, all green and gold, a pagan goddess of the forest. "I do not remember him or his mother at all, but then I was seldom at court myself until my father married Catherine Parr. She was the one who wanted us to be as a family. By then my father was too ill to take mistresses as he once did, but before that . . ."

Kate thought of Richard's words, of how King Henry's children had poisoned the king's mind against his mother until he sent her away and let her and her children rot. It seemed that could not be true at all.

Elizabeth took a long sip of her wine and stared down into the goblet. "It could be so, of course, but I knew naught of it. If Master St. Long had come directly to me with his tale . . ."

"He had too long nursed his grievance, and planned his revenge, to do that," Kate said. "I fear he was quite mad."

Elizabeth gave a bitter laugh. "Then mayhap he really was of my father's getting. All us Tudors are a little mad, I fear. I am only sorry you almost paid the price for that, Kate. You must concentrate only on your music now."

"I will, for a time. I have a score that is only half-done, and I am eager to finish it." But Kate knew now that music could never be her whole life. Men like Dudley and Cecil were sure the queen could never be truly safe, not with the Greys and Mary of Scotland, and unknown enemies like Richard St. Long, in the world. And the peace and security of England rested on Elizabeth. Kate had to do what she could to protect the queen and country she loved, the new life that was just beginning for all of them.

"You must take of yourself, Kate," Elizabeth said. "You have so many friends. Including, it seems, the Howards."

"Lady Gertrude? She was telling me about my mother."

Elizabeth's dark eyes narrowed as she studied Kate over the rim of her goblet. "Was she indeed? Well, Eleanor Haywood was a remarkable lady."

Perhaps it was the darkness, the firelight, the wine, the strange feeling of being caught in a moment set apart out of time, but Kate felt bold. "Did you know about her? My mother?" she said abruptly.

Elizabeth drained the last of her wine. "Did I know who her father was? Aye, I knew. My aunt Mary Boleyn knew, and she told her children, my cousins Lord Hunsdon and Catherine Carey. We all try to look out for you, you know, Kate. But you do not make it easy for us when you do things like chase villains down frozen rivers."

Kate felt suddenly angry. "But you did not tell me!"

Elizabeth's own Tudor temper flared in her eyes. She suddenly rose and put the empty goblet down on the table with a sharp click. "'Twas not my secret to tell. Nor was it Lady Gertrude's, but she is old and forgetful."

"I can be forgetful, too," Kate said quietly, her anger burning down as fast as it came. "If that is what you want."

Elizabeth laughed. "You may well wish to forget you are a Boleyn, Kate. We are a wild lot, prone to tempers and scandals. But we are loyal, too, and you have certainly proven yourself to be that. What *I* want is your presence here at court, to play your music for my banquets and keep watch for me on my court. You see things from where you are that other people cannot, Kate, and I need that. Will you stay?"

There had never been any question of that. Kate had had a taste of what it meant to be useful, to have excitement in her life, and she was not going to let that go. "Of course, Your Majesty. Always."

Elizabeth nodded, and her stiff shoulders relaxed under the fine brocade of her robe. "Then know that I will never allow your mother's name to be sullied, just as I will not allow that of my own mother. They are safe in their graves, as are their secrets. And now you must rest. Tomorrow you must go back to your father and work on your music, regain your strength. You shall need it."

Then the queen was gone, the door closing quietly behind her, and Kate was alone again. She slid deeper under the bedclothes, watching the shifting glow of the dying firelight, wondering what the world would reveal to her next.

Author's Note

When I started writing *Murder at Westminster Abbey*, I had lots of fun digging through boxes looking for photos and scrapbooks of my trips to England, and I got to revisit my very first tour of Westminster Abbey! It was a rainy, stormy day, and I had just arrived in London after a long overnight flight. The hotel room wasn't yet ready, and I was jet-lagged and a bit silly with lack of sleep and too much Chardonnay (I am a terrible flier!). So what could be better than a few hours wandering around in the cool darkness of Westminster Abbey, out of the rain?

For a lifelong history geek like me, the Abbey was a magical place. I spent hours at Poets' Corner, visiting Chaucer and Browning. I stumbled across Anne of Cleves, Margaret Beaufort, and Aphra Behn, and stood atop where Oliver Cromwell once lay, before the Restoration came and he was dug up again. Best of all, I found myself nearly alone for a few precious minutes at the tomb Elizabeth I shares with Mary I. I think I worried the security guard with my sobbing, but no matter—I was "meeting" one of my heroines at last!

(I also cried on that trip at the Chapel of St. Peter ad Vincula at the Tower, but that was a few days later and I couldn't blame jet lag....)

It was wonderful to revisit my memories of that trip

(and rewatch a DVD of William and Kate's wedding, just for research on cathedral details, of course!). It was also a lot of fun to delve deeply into the events surrounding Elizabeth I's coronation—I almost feel like I could have been there now, and met all the historical figures who played a part in the glittering events. (Especially Lady Catherine Grey—her story is not done yet!) For more historical background on the events of January 1559, and some great resources I came across in my research, you can visit me anytime at http://www.amandacarmack.com....

Read on for a sneak peek
at the next Elizabethan Mystery
from Amanda Carmack,

MURDER IN THE QUEEN'S GARDEN

Available from Obsidian in February 2015.

CHAPTER 1

August 1559

"Make way, you varlets! Make way for the queen!" The guards in Queen Elizabeth's green-and-white livery galloped along the dusty, rutted lane, pushing back the eager crowds who gathered to watch the queen ride by.

Along the road, the royal cavalcade seemed to stretch for miles. Hundreds of people rode with Queen Elizabeth on her summer progress, an endless stream of horses, wagons, and coaches. Baggage carts were piled high with chests and furniture, maidservants and pages clinging to them precariously as they bounced along. The courtiers on their fine horses were a kaleidoscope of bright velvets and feathers, a brilliant burst of color emerging from the brown dust of the hard, dry summer pathways.

None was more glorious than the queen herself. She rode in her finest coach, a gift from one of her suitors, the prince of Sweden. It was an elaborate conveyance, painted deep crimson and trimmed with gilt paint, lined with green satin cushions. Six white horses drew it along, the green ribbons braided in their manes and tails fluttering in the wind. Queen Elizabeth, resplendent in white-

and-silver brocade, her red-gold hair piled atop her head and twined with pearls, waved her gloved hand at the crowds who clamored to see her.

"God save our queen!" they shouted, falling over one another, tears shining on their faces. Parents held their children up on their shoulders to glimpse a real queen.

"And God bless all of you, my good people!" Elizabeth called back.

Sir Robert Dudley rode beside her on his grand, prancing black horse, seeming to be a part of the powerful beast himself in his black-and-gold doublet, a plumed black hat trimmed with pearls and rubies on his glossy, curling dark hair. He laughed as he caught some of the bouquets tossed to the queen, and he leaned into the carriage to drop them in her lap. Elizabeth smiled up at him radiantly, the very image of a summer queen, full of heat and light and pure, giddy happiness.

Kate Haywood could barely glimpse the queen's coach from her own wagon farther down the lane, but even she could see the sunburst of the queen's smile. It had been thus all summer, from Greenwich to Eltham, a procession of dances, banquets, and fireworks over gardens in full, fragrant bloom. After so many years of danger and fear, it seemed summer had truly returned to England at last, and everyone was determined to enjoy it to the hilt. Especially the queen.

Kate looked down at her lute, carefully packed into its case and propped at her feet. She had let her clothes chest, filled with her new fine gowns and ruffs, be loaded into the baggage carts, but never this, her most prized possession. It had once belonged her mother, who had died during Kate's birth, and Kate had grown up learning to play her music on it. It was her most trusted companion, and now that she was a full member of the queen's musical consort, it was her way of earning her own bread as well. It had seen much activity in the past few weeks, with Kate playing deep into the night as Queen Elizabeth danced on and on—mostly with Robert Dudley.

Kate flexed her fingers in her new kid gloves. They, too, had seen much work lately, and she couldn't afford for them to grow stiff. Once the royal cavalcade reached Nonsuch Palace, there would be much dancing again. It was said that Lord Arundel, the palace's owner, was much set on wooing the queen and had planned many elaborate pageants to advance his pursuit.

For a moment, Kate thought of her father, content in retirement at his new cottage near Windsor. She received letters from him on this progress, full of his news as he finally had time to work on the grand Christmas service cycle he had longed to finish. He also had words to say about a kindly widow who lived nearby who brought him fresh milk and new-baked bread. He seemed happy, but Kate often missed him a great deal. They had been each other's only family for so long.

And yet, he had kept her mother's secret from Kate all her life. And she hadn't yet been able to bring herself to confront him about that. She didn't know if she ever would. It made her feel so very lonely.

Kate leaned forward to study the coach in front of her wagon through the choking clouds of dust. Catherine Carey, Lady Knollys, the daughter of the queen's aunt Mary Boleyn, rode there with her beautiful daughter, Lettice, the fine new conveyance a sign of their high favor with the queen. Beside them, talking to the ladies through the open window was her brother Lord Hunsdon.

He threw back his head and laughed, his red beard glinting in the sunlight, and his sister peeked out the window to laugh with him. She caught her plumed hat just before the wind would have snatched it from her dark hair.

Whenever Kate saw Lady Knollys, she wondered if her own mother had looked something like her, with her delicate face and shining black hair—"Boleyn hair," they called it. For Kate's own mother, Eleanor, was the illegitimate half sister of Anne and Mary Boleyn. A fact Kate had discovered in a most shocking way only a few months before.

Not that the Careys, or anyone, ever spoke of that fact or acknowledged it, though sometimes Kate thought she saw Lord Hunsdon looking at her. . . .

The convoy suddenly lurched to a halt, startling Kate from her brooding thoughts. She clutched at the wooden side of the wagon to keep from tumbling to the floor.

"Are we stopping *again*?" Lady Anne Godwin, one of the queen's new maids-of-honor who sat across from Kate, cried. "We shall never get to Nonsuch at this pace! I vow we could walk faster."

Mistress Violet Melville, from her perch on the bench next to Kate, smiled and said, "Of course Queen Elizabeth will wish to stop and talk to the people whenever she can. Most of them will never see such a sight again."

Kate smiled at her. She had come to like Violet very much on their travels, for they often found themselves in the same conveyances and sharing lodgings in the palaces and manors of the summer progress. She was one of the queen's newest maids-of-honor, small and pretty, with blond curls and a quick smile. She enjoyed music and could help while away dull hours on the road, talking of the newest songs from Italy and Spain. She was also a fine source of gossip about the court, conveyed through quick whispers and giggles. Who was in love with whom. Who was seen speaking to whom.

Information that seemed most frivolous but could prove deadly useful—as Kate had often discovered lately.

Violet seemed especially excited today, for her brother served as a secretary to Lord Arundel, and she would get to see him at Nonsuch.

"And it is such a lovely, warm day," Violet said. "Who can grumble about being out in the sunshine?"

"I can," Lady Anne muttered, readjusting her silk skirts around her. Unlike Violet, she was not often very merry. "My backside is aching from this infernal jolting wagon. And your nose will grumble, too, Violet, when you get hideous freckles."

Violet just laughed and leaned out to see what was happening. Kate peeked over her shoulder to see that the queen had halted her carriage to call forth a man with a little girl in his arms. The child shyly held out a bouquet to Queen Elizabeth, who accepted it under Dudley's protective watch.

Kate felt a pang of strange wistfulness as she watched. It had been many weeks since she had seen her friend Anthony Elias, who was working to become an attorney in London. Yet she thought far too often of his smile, his beautiful green eyes. The safety she had found in his arms when she nearly died on the frozen Thames. If he ever looked at *her* as Sir Robert looked at the queen . . .

But Anthony would not. And she had her own work to do. She had to cease to think about him.

She sat back on the narrow wooden bench and made sure her lute was still safe. Music was her only pursuit.

Violet turned and gave her another smile. "Have you had your horoscope done by Dr. Dee yet, Kate?"

Kate shook her head. "I have not yet had the time," she said. She had seen Dr. John Dee's bearded, black-robed figure hurrying around the court and his apprentice, Master Constable, dashing after him with his arms full of mysterious scrolls and books. Having one's horoscope cast was considered essential by so many people at court in recent days. Dr. Dee had forecasted the queen's coronation date, as well as where she should visit on this progress. Queen Elizabeth relied on his wisdom entirely.

But Kate was sure the hour of her own birth, which had been the hour of her mother's death, could not augur well for the future. She had to learn how to make it for herself. It seemed best not to know her destiny.

"Oh, but you must!" Violet cried. "Everyone is doing it. Dr. Dee had no time to cast mine, so Master Constable did it. He said I was born under Saturn and am thus of melancholic disposition. I should marry within the year but never to someone born under Mars or great misfortune will ensue."

Kate shook her head. She thought of Violet's frequent laughter, her love of dance and song. It seemed Master Constable wasn't learning much from his apprenticeship.

"I am surprised the learned Dr. Dee would even wish to return to Nonsuch," Lady Anne said with a smirk. "Surely that would be a most bad omen for him."

"What do you mean?" Violet cried.

"Have you not heard the tale?" Lady Anne said. Her eyes were shining with the pleasure of gossip. "I know not much about it, but my uncle was there when it happened. It was in old King Henry's time, when he was married to poor Queen Catherine Howard."

Catherine Howard had lost her head in the Tower when she was barely more than sixteen. Kate remembered that dark, cold night before the new queen's coronation, when she'd knelt on the stone floor of St. Peter ad Vincula in the Tower with Queen Elizabeth, sure that unseen eyes watched their every movement as Elizabeth searched for Anne Boleyn's resting place.

"Oh, do tell us!" Violet urged. Kate said nothing, but she was intrigued.

Lady Anne smiled. "'Twas on a summer progress just like this one. Nonsuch was the king's then and not yet finished, but he was determined to bring his new queen there. Dr. Dee was an apprentice to a man called Dr. Macey, so they say, and King Henry wanted Macey's advice that summer and summoned him to Nonsuch."

Kate glanced ahead to where the queen was greeting more of her subjects, smiling and holding out her hand to them. The shimmering, brilliant radiance of the scene seemed so far away from when the old, mad king came this way with his frivolous, flirtatious young queen. Had King Henry required some dark magic from Dr. Macey that year? There had been such frightening tales of alchemy and spirits. . . .

"What happened?" Violet whispered. Her eyes were wide, as if she, too, feared to know of ungodly arts.

"A courtier named Lord Marchand accused Dr. Macey of—of *treason*!" Lady Anne hissed the last word. "He declared that Dr. Macey had predicted the king's death, which is a burning offense. He also said things unseemly about the queen. Macey was thrown in jail, and his apprentice, Dr. Dee, was cast out of court when he tried to clear his master's name."

"Was he executed, then?" Kate said, appalled.

Lady Anne shook her head. "That is the strange twist of the tale, Mistress Haywood. This Lord Marchand vanished quite utterly as if he fled some evil. No such horoscope predicting the king's death could ever be found, but poor Dr. Macey died of a lung fever anyway. Dr. Dee went abroad soon after that. And it all happened at Nonsuch. What can Dr. Dee be thinking to go back there now?"

"How terribly sad," Violet sighed. "And Lord Marchand never reappeared at all?"

"Never," Lady Anne said with obvious relish. "My uncle said some people declared a demon spirited him away at Dr. Macey's conjuring."

"A demon!" Violet shrieked.

"Don't be silly," Kate said. "How would a demon appear in the midst of a crowded court? Surely there would at least have been the smell of brimstone." Kate laughed, but she couldn't help shivering. The warmth of the summer sun couldn't quite banish the old, dark memories of the past.

The procession jolted forward again, and Lady Anne and Violet talked of other, happier matters—the newest style of ruff from France, the new Spanish ambassador, who was newly betrothed to whom. Horoscopes and mysterious vanishings seemed forgotten, especially when they rolled over the crest of a hill and Nonsuch Palace came into view at last.

Even Kate was stunned by the sight of it, despite the paintings and etchings she had seen. She had heard many tales of Nonsuch, of course—King Henry had begun building it the year his precious son, Prince Edward, was born, intending it to surpass in luxury and grandeur any châteaus of the French king. It was to be the most lavish palace in Christendom. But he had never finished it, and Queen Mary had sold it to Lord Arundel.

It was dazzling, all golden stone and rosy brick in the sunlight, rising above the lush green parks and gardens like a fairy-story palace. Octagonal towers crowned with gilded onion-shaped cupolas rose at every corner and linked with crenelated walkways, and the walls were decorated with enormous colorful stucco reliefs of classical gods and goddesses.

It was beautiful, elegant, joyful. Hardly a place where treason and dark magic could ever triumph.

Hardly a place where anything as evil as murder could ever happen at all.

Also available from
Amanda Carmack

Murder at Hatfield House
An Elizabethan Mystery

In 1558, dark times rule England—the country's greatest hope lies in the young Princess Elizabeth. And Kate Haywood, a talented musician in the employ of the Princess, will find herself involved in games of crowns as she sets out to solve the murder of Queen Mary's envoy.

"An evocative and intelligent read."
—*New York Times* bestselling author Tasha Alexander